What the critics are saying...

Recommended Read! "There aren't too many stories where the elements of plot, setting, characters, and romance come together so beautifully, but *Summer in the City of Sails* proves to be the one of those rare treats in the romance genre." ~ *Sarah W, Fallen Angel Reviews*

"Shelley Munro's name on a book is a surefire guarantee that the you are going to read a story that is completely unputdownable, and her latest release *Summer in the City of Sails* is no exception!" ~ *Julie Bonello, ECataRomance Reviews*

"This was an incredibly fun read. Summer is hilarious to a fault and turns rough, stern Nikolai on his butt...I highly recommend this book because it is written very well, with tender, passionate moments and a lot of wit and humor all set in the beautiful land of the Down Under." ~ *Marina, Cupid's Library Review*

"A thoroughly spicy book, *Summer in the City of Sails* has a charismatic appeal that lured me to each and every page. The seamless flow of the book allows the chapters to wiz by so quickly that I reached the end before I knew what hit me." ~*Francesca Hayne, Just Erotic Romance Reviews*

"*Summer in the City of Sails* is wonderfully entertaining...I found myself needing to know who was threatening Summer and why. I couldn't put the book down until I knew. This is a book I could read over and over and never tire of." ~ *Chrissy Dionne, Romance Junkies*

SHELLEY MUNRO

Summer in the City of Sails

ELLORA'S CAVE
ROMANTICA PUBLISHING

An Ellora's Cave Romantica Publication

www.ellorascave.com

Summer in the City of Sails

ISBN # 1419952544
ALL RIGHTS RESERVED.
Summer in the City of Sails Copyright© 2005 Shelley Munro
Edited by: Mary Moran
Cover art by: Syneca

Electronic book Publication: March, 2005
Trade paperback Publication: September, 2005

Excerpt from *Talking Dogs, Aliens and Purple People Eaters*
Copyright © Shelley Munro, 2004

Warning:

The following material contains graphic sexual content meant for mature readers. *Summer in the City of Sails* has been rated *S-ensuous* by a minimum of three independent reviewers.

Ellora's Cave Publishing offers three levels of Romantica™ reading entertainment: S (S-ensuous), E (E-rotic), and X (X-treme).

S-*ensuous* love scenes are explicit and leave nothing to the imagination.

E-*rotic* love scenes are explicit, leave nothing to the imagination, and are high in volume per the overall word count. In addition, some E-rated titles might contain fantasy material that some readers find objectionable, such as bondage, submission, same sex encounters, forced seductions, etc. E-rated titles are the most graphic titles we carry; it is common, for instance, for an author to use words such as "fucking", "cock", "pussy", etc., within their work of literature.

X-*treme* titles differ from E-rated titles only in plot premise and storyline execution. Unlike E-rated titles, stories designated with the letter X tend to contain controversial subject matter not for the faint of heart.

Also by Shelley Munro:

Never Send a Dog To Do a Woman's Job
Talking Dogs, Aliens, and Purple People Eaters

Summer in the City of Sails

Trademarks Acknowledgement

Prologue

"I'm not telling him. *You* tell him."

"It was your fault. You left the book in the taxi," Marty snarled back at Ross. His hands curled to fists, and it looked as though he was ready to straighten the kink in his brother's nose.

Dare Martin had heard enough. He strode into his Auckland office and shut the door behind him. The soft thud of wood sliding home muted the chatter from the early dinner crowd out in his restaurant and acted like a bomb explosion on his cousins. They whirled to face him, their familiar features bearing expressions ranging from uneasiness and trepidation to outright fear. He stepped away to stop himself from grabbing their dumb-ass heads and banging them together.

"I hope you're fooling around." Dare's low growl displayed irritation, but the sound was mild considering the touchy subject. He dropped into the high-tech leather chair that sat behind the rimu-veneer desk and leaned back to observe them closely. They'd better be kidding, or he'd give them old-fashioned cement boots and drop them in the blue waters of the Hauraki Gulf. The book held an important place in his plans to take over the Ngataki family business. Hell, important be damned. It was bloody essential. "Where's the book?" His normally lazy drawl flattened to crisp and no-nonsense.

Marty backed up and edged to the door, his chubby face paling to reveal a mug full of freckles. "Ross left it in the cab. We realized we'd lost…ah…left it and grabbed another cab to follow. When we caught up with the driver, he said there was no package on the backseat of his cab."

"Yeah, it wasn't there," Ross said.

Marty glared at his brother then continued. "When we followed the cab, we saw him drop off at the library on Wellesley Street. A woman got out with a loada packages. I think she thought our package belonged to her and took it with her."

Pissed yielded swiftly to fury, but apart from lifting his hands to grip the edge of the desk, Dare kept his expression impassive. "I *want* that book."

"We couldn't find her in the library, but turns out the bird works there. We saw her leave and followed her home to Bottle Top Bay, boss," Marty said.

"Yeah, we know where she lives. Young bird, she is. Nice tits." Ross' brows waggled up and down, and he smirked the dopey grin that never failed to prod Dare's temper.

"If you know where she lives then get the friggin' book back!" Dare roared, letting rip with his frustration. Goddamned bloody relatives. "I don't give a rat's arse how you do it. *Just get it back.*"

"Sure, boss." Marty's beefy hand reached for the wooden doorknob. "The house is isolated—just the one next door. Breaking in won't be a problem." He spoke so quickly his words ran together into one, a sure sign he sensed how close they were to bodily harm.

"Yeah, no problem, boss," Ross said, his bearded chin bobbing up and down in agreement.

Dare sucked in a deep breath. A Goddamned bloody farce, that's what this was. No wonder he'd found a gray hair this morning. After another calming breath, he flipped a red hardbound book open and reached for his engraved silver pen to add a notation to the margin. A soft shuffle of shoes made his head jerk up. "You still here?"

"Need a car," Ross muttered.

"Steal one." Dare seethed as he delivered the obvious answer. The blow his cousin had copped during that brawl last year had left him two sandwiches short of a picnic. "And don't get caught because I won't bail you out."

Dare gripped his silver pen tightly and concentrated on his bookwork. Lumbering footsteps followed by a click as the door shut indicated his cousins had left. Dare tossed the pen down in disgust and leaned back. His chair slid smoothly into a reclining position.

He had a dream, a vision of power and how the future would pan out.

Nothing was going to get in the way of his dream.

Chapter One

"I want you to look after Summer."

Summer's bare feet froze outside the door to her Uncle Henry's study. Her hand slid from the brass doorknob. A babysitter? Indignation stabbed her mind, robbing her of the sense of accomplishment she'd felt only seconds earlier. At age twenty-two, why did they think she needed a babysitter? Her eyes narrowed as she placed the package she carried on a wooden pedestal table then pressed closer to hear the details.

"Do I look like a babysitter?" a masculine voice snapped. "Try the yellow pages."

Summer nodded emphatically, giving a silent cheer for the owner of the low, husky voice. *Way to go, mister.* But while she waited for Uncle Henry's comeback, she fumed. She knew exactly where the idea had originated. Her family. Or more specifically her mother who thought danger lurked behind every corner in sinful Auckland City.

"Think of it as a favor," Uncle Henry said.

"No."

The blunt, uncompromising answer made a smile surface. She liked this man. And she agreed with him. One hundred percent. Yes, she'd been a sickly child, but she'd outgrown the bad asthma attacks. As long as she used her preventer, there was nothing wrong with her health. Summer glanced down at her bust and hips, her expression turning rueful. Thanks to her mother's excellent cooking, her body — well, the polite word was "curvaceous".

"Nikolai," Uncle Henry groaned. "My sister will make my life miserable. She'll hunt me down on my honeymoon."

Summer suppressed a snort as she flipped the end of her French braid over her shoulder. Why did Uncle Henry think she'd come to Auckland, the city of sails? Although her mother meant well, she was overprotective, especially when it came to the baby of the family. And now she was doing the smothering thing by remote control, all the way from Eketahuna. If Summer allowed this, her bid for freedom would end before it started. It was time her family let her make her own mistakes and let her fix any stuff-ups by herself.

When her boss at the Eketahuna Library had suggested further training in big, bad Auckland City, the possibilities had made Summer breathless. Eager. At last, a chance to spread her fledgling wings. Despite her parents' protests, Summer had grasped the opportunity with both hands.

And she wasn't about to let anyone take the experience away from her.

"Tell someone who cares," Nikolai said. "With my track record, I'm the last person you should ask."

A shiver goose-stepped down Summer's spine. That voice… His voice did things to her. She thought about easing the door open a little further to check out the body that matched the sexy rumble. Meeting men was high on her to-do list. No time like the present.

"I didn't want to do this," Uncle Henry muttered, "but I'm a desperate man. *You owe me.* That time I saved you from the broad in—"

The heartfelt Anglo-Saxon curse made Summer's brows shoot toward her hairline. She hadn't heard her brothers use that one before.

"All right, dammit! I'll check on her now and then, but if I see one girly tear, I'm outta there. And our debt is square once you get back."

"That should do it," Uncle Henry hastily agreed. "Just check to make sure her car is there and get a visual every couple of days."

Get a visual? Summer thought, puckering her forehead. Good grief. Nikolai was one of Uncle Henry's military friends. He'd take his duties seriously. This was not good.

"All I want is a peaceful honeymoon."

"All you want is to get laid," Nikolai muttered.

Uncle Henry chuckled—a smug masculine sound that made Summer ache to deck him on Veronica's behalf. "Yeah, that too."

Right, that did it. If she allowed this, she'd never escape her family's well-meaning influence. Yeah, she loved them, knew they loved her in return, but enough was enough.

Summer shoved the door open and strode through. "I'm back. Oh—" She stopped in front of her uncle's large wooden desk. Her hand fluttered to her left breast. "I didn't know you had a visitor."

"Summer, this is Nikolai Tarei. He's my closest neighbor."

Summer's gaze had already snapped to the man with the sexy voice. Physical awareness floored her, made her tongue stick to the roof of her mouth. Luckily, her brain continued to function and nothing impaired her twenty-twenty vision. Oh, boy! Tall, dark and sinfully sexy was welcome to guard her body *any* time.

Her uncle stood and rounded the desk to stand at her side. "Nikolai, my niece Summer. She's up in Auckland to do a six-month course at Central Library."

Nikolai shoved away from the wall and stepped across the faded blue carpet. "Pleased to meet you," he said, holding out his hand in greeting.

Summer realized her mouth gaped and snapped it shut. She stuck out her hand, and instantly it was engulfed in his warm grasp. Her heart tap-danced, did a jig—the whole works. She fought the urge to jerk her hand away. One thing stood out in her mind. This wasn't the right man to practice *Miranda's Tips to Flirting* on.

He finally released her hand and stepped back. Summer's avid gaze followed as if attached by an umbilical cord. Big. Actually, make that huge. He towered over her by a good six inches. Broad shoulders gave his black T-shirt quite a workout. Summer took in his shoulder-length unfettered hair, the stubble shading his jaw. Under no circumstances would she call him tame. Dark eyes that reminded her of the richest, most expensive chocolate skimmed her face, her body, then settled back on her uncle.

Stupidly, Summer felt the sting of rejection, but she told herself it didn't matter. Nikolai Tarei reminded her of her two brothers—extremely capable and overprotective. And one look told her it was likely he bore the bossy gene. She didn't need another brother-figure looking over her shoulder, vetting boyfriends, putting a dampener on her quest for independence. Not when she intended to let loose and live a little.

"I wanted you to meet Nikolai before I left. If you have any problems you can call on him," Uncle Henry said. His cheerful, gruff voice made Summer stiffen. Trying too hard. Did they think she was stupid?

"Most people would call that babysitting," she said, baring her teeth in a smile. Summer intercepted the brief glance the two men exchanged—the quirk of brow, the silent grimace that said, "You deal with her".

Oh, for goodness sake! "I'm not expecting any problems," she said. "I'll be too busy." She paused a beat. "Going out on the town."

Uncle Henry spluttered. His mouth opened and closed several times.

"I have to go. I'm expecting a call," Nikolai said.

Summer choked back a laugh. In military terms that qualified as a strategic retreat. Wise man. She watched him saunter to the door and frowned. What should have been a loose-limbed stride had a distinct hitch, but his black jeans covered any evidence of the injury.

"Coward," Uncle Henry muttered.

Summer turned her gaze on her uncle. "Did you say something?"

"No."

Summer heard a distinct snicker and whipped her head around.

Nikolai edged away, moving closer to the door. "Henry, see you when you get back. Give my love to Veronica."

"Right." The two men shook hands. "Thanks."

The silent communication thing again. Summer watched Nikolai walk through the door and limp down the passage. Appreciation bloomed along with a grin. The man had a mighty fine rear end. He might be her babysitter, her jailer, but that didn't mean she didn't appreciate the view.

She turned to her uncle. "What's wrong with Nikolai's leg?"

"Knee injury."

"On active duty?"

"Yeah."

Suspicion made Summer narrow her eyes. "Do Dillon and Josh know him?"

"Your brothers? Maybe."

A tight sensation gripped her chest. "Don't tell me he's Special Air Service."

"Okay." Uncle Henry blinked rapidly. "I won't."

* * * * *

Nikolai limped down the uneven front path, heading for the gate in the boundary fence between his and Henry's property. He would have stomped if it hadn't been for his blasted knee.

A babysitter.

Hell, like he needed that sort of responsibility.

His foot skidded on a pile of damp grass clippings. Pain, sharp and jagged, lanced from his knee up his thigh. Nikolai glared at the green hose that spurted water into Henry's rose garden. He sucked in a pained breath, cursed and staggered to the gate, leaning his weight against it while he rode out the pain.

Babysitting! Hell, Henry should know better. Incapacitated the way he was now, he was about as useful as a gun without bullets.

Nikolai tried a little weight on his knee and decided he'd make his kitchen without keeling over. The gate creaked open. He should have taken that damned painkiller before he went to Henry's. At least then, he might have had an excuse for agreeing to Henry's blackmail. But no, he'd been drug-free, clear of mind and in total control. Yet he'd still managed to find himself looking after a green girl just out of high school.

He gritted his teeth as he limped the last few steps to his front door. Nikolai shouldered the door open, and headed straight for the kitchen and the bottle of pills. Five minutes later, he dropped into his recliner chair and stared out at his overgrown garden, past the knee-high grass and the scraggy shrubs. He watched Summer carry a suitcase from the house and toss it into the rear of the car. Henry followed with a smaller bag and a suit in a protective cover. Nikolai saw Summer say something, heard Henry's booming laugh through the open window. His throat constricted with a feeling he didn't want to analyze when Henry swept his niece into a bone-crushing hug.

Hard to believe his friend and mentor was married after years of the single life. Nikolai snorted. That was the kicker. Henry had sworn he'd never marry then taken one look at Veronica and fallen hard. They'd married secretly last week and were off on a cruise this evening. Hopefully, marriage would work for Henry. It sure as hell hadn't for him.

Nikolai thrust aside past memories to study Summer again. Average height, long brown hair in a plait, on the chubby side, and a dazzling smile that made a man look twice despite the god-awful gray sack thing she was wearing.

His charge until Henry returned. Nikolai leaned back in the chair and closed his eyes. Hopefully, he'd never see her more than once a week. It couldn't be that bad.

* * * * *

A noise woke Summer. One moment she was dreaming of playing rugby with the All Blacks and the next her eyes sprang open, the fine hairs on her arms prickling in silent alarm. She froze, exhaling slowly while she listened.

There it was again—a muted sound that could be a footstep. Summer slid from bed, knowing she'd have to investigate or she'd never get any sleep.

Voices whispered down the passage outside her room. Summer froze. A light flashed briefly then shut off.

"Must be in one of the bedrooms."

The guttural whisper snapped Summer to attention. She crept noiselessly toward the window. The shutter clicked as she opened it. Loud enough that she froze again.

"I'll check in this room and the bathroom. You take the other two rooms."

"What about the girl?"

"You heard the boss. Do whatever's necessary to get the goods."

"Right."

Two of them. That didn't sound good. Healthy fear made Summer spring to action. She shoved the window open wide, no longer worrying about attracting attention. Footsteps sounded right outside her door. The door handle grated as it turned. Summer slithered out the window feetfirst. The sill dug into her stomach while her feet dangled two feet above Uncle Henry's prized rose garden. Not the best position to be in, but not as bad as being accosted by strange men in the middle of the night. Summer wriggled further over the windowsill and let go.

Rose thorns sliced at her calves, her thighs. Summer bit her bottom lip. Shit! That hurt. Well that would teach her to wear a skimpy nightgown to bed rather than the flannelette pajamas her mother had packed. She extricated herself from the grip of Tom Thumb, Uncle Henry's favorite rosebush, and limped toward Nikolai's house. Pique made her grimace and think in curses. Just her luck. Her first night alone, and she needed help. A great start to her bid for independence.

"She's not here."

Summer glanced over her shoulder and once again cursed her nightgown. The pale material stuck out like a Jersey bull in her mother's vegetable garden.

"She must be here."

Summer changed direction. She'd have to go around the back of Nikolai's house. She stepped up onto the verandah and almost fell through a broken board. Damn and blast.

"The window's open. Look out in the garden." The intruders' voices carried on the night air.

An open window beckoned, the sheer net curtains fluttering in the soft breeze. The voices moved closer, and Summer didn't hesitate. She dived through the window.

Something tackled her, sending her flying. Summer landed on her back in the middle of a mattress. The air hissed from her lungs as someone pinned her in place.

"Don't move," a harsh voice said next to her ear. A hand moved down her arm and across her chest, freezing when it came into contact with her breast. This time, the succinct Anglo-Saxon curse didn't raise so much as an eyebrow. The body pressing her into the bed moved, but not enough for her to draw a good lungful of air. A bedside lamp switched on. She blinked at the surge of bright light.

"You." Nikolai glared down at her. "What the devil are you doing in my bedroom?"

Summer swallowed. His hand was warm, and she felt her nipple hardening under his touch. Humiliation at her body's betrayal made her tense even as she savored the spike of sensation.

"Um…would you mind taking your hand off my breast?" The way her nipple was cozying into his palm—talk about a newsflash. Being this close to the man was unnerving, especially since he was the enemy. She refused to think about how good it would feel if he rearranged their bodies a fraction. Nope. She wasn't going there.

The furrow between his brows deepened. "Isn't that what you're here for?"

The innuendo made Summer stiffen even more. "Someone's broken into Uncle Henry's house."

"Why didn't you say so?" To Summer's intense relief, Nikolai moved off her. "Have you rung the police?"

"No. I…" Summer's voice trailed off as she took in the broad expanse of his naked chest. Oops, naked all over. Her gaze jumped northward again, but the vision of masculinity remained seared to her retinas. *He looked so much better without clothes.*

Nikolai rolled his eyes with the same masculine impatience her brothers exhibited when they thought she was acting blonde. "Never mind. Get in bed and stay warm. I'll take care of things."

He yanked on a pair of jeans and limped from the room before she could tell him what she thought of his verbal pat on the head. No way was she staying in his bed and missing out on the fun. She sprang from the mattress. This was more adventure than she'd ever imagined, and it was only her second day in Auckland.

Summer crept down the passage, feeling her way cautiously through the dark and unfamiliar house.

"I thought I told you to stay in bed."

Summer jerked as his warm breath tickled her ear. Oh, boy. Who would have thought an ear was an erogenous zone? She bit down on her bottom lip, frowned then grinned as a brainwave struck. "I heard a noise outside the window." Luckily, it was dark since she couldn't lie to save herself. And her body was broadcasting lustful messages a blind man could decipher. Full participation in this adventure would give her something else to think about, help her gain a semblance of control—she hoped.

"All right. Stay with me," he ordered. He moved off, sliding through the darkness with the ease of a soldier on night maneuvers.

Summer blundered after him and kicked a table leg. The clatter made Nikolai curse. She blinked. Another new one to save for later—wait until the next time her brothers tried to tell her how to live her life. She'd stun them with her brilliance.

"Can't you be quiet?"

"I can't see."

Another muttered curse. "Here." He seized her hand. "Hold onto me. And keep up."

Summer felt a royal salute coming on until he attached her hand to the waistband of his jeans. When she touched warm masculine skin, every militant urge in her mind stalled. Her fingers curled about the body-warmed denim. She sucked in a deep breath, her senses reeling and her body humming—from toe-tips to the top of her head. Bits in between tingled and plunged, and swooped like a high-speed lift traveling to the ground floor. *Oh, boy.*

Nikolai opened the front door and slid outside. Summer stumbled after him, her mind engaged on sensation, the way her silk nightgown caressed her curves, rather than the urgent need to reconnoiter. He stopped without warning. Summer didn't, and her nose flattened against his shoulder blade. A soft whoosh of air escaped from between her parted lips.

Nikolai's hands snaked out, steadying and preventing her from falling. "Mind the step. I haven't got round to fixing it yet."

The step? Her next intake of breath was a mistake. It was full of Nikolai. Sandalwood soap and Nikolai, and it was a very combustible combination. Who'd have thought?

In the distance, a siren sounded.

"Help is on the way." Satisfaction oozed from his voice.

"Are they still in Uncle Henry's house?"

"Yeah. Can't you hear them?"

Hear them? She couldn't hear anything apart from the thud of her heart. It was a wonder he didn't hear the rapid tattoo, him standing so close and all. Her breath caught. Did he realize his hand had slid down to her butt? It wasn't her most attractive feature and frankly, she thought there were better places if he wanted to explore.

"Damn. They must have heard the siren."

Summer turned her head in the direction he was looking. Two shadowy figures sprinted across her uncle's lawn, past the fishpond out front and disappeared from sight around the corner of the house. Seconds later, a car engine roared.

"Hell of a cheek," Nikolai muttered. "Look, they're going to drive back down the road as if they have every right. Smart. If they were speeding that would look suspicious."

A car pulled into Nikolai's driveway. The siren stopped.

"Stay there."

Another order. Summer thought about it, then decided she didn't do orders. The police would want to interview her. After avoiding the hole, she stepped off the wooden deck.

"Nik. How's it going?" Two men leapt from the car, and the three of them indulged in a complicated handshake followed by a round of shoulder clapping that would have flattened a normal person.

Summer came to a sudden halt. They didn't look like any policemen she'd ever seen. Her eyes narrowed, and she must have made a sound. The two strangers whirled about. Their faces, tight and ready for action, gave them away. They were definitely not policemen.

"Who's the babe?" Although the voice was soft, the words carried.

Nikolai sighed heavily but didn't look in her direction. "I thought I told you to stay put?" He limped up the path to her and tugged her by the arm until she stood in front of him. Summer felt his body heat sear the length of her back. His arm wrapped around her as if he thought she might try to escape. Pressed to his body and with his arm weighing down on her breasts, she could hardly breathe. "This is Henry's niece."

There was a moment's silence, then one of the men whistled. "Not a babe then?" The soft words held a question.

Nikolai tensed.

Summer struggled to free herself of his grip, and Nikolai let go the instant she wriggled. Enough. They couldn't pretend she was invisible. She was right in front of their eyes. "Are the two mutually exclusive?" she demanded.

"Of course not, ma'am," one of the men said.

She glared and stuck out her hand. "Summer, not ma'am."

"Jake," the man said.

Interesting. His hand was as warm as Nikolai's but didn't produce the same tingles. A soft growl came from the man behind her. Jake grinned as he slowly let go of her hand.

The other man beside Jake claimed it almost instantly. "Louie," he said. "Pleased to meet you, Summer." His low drawl was distinctly flirtatious, and Summer felt an answering grin gather momentum.

"*Louie.*"

Startled, Summer's gaze snapped to Nikolai. His face bore a feral warning while his tone promised reprisal. Against what Summer didn't know, but Louie did and he heeded the caution.

"Shirt," Nikolai snapped.

Jake and Louie grinned at each other. They did the communication thing, then Jake shrugged, whipped off his cotton shirt and held it out to Summer. She stared at the shirt. What did they want her to do with it? Wash it?

"Hell." Nikolai grabbed the shirt and thrust it against her chest. "Put it on. Before we drown in the drool." A snicker drew Nikolai's wrath. "What?"

"Nothing," Jake said.

Nikolai nailed her with a glare. "We'll go and check out Henry's house. Make sure they've gone."

Summer nodded, and when they moved off, followed them.

"Stay," Nikolai said.

Summer stopped. She frowned at the departing men, then looked over her shoulder. Nope, Nikolai didn't own a dog.

And she didn't have fur.

Summer crept down the footpath after the three men, careful where she placed her bare feet. Her body ached in all sorts of interesting places, but she didn't intend to miss a single bit of this adventure.

Chapter Two

The girl would drive a sane man to drink if she didn't entice him into bed first. How the hell had he ever thought her unremarkable? Jake and Louie hadn't missed a thing. It seemed he was the only one slow on the uptake. And that made this babysitting assignment a mite trickier proposition than he'd originally thought. Especially, when he had the urge to run his hands over her breasts and down her body in a little one-on-one investigation. His cock twitched in total agreement with the idea. Nikolai cast a furtive glance over his shoulder and cursed. Jake and Louie stilled.

"What?" Louie demanded in an undertone.

Nikolai sighed. "Nothing. You two go ahead. I'll handle it."

Jake glanced back, the ever-present humor turning up into a flagrant grin. "The babe?"

"Henry's niece," Nikolai gritted out. The plan was to look after the girl, not get down and dirty as his cock was so busily planning. *He was a babysitter.*

Louie smirked. "Whatever."

They slid away, blending into the darkness without another word while Nikolai went to deal with Summer Williams.

"I'm not in the SAS so I don't have to follow orders." She folded her arms across her chest, and Nikolai couldn't help but notice her spectacular curves. The girl obviously didn't pick at lettuce leaves for dinner. She'd look great decked out like a fifties movie star. But she'd look best of all naked— Whoa!

"Button up the shirt," he ordered, averting his gaze and mentally telling his body to cool it. Henry's niece was way out of his league. Too young. Too naïve. And probably a virgin to boot. "You'll catch a cold."

Her blue eyes shot fire. "I'm not in the army. I'm not part of your unit."

"Who said I'm SAS?"

"Uncle Henry."

Nikolai glided closer, right into her personal space, intimidation on his mind. He sucked in a deep breath. Mistake. Big time. Her delicate feminine scent teased him, distracted him.

Flowers.

Woman.

Bad move. The boys were right. He *was* thinking babe. He struggled with concentration, resisting the urge to shuffle like a raw recruit. Damn, his jeans were starting to feel like a suit of armor. *Think cold showers.*

"I don't think so," he muttered, contradicting her answer. Shit, if he carried on like this for much longer she'd notice his body's reaction. In a desperate act of self-preservation, Nikolai pictured the gruff, no-nonsense Henry. It didn't help. He took a hurried step back, away from temptation. "Henry wouldn't tell you stuff like that."

This time she closed the distance between them. "My brothers are SAS. I can spot a military man from a hundred feet away."

She sounded so ferocious Nikolai's curiosity was piqued. He might be SAS, but he wasn't contagious. "What's wrong with the army? Henry's military."

"Don't you mean what's right with them? They're bossy, opinionated, macho, pigheaded, think their way is the only way, shoot first and ask questions later, scare away boyfriends— Did I mention bossy? All for my own good, of course!"

Nikolai watched her impassioned face and couldn't help laughing. "Why don't you save the character assassination for your brothers? Or Henry. Remember me? The man you ran to for help." Just as well she disliked the military type. Since she'd made her opinion clear, he'd keep out of her way, apart from the promised weekly check for Henry. Yeah, he could do that. Better for both of them that way. Besides, Nikolai didn't think Henry would appreciate the thoughts that were currently running through his head. Hell, he'd flatten any guy who dared think about his niece like that—if he had one. His jaw flexed. That included Jake and Louie. *Hell, especially Jake and Louie.*

She planted her hands on her hips, dragging his reluctant gaze to her curvy body again. "The two men are gone," she stated. "I want to see the damage then go to bed. I have a busy day tomorrow."

Disappointment surged through Nikolai as quick as machine gun fire. He'd liked the look of her in his bed. The feel of her...hell! Preservation kicked in big time. The girl was young—too young—and probably hadn't even been born when he attended high school. How many times did he have to tell himself that before the facts sank into his thick head? Besides, he'd failed with Laura. He'd lost both her and their baby.

No point making the same mistake twice.

Summer was right. He was committed to his job, and that didn't leave room for anything else. Once this bum knee mended, he'd be back in the thick of the latest war brewing. "All right. We'll check out the house then leave you on your own." He took her arm and guided her down the footpath toward Henry's house.

The front door to the house stood wide open. Nikolai heard Jake and Louie murmuring in low voices near Henry's study, so he knew it was safe to take Summer inside.

Nikolai directed her to Henry's study, which had been ransacked. Books dotted the floor, ripped from shelves and tossed haphazardly in all directions. Broken glass from picture frames crunched underfoot, and a coffee table and chairs were overturned. He stopped Summer at the door. "Your feet are bare. Watch the glass. I need to know if anything is missing."

"How can I tell with this mess?"

"Thieves usually take valuables that are portable. Electrical goods. Jewelry. Money. Do the best you can. Take one room at a time."

She wandered off so he limped over to Jake and Louie, skirting the same glass he'd warned Summer about. "Point of entry?"

Jake eyed the direction in which Summer had gone. "They forced the laundry window."

Nikolai's nod was curt as he watched Jake eyeball Summer. "I doubt Henry keeps anything of military value here, but we can't dismiss it totally."

"Nothing obvious missing." Louie shrugged. "They've tossed the study and the bedrooms, but ignored the kitchen and dining room. You gonna contact Henry?"

"Nah." Ribald amusement surfaced at the idea. He could hear Henry's curses already, and none of the language sounded printable. "I know better than to interrupt a man on his honeymoon. When he gets back is soon enough."

Jake righted a chair and straddled it. "Do you want us to stay?"

The glint in his friend's eyes made Nikolai sober. Edginess took over. Nikolai straightened to his full height and faced off with his mate. The attempt at intimidation didn't wipe any of Jake's smirk away. Nikolai decided he'd ignore the whole subject and pretend he didn't know what Jake was getting at. "You might as well head off. I doubt they'll be back now."

Louie grinned, and leapt in to pick up the gauntlet. "You and the babe be okay on your own? You don't need chaperons?"

Both of his friends chortled at that one.

Nikolai bared his teeth but there was no grin involved. "Thanks for coming," he gritted out. "Appreciate the help."

The three men walked to the door together, his two friends chuckling loud enough to scrape Nikolai's feelings the wrong way. Never mind that he'd be leading the joking if it was one of them in the same position.

"How's the knee?" Jake asked.

"Better. I start physio next week."

The phone rang, and all three men froze.

"Damn funny time for the phone to ring," Louie muttered.

Nikolai headed inside at a run, ignoring the pain signals traveling from his knee. The ringing stopped.

Louie followed. "Too late. She's answered it."

"Summer!" Nikolai hollered.

Summer appeared at the end of the passage, and he saw her pallor even with the distance between them. When she saw him, she ran toward him. An instant later, he held her trembling body in his arms. "Who was it?" he asked, already suspecting the answer.

"I don't know. They said they'd be back." Summer shivered.

Nikolai tightened his hold as if he could stop the shaking by sheer willpower. "Anything else?"

"That I wouldn't have guard dogs all the time."

Nikolai waved off his hovering mates. "We'll be fine. Catch ya tomorrow."

Louie nodded, "Ring if you need us."

"I think Nikolai has things under control," Jake said deadpan.

Nikolai glared at his friend, and indicated the door with a jerk of his head. "Good night."

Summer tugged away from his touch. Her eyes were wide and blue, and they shimmered in the light. Nikolai braced for tears and the accompanying uneasiness that weeping females brought. Hell, he hated it when they cried. Laura used to excel at tears on demand. It had taken him a long time to work that out, but experience still hadn't taught him how to cope with the outpouring of feminine emotion.

"Where did they get in?" she demanded.

Nikolai did a double take. Not one tear in sight now. Instead, fury vibrated through her body, rage making her eyes glow with an inner fire. "Ah, the laundry window."

"Would you mind boarding up the window while I finish checking through the rooms?"

"No problem." Bemusement shaded his tone.

Her head dipped in a no-nonsense nod as she stepped away from him, heading for the lounge.

A flash of tanned legs drew his gaze, making him curse softly. "What happened to your legs?"

Summer slowed and glanced down at her bare legs with indifference. "I jumped out my bedroom window. Uncle Henry's rose garden is below."

Nikolai swallowed. He was trained to deal with medical emergencies out in the field, but it was different, worse somehow, when it was Summer. Angry scratches marred the creamy perfection of her lower limbs. The right leg appeared worse. The scratches went all the way up her leg, disappearing under the flimsy hem of her nightgown. Closer scrutiny showed thorns protruding from her calf. "That must hurt. Why didn't you say something?"

She lifted one shoulder in a shrug. "I'll live."

"Where does Henry keep the first-aid kit?"

"You sound like my mother," she snapped. "Stop fussing. I'll grab the kit when I've finished checking all the rooms."

Nikolai didn't know whether to laugh or groan. The lady had enough prickles to rival a rose bush as it was without borrowing from nature. "How are you going to get the thorns out by yourself?"

"I'll look in the mirror."

"Wouldn't it be easier if I did it?"

She eyed him with clear mistrust. "I am not letting you look at my butt."

This time he couldn't restrain a grin, her trepidation feeding his determination to follow through. "Seen one butt, you've seen them all."

"This is a stupid discussion." Summer took three steps into the lounge. "Let yourself out when you've finished in the laundry."

Nikolai blinked at her retreating back. It had been a long time since he'd been dismissed that way. And by a young slip of a girl. "How do you know I wasn't involved in the break-in?" he asked in a soft voice, the words bursting from him before he gave it a second thought.

She stilled then whirled about to glare at him. "That's not funny."

"You don't know me."

"Is this a lecture? A life lesson? I might come from the country, but I'm not totally stupid. Uncle Henry trusts you, and that's good enough for me." She stormed past the den.

Nikolai stalked noiselessly after her, admiring the feminine roll of hips as she strode away. His gaze drifted up to her stiff shoulders then returned to her butt. Nope. Nothing wrong that he could see.

She paused to right a stool, and as she reached for the chrome leg, Jake's shirt and the nightgown rode up. Nikolai's breath hissed out.

"Right, that does it," he snapped, tearing his gaze from her body and fixing it on her indignant face the instant she turned to glare at him. "Where's the first-aid box? Those scratches go all the way up your leg. They'll get infected if they're not treated."

Summer studied his face. She sighed, and then huffed hard enough to blow her fringe away from her eyes. "You're not going to leave without a fight, are you?"

"Nope."

Stubborn, stubborn man. "I heard Uncle Henry ask you to keep an eye on me. Are you going to be like this the whole time he's away?" Yep, determined and stubborn, Summer decided, answering her own question. "I think this is an extreme plan to see my naked butt."

She looked up in time to catch him blink, then his mouth curved up at the corners in a slow grin. Her heart sped up without warning, and her face heated enough that she needed to fan her cheeks, but she kept her hands clenched firmly at her sides. This was not the man to try out her best flirting moves on. "How old are you?"

He picked up the conversation beat without hesitation. "Thirty-one."

Good, another black mark to add to the dreaded bossy factor. He was *way* too old for her. The article in *Miranda* magazine suggested a five-year age gap was good, and she agreed. Besides, she didn't want to tie herself to one man, and the more her family interfered, the more determined she was to have fun and make up for lost time. Clear relief at his advanced age made her chirp, "I'm twenty-two."

"Is the first-aid stuff in the bathroom?"

Stuck record. Clearly, he wasn't going to back down. She sighed, "Yeah, in the bathroom cabinet. Wait there. I'll get it."

"You're going to have to lie down. Your bedroom is probably the best place."

It didn't sound the best place to her. Especially when she pictured her small single bed and the lineup of stuffed bears. Then she imagined Nikolai touching her, gazing at her rear end. She shuddered inwardly. No! And that was a big fat no. Dirty laundry covered the floor, still lying where she'd tossed it earlier. Underwear... She shook her head emphatically. "I don't think so."

"God, you're stubborn. Just like Henry," Nikolai muttered right behind her. "No more arguing or I'll paddle your butt."

Summer spun about and fluttered her lashes at him. Right, that did it. She'd scare him off with underhand tactics. "Oh, kinky. Sounds like fun."

They stared at each other.

Nikolai cleared his throat loudly. "I'd be gentle with you."

A shiver rippled through her body and it had absolutely nothing to do with the temperature in the dimly lit passage outside her bedroom. "Yeah, but would you respect me in the morning?"

He froze then chuckled. "I thought we'd established that I'm too old for you to hone your skills on."

Summer forced herself to move. What the heck was wrong with her? She wasn't usually like this. "We discussed it, but I wasn't aware we'd come to an agreement." Oops, what had happened to the naïve country girl from Eketahuna? And the decision that he was too old for her?

Nikolai brushed past her, heading for the bathroom. She heard the bang of a cupboard as it closed, the slide of the medicine cabinet then the slow, careful footsteps as he limped back. Her insides clenched in anticipation.

"This your room?"

She nodded, eyeing him warily. This whole situation was way out of control. She wasn't going to let him look at her butt, was she?

He shouldered the door open. "On the bed."

An order. Summer remained at the doorway to her bedroom. The room was a lot smaller than she remembered and a lot messier, too. Her gaze darted to the filmy underwear that littered the floor. The piles of bright, in-your-face colors lying on top of the green carpet looked like flowers in a meadow. Not one pair of plain white granny pants in sight. Summer tried to take comfort from that fact.

"I wonder what they were looking for," she said. Conversation. That's what she needed—something to distract both of them. "Do you think they were after goods to sell, because I haven't found anything missing yet? And 'they'll be back' sounds like a line from a second-rate movie."

Nikolai stepped over a turquoise-colored bra with barely a pause. "Don't try to change the subject. On the bed."

The fixed expression and unyielding jaw told her it was useless to argue, while her innate common sense suggested she close her eyes and think of…England.

While she hesitated, Nikolai straightened the covers then gestured impatiently. Summer hesitated by the edge of the bed. He quirked a brow, and she huffed out a put-upon sigh. She stretched out, face down on the bed. Silence filled the room, and Summer's senses jump-started into hyper-drive. The groan of the first-aid box snapped like rifle fire when Nikolai opened it, the rustle of plasters and bandages, the return volley. The mattress depressed on one side as he sat beside her. Heat gathered in her face. He was staring at her butt. She knew it.

The silk of her nightgown rustled as he lifted it. Cool air brushed across the tops of her thighs.

"Hell, Summer. Why didn't you say something earlier? That must hurt."

He was looking at her legs. Fingers curled into the duvet cover while she bit back a moan. Beneath the silk fabric of the nightgown bodice, her nipples tightened while a gush of liquid warmth between her legs made her heart stutter in distinct alarm.

His fingers traced over her left calf then up her thigh. The warmth in her face sprinted downward and spread until her body burned with an unrelenting heat. Summer squirmed inwardly. Thank goodness, he couldn't see her face, or he'd know how turned-on she was, how much she wanted to explore his body and get down and dirty with him. Despite her virginal state, she was learning she lacked nothing in the imagination department.

"Can you hurry the process?" She wasn't particularly proud of the begging tone, but desperation left little room for dignity.

She heard him rummaging through the first-aid kit again. A metallic clink sounded.

"This is going to hurt," he warned.

Not half as much as her pride. His fingers skimmed over her thighs again. She shivered. Please let him hurry. She didn't think she could take too much of this torture. Actually, the pain wasn't too bad. At least it helped her concentrate on something other than Nikolai's touch.

"There. All done." The tweezers clattered against the kit as he put them down. "A little antiseptic and you'll be fine. I'll check the scratches for infection tomorrow."

"I don't think so," she muttered. "One free look at my butt is all you get." She turned over and sat up, tugging the silk nightgown down as far as it would go and resisted the urge to look at him. He had the gall to laugh—a low, sexy laugh that sucked at her insides.

"Will you be all right sleeping in here for the rest of the night, or do you want to sleep at my house in case they decide to come back?"

Her gaze shot to his then. Exactly what was he offering? Pressure in her lungs reminded her to breathe. "I'll sleep here." The flexing of his jaw indicated he intended to argue the point. "You gave me an option and I've answered. I'll be fine here. Despite the phone call, I doubt they'll return tonight."

He hesitated, and Summer decided it was time to assert herself before he started pushing her around. "I'll lock the windows and doors."

"I'll stay here tonight," he said as though she hadn't said a word.

"In my bed?" To her immense frustration, her sentence ended on a squeak.

Nikolai glanced at the bed then back at her. His lips kicked up in a faint smile. "Does it look as though we'd both fit in that sorry excuse for a bed?"

Irritation made her snap, "There's no need for sarcasm."

"I'll sleep in Henry's room."

"Fine. You're going to do what you want no matter what I say." She stalked to her bedroom door and arched her brows in a silent order for him to leave. When he made no effort to leave, she spelled it out bluntly. "Good night."

The instant he cleared the doorway, she slammed her bedroom door shut. Summer heard a chuckle before his slow, uneven retreat. Good. He's gone.

As she picked up a hairbrush and a tube of lipstick, Summer shoved Nikolai from her mind. Or tried to. Everywhere she looked, she was reminded of him. The first-aid kit still sat open on her bed. Used pieces of cotton wool and a tube of antiseptic ointment were in plain sight, the impression his body had made on her bedspread jolted her back in time. Lord, she could even smell the spicy scent of the soap he used.

Summer stomped around her bed and picked up a discarded drawer. She scooped up piles of silky lingerie and dumped them inside. She gathered a pile of books that the intruders had tossed on the floor, along with the ring binder that contained her study notes. When the room looked slightly more habitable, she decided to go to sleep. She crawled under the covers and flicked off the bedside lamp. Ten minutes later, she was still wide-awake. Summer reached over and turned her lamp back on. She'd read. That's what she'd do.

She fished inside the straw basket by her bed until she found a parcel wrapped in brown paper amongst the rest of the junk. Ripping the package open, she smiled and turned the first book over. Her smile faded. She pulled the second book from the parcel and looked at the title. Then the third.

This wasn't her package.

These weren't her books.

A frustrated scream lodged in her throat, but she bit down on her tongue and glared at a book on fly-fishing. She would have let the screech loose if it wasn't for the fact that the smallest peep would bring Nikolai storming in.

A card fluttered free from one of the books. It read, *Special order for Alistair Martin.*

So much for the reading idea.

Summer groaned. She hoped Alistair Martin appreciated her hot romances from Ellora's Cave. Meanwhile, she'd have to think up some other way of wiping Nikolai Tarei out of her mind.

Chapter Three

Nikolai haunted her thoughts all day just as he'd inhabited her Technicolor dreams. The naked visual of him she'd stored in her brain combined with all the sexual how-to articles she'd read produced a truly stunning fantasy.

Two people slow dancing, their arms wrapped around each other. She and the big, bad SAS man. Slowly undressing. Letting clothing fall to the ground while they continued to move to the music, rubbing against each other, pausing to slide lips across each newly bared body part. Summer's breasts tingled as Nikolai slid his mouth across the upper slopes and curves then tugged at a straining nipple through the silky fabric of her lemon-colored bra. He pulled away, leaving a circle of wet fabric.

"Do you like that?" he'd asked.

Summer considered. "I'm not sure. You'd better do it again."

Nikolai laughed softly, his dark eyes gleaming. "We can't have that. A girl should have an opinion about something this important." And he'd bent his dark head again, sucking the tip of her other fabric-covered nipple into his mouth.

A sensation of heat engulfed her whole body. Summer gripped Nikolai's shoulder. "I need... It might be better if I took this off. I wouldn't want you to get fluff-balls."

Two dark brows shot upward toward his hairline as he released her nipple to stare up at her. "Fluff-balls?"

"You know, like fur-balls in cats."

"You know, I think you're right." His hand went behind her back, and with one casual flick, her bra fell open. "And while we're at it, maybe we should get comfortable. How does the bed sound? We can try the kitchen table next time."

Next time. Was he teasing? Summer tipped her head back to study his face, her pulse kicking up a notch at the sensual promise in his slumberous eyes, his smiling lips.

The rest of their clothes dissolved and suddenly cool cotton sheets were at her back, and Nikolai leaned over her, his tanned fingers exploring her breasts. Summer stirred restlessly, her breasts aching for his touch. When he finally got around to touching her nipples, he pinched them hard. The corresponding jolt between her legs made Summer cry out.

"I'm going to make you so hot for me you'll beg," he whispered against her belly. "I'm going to make you wet and hungry. Your pussy is going to cry for my possession." Nikolai kissed her quivering belly, and used his tongue to trace around her belly button. "I'm going to lap at your juices and tease your clit like this." His tongue darted inside her navel then he licked around the rim. His demonstration hiked her heart rate. Excitement and anticipation warred as his hands alternatively soothed and plucked at her breasts, and his mouth explored her belly button. Between her legs ached. She stirred restlessly, writhing and squirming as her hips lifted. Liquid honey flowed from her cleft. Her breath caught as Nikolai moved lower, his hot breath stirring the short hair on her mound. His tongue traced around the heart-shaped thatch, leaving a gleaming wet path in his wake.

Summer's legs splayed, and she lifted her hips shamelessly, silently begging for him to touch her intimately. She felt so wet. So needy.

Nikolai parted her legs even further, baring her to his eyes.

"You're so wet for me," he whispered. His breath washed against her swollen clit. He blew against the tiny nub, and an intense shiver racked her body. "But you haven't begged me yet. Ask, Summer. Ask me to give you pleasure. Tell me what you'd like. My mouth. My cock." Nikolai looked up at her then, their gazes colliding. His dark eyes compelling, dominant and so heavy with heat and promise that another shudder swept her body. "Tell me you want me," he whispered.

"Please, Nikolai. Nikolai, I need you inside me. Please ease the sweet ache. Nikolai. Please."

She'd woken tingling, shuddering and so hot that a slow, cruising finger across her engorged clitoris had thrown her headlong into a toe-tingling orgasm. Now she craved the real thing, with a real Nikolai instead of a dream figure.

Oh, yeah. Summer flapped her hand in front of her hot face and shoved a returned library book from her trolley on the shelf. But she refused to replace her well-meaning family with a bossy boyfriend. She sighed. Perhaps she'd better buy that magazine she'd seen with the article about sex toys. Then she could make an informed choice in the adult shop she'd seen in Papakura. Sex toys were obviously the way to go until she met a worthy man, one that wouldn't boss her around and lay down the law.

"Wake up, Summer," the head librarian snapped, appearing out of thin air from behind the animal husbandry section. "You've shelved that book in the wrong place." The thin, dark-haired woman plucked the book from the section on agriculture and thrust it at Summer. "Find its correct home then you may leave. I trust you'll pay more attention tomorrow."

"Sorry, Mrs. Ferguson," Summer murmured. Something else to blame on the big, bad SAS man. She shoved the book on the science shelf and stomped off to grab her orange straw basket and car keys.

She hoped this Alistair Martin was home because she wanted her books. Needed them. It was enough to drive a girl to write her own romances. In fact, she'd started composing chapter one in her head last night. The idea would have worked if the hero hadn't turned into the image of Nikolai. Her character had appeared with a distinctive bossy streak along with a hot body. Suffice to say, her sleep had been restless.

Summer fired up her rattle-trap car and backed from the parking space. She needed her hot and steamy romances. Fly-fishing just didn't do it for her. She drove down Queen Street, heading for Parnell.

"Number fifty-five, fifty-seven... A restaurant? That can't be right." Summer glanced at the card again. Definitely fifty-nine. A vacant car park decided the situation. She zipped into the parking space then scooped up the books and climbed from her car.

The restaurant was beautiful. Classy. At least to the eyes of a girl from small town Eketahuna. Her heels clicked over the mocha-colored tiles and intricate mosaic insets until she stood in a small reception area. Over to her left, there was a bar area with plush chocolate carpets and built-in leather seating. Two couples sat in a booth, drinks in front of them, while four businessmen stood at the bar.

A stylish woman appeared in front of Summer. "Hello. Table for one?"

"Yes, please." Summer decided a drink was a good idea.

She followed the woman to a table in an outside courtyard. Cacti and succulents in ceramic planters were arranged around the cobbled patio. Red and green umbrellas provided shade while music with a decidedly Spanish feel gave an exotic ambience. Summer half expected a man in a swirling black cape with a rose clamped between his teeth to appear at any moment.

The woman seated Summer then produced a menu. "Your waitress will be with you in a moment."

"Thanks. Actually, you might be able to help. I'm looking for a man—" Summer paused at the expression on the woman's face, then laughed. "That didn't quite come out the way I meant. I mean I'm looking for a particular man. Alistair Martin. I don't suppose you know where I could find him? I wasn't expecting a restaurant at this number."

The frown on the woman's brow cleared. "You mean Dare. You're in luck. He's in the office at the moment. Can I tell him your name?"

"Summer Williams."

"I'll let Dare know you're here."

A waitress took her order and reappeared with a plate of bread and dips along with Summer's orange juice. While she waited for the man to appear, Summer amused herself people watching. A group of university students over to her right had read the same article on flirting she had. A blonde girl flicked her hair over her shoulder and smoothed the nonexistent wrinkles in her tight-fitting red top. Summer drew in a breath, enlightenment making her grin widen—lots of meaningful eye contact and mutual smiling happening there. So, that's what the article meant by body preening.

"Miss Williams?"

Summer started and spun about. The man bore an amused yet quizzical expression on his handsome face. "Oops, caught me eavesdropping," she said with a laugh. "Call me Summer."

Of course, she would look a fool in front of an eligible man. At least she hoped he was eligible because he pushed more than one of her hot buttons—an excellent distraction from the big, bad SAS man. Her gaze darted down his suit-clad body to his left hand.

No ring.

Her breath eased out. The lack of ring didn't mean he was free of feminine entanglements, but it was a step in the correct direction.

His teeth flashed a dazzling white as he grinned, "I'm Dare Martin. May I join you?" He indicated the empty chair at her table.

"Of course." Summer's hands rose to touch her cheeks. "You weren't meant to catch me doing something so uncouth. It's put me at a distinct disadvantage."

Dare laughed again, his gray eyes twinkling. "It's refreshingly honest. I believe you wanted to see me. I hope you're not after a job because I leave all the hiring to my manager."

"Oh, no. Nothing like that," Summer said. "I think I have something that belongs to you." She bent to hunt through her basket, pulled out the brown paper bag containing Dare's books and passed it to him. "I hope you have my books. It was a huge disappointment last night when I found I had the wrong parcel. I don't know how it happened."

Dare glanced inside the bag then looked up at her, a pleased expression on his face. "I think I could kiss you," he said.

Summer's gaze traveled to his lips. He didn't mean that, did he? Because she quite liked the idea.

"I rang the bookshop this morning, but they were adamant they gave me the right books." He signaled a passing waiter and ordered a drink. "Would you like another drink?"

Summer nodded. "Thanks. I suppose it was rather a shock to get a parcel of romances when you expected fishing books."

"You could say that. Look, I really appreciate you taking the trouble to deliver my books in person. I'm afraid your books are at my home, and I'm busy tonight. How about if I deliver them to you tomorrow?"

Another night without a decent book. Summer suppressed a sigh. She'd have to think up another activity to put Nikolai out of her mind, even if that meant cleaning the oven.

"I don't suppose you're free tomorrow afternoon?" he asked, breaking into her thoughts. "I'd like to buy you lunch to repay your kindness."

That should do the trick, Summer thought, and help push that Nikolai right out of her mind. "You don't need to do that."

"Of course I don't." His gray eyes flittered across her lips then rose to meet her eyes. "But I'd like to. How does midday sound? Actually, you'd be doing me a favor. I want to scope out a competitor, and I won't stick out nearly as much if I have a dining companion."

"You know how to turn a girl's head," Summer said dryly. Her stomach tingled pleasantly as his gaze drifted across her face again. It felt as though he was touching her, kissing her lips.

Dare burst into delighted laughter. "What I meant to say was that your beauty will dazzle the waiters, and they'll be too mesmerized to pay any attention to me while I'm in spy mode."

"Smooth." Summer flicked her French braid over her shoulder and grinned. Oh, this flirting thing was fun. "Very smooth. I'd love to have lunch with you. Where are we going?" Under the table, she crossed the fingers on her left hand tightly, hoping he'd name a smart restaurant, somewhere to show off the brand-new outfit she'd purchased during her lunch hour today.

"There's a new restaurant opening on the banks of the Waikato River, toward Hamilton. Where do you live?"

Yes! She just hoped there wasn't too much silverware to bamboozle her. She'd better check the etiquette books tomorrow and brush up. "Not the Liberty Jones restaurant?"

"The very same."

Perhaps she should see if she could book in a hair appointment, too. "I live in Bottle Top Bay, near Papakura, so it's on the way. Number twenty. It's a big white house."

His gaze did a final cruise across her face before he checked his watch. "I really do have to go, but I'll be counting the minutes until tomorrow." He rose and moved around the table until he stood by her chair. Dare picked up her hand.

Summer met his gaze and felt trapped like a butterfly in a web. She couldn't have looked away if she wanted to. Her stomach churned in excited anticipation, much like the time she'd sat in the front car of the roller coaster waiting for the ride to start.

Dare sobered, a flash of something indefinable flickering across his face before he bent to press his lips against the back of her hand. A quiver shot down her arm, and she bit back a sigh. Talk about romantic.

"Until tomorrow," he murmured.

Summer nodded dumbly. "Tomorrow."

He released her hand slowly, and with apparent unwillingness.

"You won't forget my books, will you?" Summer blurted. *Oh, boy.* Part of her wished he'd leave before she made a big fool of herself and he rescinded his invitation. The other part wanted him to stay right where he was so she could practice her flirting.

Dare released her hand. "I won't forget, but you won't have much time for reading. I'm going to keep you very busy." He smiled then strode off without looking back.

Once he'd left, Summer gave up trying to look cool and poised, and energetically fanned her face with the menu pinched off the next table. She stared at the doorway where Dare had disappeared and grinned. "Fancy that. No time for reading." She fanned her face with renewed vigor. "Be still my heart."

* * * * *

The last week had flown. Summer parked her car in Uncle Henry's driveway and leaned over to grab a pile of shopping bags. Today, during her lunch hour, she had made another serious dent in her savings account.

"Making up for lost time," she sang, doing a little shimmy as she exited the car. When she slammed the car door shut, one of the bags slithered to the concrete footpath. "Bother."

"Let me," a husky voice said from behind her.

Nikolai. Summer froze for an instant, knowing he'd come to check up on her. Resentment flared, but she tamped it down. Nikolai had waved whenever he'd seen her, but he'd kept his distance. Perhaps she shouldn't prejudge him today since he didn't appear to be taking the babysitting gig too seriously.

"Thanks." Summer indicated the bulging bags she held with a jerk of her head. "I've been shopping."

"What have you done to your hair?"

Summer juggled her shopping parcels so she could turn to look at him. Holy cow. One look at his face and her instincts screamed danger. She swallowed but refused to look away. "I had it cut."

"I can see that." Nikolai sauntered closer and picked up a lock of her hair between two fingers. He fingered the curl with care. "It's blue."

"Yeah." Summer found she had to swallow again. "It goes with my eyes."

Shelley Munro

Their gazes met and held. Summer felt the leap of her pulse and knew she had to do something before she melted at his feet.

"You're just the babysitter, not my father." Not that Summer ever in a million years imagined a parent who looked like Nikolai.

His mouth twisted. He let go her hair and stepped back. "I feel old enough to be your father."

Summer let that one go, while she silently reminded herself she was interested in Dare. Nothing about Nikolai attracted her in the slightest. "Did you want something? I have a date, and I'm running late." She glanced at the oversized watch on her wrist. "Very late."

Nikolai stepped back again, putting even more distance between them. His face had frozen, wiped of every emotion. Summer had no idea what he was thinking and suddenly she wanted to know.

"Just checking to see you haven't had any problems since the other night. Don't let me keep you."

"No problems. Not one." Summer crossed the fingers of one hand behind her back to negate the small fib. No problems that was, except the phone caller who specialized in heavy breathing. If she told Nikolai, he'd take over, and she would lose what little freedom she had. She heard the sound of a car approaching and whirled about with dismay. "Bother. That's Dare now."

"Go and do whatever you need to do. I'll tell the boyfriend you're running late."

"Thanks." Summer sprinted for the door, then came to a sudden halt and spun to glare at him. "You're not going to interrogate him." Her brows drew together in warning. "Are you?"

"I don't have to stay. I have things to do."

Now she'd offended him. "Sorry. I— Never mind. Thank you. I'd appreciate you staying. Tell Dare I'll be ready in fifteen minutes."

Nikolai watched her race through the front door, not even stopping to unlock the door because she hadn't locked it when she left this morning. A snort escaped. Naïve. Innocent. He shook his head as he caught a flash of blue right before she disappeared from sight. And this time a smile tugged at his lips.

Blue hair.

She was right about one thing—it did match her eyes.

Behind him, the car pulled up. Nikolai leaned against the fender of Summer's battered Mazda and watched a man climb from the late-model BMW.

He hated the man on sight.

Dare was a city man, slick and well-groomed in his fancy duds—a suit no less, even in the humid summer weather. Nikolai glanced down at his worn jeans and paint-splattered T-shirt then shrugged inwardly. Why the hell was he comparing himself with the bantam rooster? His job was to keep an eye on Summer.

That was all.

He pushed away from the car, stood to his full height and held out his hand. "You Summer's date?"

The man nodded but didn't accept the hand Nikolai held out.

"Nikolai Tarei," Nikolai said. "Summer's running late. She'll be out in ten minutes." His brows rose fractionally when the man continued to stare at his outstretched hand. Yeah, it was covered with paint, but that was because he'd been painting.

Finally, when Nikolai was ready to give up and drop his hand to his side, the other man smiled, accepting the handshake. "Thanks. I'm a bit early. I'm Dare Martin."

The man's hand felt soft and pampered when it touched his, and Nikolai wondered what Summer saw in him. He was pretty enough. Had a few bucks in his back pocket, too, if the car was any indication. But Nikolai knew Henry wouldn't approve. And from what Summer had mentioned about her two brothers, he guessed they might have a few problems with her date, too.

"You related to Summer?"

Nikolai retreated to lean against the car again. He folded his arms across his chest and looked the man right in the eye. "No."

"Hi, Dare! Sorry I'm so late. The meeting went late after work and then I had to deliver your package for you. The traffic at Spaghetti Junction was at a crawl." The nasty glare Summer sent him as she hurried past let him know she'd overheard. She sauntered right up to Dare, placed her hands on Martin's shoulders, and stretched up to plant a kiss on the man's lips. Oh, yeah. She'd heard all right, and was making her disapproval clear.

Martin's hands curled around Summer's waist with a possessiveness that Nikolai would need to be blind to miss. A roaring protest filled his mind, screeching for release. Nikolai's hands dropped to his side and fisted.

Son of a bitch.

He did a double take. His eyes narrowed while shock punched him in the gut. What the hell was the girl wearing? He eyed the long expanse of tanned leg beneath the short hem of the tight black skirt, the strappy heels on her feet. Then his gaze lifted and paused to savor the two inches of creamy skin at her waist before he hit cloth again. What had happened to the baggy sack thing?

When Summer turned to face him, his mouth emptied of every trace of spit. Her black top was sheer and lacy. And low. His gaze fastened on the swell of luscious curves before he had time to veto the move. She might be nine years younger than him, but she was fully grown. Not a shred of doubt there. Nikolai swallowed and forced his gaze northward to meet the challenge in her blue eyes.

"Ready to go, sweetheart?" Martin said.

Summer turned to Martin and nodded. She allowed the man to place his arm around her waist, his fingers to skim over her bare flesh. The hair at the back of Nikolai's neck prickled until he felt like a Doberman guarding its territory. He wanted to rip Summer from Martin's arms then attack. Summer was his and he —

Whoa!

Nikolai's thoughts screeched to an appalled halt. Where the hell had that come from? He was useless at male/female interaction. Laura had told him often enough. Every time Laura had needed him, he'd managed to let her down, usually because of his work, which was why he was keeping away from relationship stuff. Nikolai shook his head to clear a sluggish brain that pounded with regrets at past mistakes. He'd told Henry this assignment was a bad idea.

Martin escorted Summer to the passenger side of his black BMW and helped her inside before closing the door. From where he stood, Nikolai got a free showing of smooth thighs and fire-engine red panties. He'd be willing to bet Martin got the same show.

Martin offered a curt nod in Nikolai's direction before rounding the bonnet of the BMW and climbing into the driver's seat.

Nikolai scanned the registration plate and committed the number to memory. He wanted to tell Summer not to be late home, but dumped the thought before he uttered it. That might be taking his duties a little too seriously. The blue sedan he'd seen driving up and down the road might belong to one of the neighbors or a visitor. It was probably nothing to worry about.

Nikolai watched Summer grin at the clotheshorse, felt the instantaneous tightening of his gut. The man looked back all right, but his eyes didn't smile with genuine emotion, and his expression didn't quite match his curving mouth.

Instinct kicked in, making Nikolai tense. Something wasn't right. He wrenched his gaze from the man's hand pawing Summer and concentrated on Martin's gray suit. A growl built at the back of his throat.

Hell, who was he trying to fool?

It was good, old-fashioned jealousy at its most simplistic. Ever since he'd seen her in that silky nightgown, his thoughts had veered from the right and proper. No matter how many cold showers he took, the memory stubbornly remained. Perhaps he needed a night on the town with Jake and Louie—along with some feminine company. He obviously needed to get laid.

The low rumble of the motor jerked him from his reverie. Forcing a grin, he lifted his right hand in a wave. The clotheshorse reversed his car and took off in a spray of gravel. Summer never looked back.

Nikolai's smile faded the minute the BMW disappeared from sight. He shoved away from the Mazda and limped up the path to his house. Time for a few phone calls—a little private investigation. He didn't have to take action, but at least he'd get rid of the edgy sensation that kept the back of his neck itching.

He'd promised to look after Summer, and he'd be failing if he did anything less.

* * * * *

Nikolai paced the length of his moonlit kitchen and peered out the window for what seemed like the hundredth time. He checked his watch. The hands glowed in the dark and told him the bloody thing was still working as five minutes had elapsed since the last time he'd looked.

Summer wasn't home. It was after midnight, closer to one. What the hell kind of time was this for a date to go to? Surely, she'd be home soon?

Nikolai hobbled another circuit of his kitchen before freezing like a panther scenting prey. What if she wasn't coming home? What if she was spending the night with the clotheshorse?

He cursed low with feeling. He'd told Henry this babysitting lark was a big mistake. Just as he'd decided he'd have to start looking for Summer, he heard a car pull up.

About bloody time.

He strode to the window to peer out between the slats of the blinds. The BMW idled in front of Henry's. From his vantage point, he saw two silhouettes merge into one. Instant fury lashed his body. His hands fisted, and he took two steps toward his front door before he realized confrontation, especially in his state, was the last thing he needed. Look how Summer had reacted earlier when the clotheshorse had come to pick her up. She'd kissed the man because she'd overheard him talking to Martin, or rather, not talking to Martin.

Nope, he needed to approach this situation with clandestine stealth, especially since he'd started to investigate Martin. Nikolai glared at the single silhouette. God, how long could one kiss take? His hands gripped the windowsill. They'd need to come up for air soon.

He snapped his eyes shut, blocking the sight. If he played the voyeur much longer, he'd be out there dragging Summer from the car. And that would be a monumental stuff-up. Nikolai counted to ten, dredging deep for control and deeper again for patience. Catch-22. Damned if he did and damned if he didn't. His eyes opened again. Ah, that was better. He loosened his grip on the windowsill and flexed his hands.

The car interior light was on and the passenger door open. Summer slipped from the car. Nikolai's heart thudded anxiously. Was Martin going to stay at Henry's tonight?

The car started, and Nikolai released the breath he didn't realize he'd been holding. Every instinct inside screamed at him to go to her, but he didn't.

She was safe.

It was best he keep his distance, or else they'd really be in trouble.

Chapter Four

Summer hummed softly as she padded about the kitchen. She plugged in the coffeemaker, and then poured a round of batter in a hot frying pan. The melted butter sizzled as the batter hit the pan, and the scent of freshly ground beans filled the air as the coffee started to drip into the carafe.

A thump on the front door made her frown.

"Come in," she called. When the small bubbles in the batter started to pop, she deftly flipped the pancake to cook the other side.

"The front door wasn't locked."

Summer grimaced. Nikolai, of course. She knew that voice without looking. "And a good morning to you too."

"The front door wasn't locked," his voice rose to a dull roar.

Summer sighed, removed the pan from the heat and turned to face his wrath. "I heard you the first time."

"This isn't Eketahuna."

Summer looked out the kitchen window at the gulls flying lazily over the estuary. "It's not exactly crime central either."

"You had a break-in the other night. God." He dragged a hand through his hair, negating his prior use of a comb.

Loose hair, she noted with interest. He looked...sexy and very jumpable with that just-out-of-bed look and the dark stubble shading his jaw.

"Are you listening to me?"

Oops. He was starting to sound like her brothers. Best she pay attention. "Sure, I'm listening. The door wasn't unlocked all night. I've been out for a walk this morning." She picked up a plate and slid the pancake from the pan. "It's a lovely day out there. Want breakfast?"

"Stop changing the subject."

Okay, so he was a bit smarter than her brothers, but that didn't mean he could boss her around. "Nikolai, I realize you're merely watching out for me, but you don't have to guard me 24/7. I'm not stupid. The door was locked while I was out last night. The door was locked overnight. Subject closed. Would you like some breakfast?"

He frowned then nodded. "Is that coffee I smell?"

"Sure is. Help yourself while I finish cooking the pancakes. Do you know where the cups are?"

"Yeah."

Summer turned back to the stove. Funny, since his arrival, every single bit of calmness had been replaced by an edgy awareness. Her heart pounded, her mouth felt as dry as unconditioned hair and she was jumpy. The interesting thing was that the sensation was quite different to what she felt when she was with Dare. She sneaked a glance over her shoulder, took a second to admire his jean-encased butt, then flipped her pancake. What was it about this man that made her thoughts turn to sex?

She knew without even thinking that becoming more closely involved with Nikolai was a mistake. He'd want to rule her life. She'd be escaping one prison for another.

"Do you want coffee too?"

He spoke from right behind her and she jerked. The man moved like a cat and crept up on a girl without warning. She sucked in a deep breath to help resettle her heart then looked at him. "Please. White, no sugar."

Summer turned her attention back to cooking the pancakes. Pour, cook, flip. Simple, except if your hands shook. The bubbles popped, and she flipped a little too vigorously. The pancake landed half in the pan and half on the element.

"Damn." She tried to retrieve the pancake without mangling it too much.

"Can I help?"

Summer whirled about and nailed him with a glare. "Quit sneaking up on me. You're not out on maneuvers now." She used her spatula to point at a wooden chair. "Sit."

"Yes, ma'am."

Her eyes narrowed as she studied his face. "Stop that. What are you doing here anyway? I thought all you needed was a visual."

The man squirmed—he actually wriggled about uneasily and refused to meet her gaze. Her antenna shot to high alert.

"What?" Summer tapped her right foot while she waited for an answer.

A trace of red appeared high on his cheekbones. Summer would have bet his ears had turned red as well, but since his hair covered them, she couldn't confirm. He rolled his shoulders in a nonchalant shrug. His attempt at casual didn't fool her.

She advanced on him, waving her spatula like a weapon. "What have you done?"

His broad chest lifted when he dragged in air and momentarily distracted her. She mined her imagination for ideas on what he'd look like without the body-fitting T-shirt, then when she felt the lick of heat through her body, she called up something cold. Icy cold to cool the latent heat that shot to her pussy. She really needed to check out some toys since she refused to jump into bed with just anyone to soothe a healthy sex drive. Well, at least, she thought she was normal. With two guard-dog brothers, a sex life was downright difficult.

"I called in a few favors to get the clothes—ah, Martin investigated."

"You did what?" The end of her sentence came out as a shriek, but she was too incensed to care. "Why?" She waved the spatula in front of his nose and missed by a whisker.

Nikolai erupted from his chair, grabbed her upper arms and wrestled the spatula from her grip. Summer kicked him in the shins. Hard.

The next minute, she was plastered against his chest with both of them breathing hard. Her breasts squashed against the hard planes of his chest, and the slumbering inferno inside Summer roared into life again. Her nipples peaked against her silky shirt. The physical reaction made her furious. She fought for freedom, squirming and wriggling until she was gasping for breath.

"Let go of me." The brute. How dare he manhandle her? How dare he interfere in her private life? Her love life was none of his business.

He settled the dispute by yanking her even closer so she felt *every* muscle in his body, all the way down. Some of the muscles appeared to grow. She froze and mortified color heated her cheeks. She would not look down. *She would not look down.*

Summer looked down. His cock bulged in his jeans, showing she wasn't the only one with a sexual appetite. A gasp escaped, and the fiery heat in her face escalated.

Nikolai chuckled—a smug masculine sound. "Yeah. Now, if I let you go, are you going to behave yourself?"

Summer gave a clipped nod, and Nikolai loosened his hold. She promptly balled her hand into a fist and plowed it into his stomach. The air exploded from his lungs with a satisfying hiss.

"That's for being nosy," she snapped.

An instant later, she was plastered against his body again. His lips moved and she realized he was speaking. Summer tried to hold onto her righteous anger, tried to concentrate, but she had trouble ripping her gaze from his beautiful lips. *Go figure,* she thought hazily. Who'd have thought she'd find his lips so interesting, especially since they mostly growled at her.

"Are you listening to me?"

Her head wobbled with the force of his shake. "It's a little difficult when I can't breathe. I'm starting to feel light-headed."

It was his proximity causing that all right! His cock dug into her belly. Gave a girl all sorts of interesting ideas. She traced his lips with her gaze. Would they feel soft? Hard? Or somewhere in between? Did she dare kiss him? All in the name of research, of course!

Summer stretched up on tiptoe even as she formulated the thought and pressed her lips to his. He froze, and she laughed inside, delighting in his reaction.

Flummoxed.

She'd managed to surprise the big, bad SAS man.

Her arms crept up behind his head, her fingers running through the long, silky strands of his hair. He groaned, drew her closer and took over the kiss. Which was a good thing since she'd reached the upper limits of her experience.

Summer pressed closer and felt the steady thud-thud of his heart. His hands smoothed their way from her upper arms to cup her face. Summer realized she was no longer held captive, that she remained plastered against his body of her own volition.

His tongue flicked across the seam of her lips, traced her bottom lip and then her top. Corny though it was, Summer saw fireworks explode behind her closed eyes. Bright flashes of orange and blue, electric yellow and fiery red burst inside her mind.

"Open your mouth," he murmured, his voice low and husky.

Oh, yeah, Summer thought. *That's what* Miranda *magazine had recommended.* She surrendered to the suggestion and tasted the vanilla spice of her favorite coffee along with the heady taste of Nikolai. His tongue delved into her mouth, thrusting and parrying then retreating.

Summer trembled. Lordy. *Miranda* knew what they were talking about. This was absolutely the best part...so far. She tried to recall the next step, but it was too difficult to concentrate. Going with the flow seemed much easier.

Nikolai froze when Summer gave a soft moan, and he came to earth with a bump. Hell, he had his tongue down her throat. How the hell had that happened? He eased back on the kiss, but wasn't able to stop himself having another quick taste of her top lip. Man, she tasted good. She felt good too—soft in all the right places. No bony hips on this girl. Just lots of luscious curves…

He dived in for one last kiss before he eased away with real regret. His gaze went to her lips. They were red and glistened from his kisses. For a moment, he was tempted to let go of all good sense and kiss her again, then guilt let rip with a swift kick to his conscience. *Get a visual*, Henry had said. So what did he do? He went one better and copped a feel.

Man.

Age wasn't just slowing down his body. It was doing something nasty to his brain as well.

He plastered his hands firmly to his sides. "I…ah…"

Summer sauntered over to the stove. As he watched the sway of her hips, he tried to untangle the knots in his tongue.

Apologize.

Promise her it wouldn't happen again.

She turned and beamed at him. The knots in his tongue turned on themselves, creating double knots. In the end, he gave up, and watched her instead. He'd never been one for talking anyhow. He was more the action type.

"You ready for the pancakes?"

"Yeah. Thanks." Did that mean she'd forgotten about his nosing around in the clotheshorse's background? Nikolai studied her carefully. Her mouth wore a soft, sexy smile but when their gazes collided, he noted a steely hardness in her blue eyes.

The same look he'd seen in his own mirror when he was about to embark on a mission—determination and the grit necessary to get the job done. Nikolai looked away. He wasn't going to bring up Martin first. He'd wait for Summer to bring up the subject.

Nikolai stepped over to the sturdy wooden table at the far end of the kitchen and sat on the closest chair, glad to take the weight off his knee. He picked his coffee mug up. Part of him noticed that the table bore a cloth these days. One of Veronica's little touches, along with pots of herbs on the windowsills. Henry's life was in for more changes, but somehow Nikolai didn't think he'd worry too much. He'd never seen a man so smitten.

Summer pulled a heaped plate of pancakes from the oven.

"Do you want me to set the table?" he asked.

"No, stay where you are."

She was pure feline grace as she walked toward him. A groan built at the back of his throat, his hands tightened around the coffee mug. Man, he was toast if Henry found out about him sticking his tongue down Summer's throat. And perish the thought if he ever found out about his latest fantasies.

The plate of pancakes dropped lightly to the table, then another platter of crispy bacon. Summer turned away and headed for the pantry. Her hips swayed in a pert wiggle that made him desperate to explore those curves in far greater detail. She returned with a jar of maple syrup in her hands and caught him in the act. Instead of acting flustered, or shy or embarrassed, she winked. *Winked, by God.* His brain changed from park to drive in two seconds flat, and Nikolai half rose from his chair. Then a second later, he hit reverse with a loud shriek of brakes. He dropped back to the padded cushion on the wooden chair with a soft thud. Something akin to shock ricocheted through the rational part of his mind.

Summer was nine years younger than him—still a babe in terms of experience. He had no business kissing her, no business lusting after her. He'd stuffed up every relationship in his life so far, from the parental one to Laura. Hell, even his latest mission. It was best if he didn't leave the starting gates this time. In the future, he'd stick to the visuals he'd promised Henry and keep his hands off. In future, he'd treat Summer Williams like a no-fire zone.

But even as he made the decision, he couldn't tear his gaze off the sway of her hips under the black denim skirt, and before he even gave it a second thought, his gaze moved on to her rounded breasts. His eyes widened. Whoa—no bra.

Someone ought to give that girl a good talking to. He swallowed, opened his mouth then shut it again so quickly his teeth clunked. Nikolai averted his gaze. He was not going there. Definitely not. He'd eat breakfast, say his piece about Martin then leave Summer to do what she would with the intel.

After Summer brought up the subject.

Summer slid an empty white plate in front of him, and handed Nikolai a knife and fork. She dropped into the chair opposite and stretched out her legs under the table.

Nikolai jolted at the brush of her legs against him and thanked God he hadn't gone with the pair of shorts he'd first picked up. He moved his legs aside and exhaled slowly.

"Bacon?" Summer asked.

He nodded. Instead of handing him the plate, she speared a piece of bacon with a fork and leaned toward him to place it on his plate. Her flimsy blouse gaped at the neck, exposing creamy curves. Spectacular, mature curves with dusky nipples. His gaze fixed like superglue. Immediately, heat suffused his body, muscles tightened all over, in places that had no business reacting. His cock ached like hell as blood pooled low, priming him for action.

"Ah, that…that's enough bacon."

She smiled, an innocent siren's smile that wound his insides so tight he thought he might shatter like the workings in his grandmother's clock that time he'd turned the key too much.

"How many pancakes?"

Nikolai nodded.

The siren's smile brightened, beckoning him closer, luring him and generally creating havoc of his earlier resolutions. Damn, he wanted to play so much his hands shook.

She laughed softly. "I'll give you two to start with."

This time she picked up a pair of tongs and deftly transferred the pancakes to his plate. He caught another glimpse of her breasts, and his dick tightened with painful intensity.

Nikolai grabbed the wrist that held the tongs. "Cut it out," he snapped.

"What?" The smile that bloomed on her soft, wide mouth was innocent, but the glint in her blue eyes didn't come close.

Nikolai's gaze was snared once again by the rise and fall of her breasts. "You know what I'm talking about," he snarled. "Don't do it."

Ohhh! This was fun. Summer fought the blooming grin with all she had. His hand shackled her wrist, holding her firm, yet he tempered his strength, not inflicting pain. She looked up and stared into the swirling depths of his dark eyes. Her breasts tingled when she faced the stormy heat that burned in his gaze. She moistened her bottom lip, reliving the taste of him, the sensation of his lips against hers.

Then Summer closed one eye in another wink. "Would you like syrup with that?"

Nikolai swore, his curse another original that she took mental note of to drag out later when her brothers were around trying to interfere in her life.

"Martin's family is involved in crime." The statement was delivered in a flat tone as he let go of her wrist. He leaned back in his chair and waited.

Summer frowned. "A crime family? What do you mean?"

"His family fronts an organized crime ring. Stay away from Martin. He's bad news." He picked up the bottle of maple syrup and drizzled it over his pancakes, then calmly began to eat.

Summer blinked. She should be angry, but she didn't think Nikolai was the sort of man who'd make up a story like this. Truth and honor radiated from him. She glanced at his bent head and frowned as she listened to him crunch on the crispy bacon. "Nikolai, I'm not stupid. If I had the slightest clue that

Dare was involved in something illegal, I'd run a mile. You can't tell me he's part of a crime family then not give me details. Spill."

"You told me not to interfere." He cut into his pancakes with a precise incision that would have done a surgeon proud. His jaw moved as he chewed stoically, ignoring her questions.

Summer had a mighty urge to hit him or at least grab him by the shirt and give him a good shake until answers spilled from his mouth. Cripes, and men thought women were unpredictable. She reached over and made a grab for his hands. "*Stop*."

Dark brows rose toward his hairline but he didn't pretend he didn't know what she wanted. "I can't tell you where I got the intel, but the source is good."

Summer gritted her teeth. Shaking was looking good. "What else did they say?"

"Rumor is that Martin has taken over from his father and is intent on putting his own stamp on the business."

"What sort of business? He's a restaurateur. The family owns several restaurants in the Auckland region."

Nikolai picked up his knife and fork again. "Good places to launder money."

"All right. What say the rumors are true? Why haven't the police done anything?"

"Because they're too clever to get caught."

An idea sprouted in Summer's mind. She tossed it around, looked at it from several angles and decided it was a keeper. "I wonder if the police have anyone undercover."

His eating utensils dropped onto the china plate with a loud crash. His hand whipped out to snare both her right wrist and attention. "*Don't even think it*," he snarled. "It's a damn-fooled idea."

"But if the man's a criminal—"

"No." His eyes were hard, his expression flat.

Big, bad SAS man mode, Summer thought with an inward sigh. She looked pointedly at her shackled wrist. "Are you going to let me go any time soon?"

Nikolai dropped her wrist as if he'd been scorched by fire. "Henry should have locked you up," he snarled, glaring at her. "Throwing away the key would have worked too."

Summer glared back. "He did the next best thing—he gave me you." And thank the Lord he did. Teasing Nikolai really got the adrenaline going, sort of like an energy breakfast drink.

Nikolai didn't dignify her return fire with a reply. "So we're agreed. You're not going to see Martin again."

Okay. Enough was enough. "I like Dare. He's a *gentleman.*"

"So my manners and clothes could use a bit of work. At least with me, what you see is what you get."

Summer gave up trying to eat. "I can't brush off Dare without a good reason."

"Women do it all the time."

"I'm not most women."

Nikolai rolled his eyes. "Hell, you're not wrong there. No wonder Henry wanted a babysitter for you."

"Look, Dare and I have gone out a couple of times. So what? We're just friends. Unless I see the proof with my own eyes, I'm going to keep seeing him."

"From what I saw, you're more than friends."

Summer stilled. "What are you talking about?"

"The lip-lock last night."

Her eyes narrowed to slits. "Were you spying on me?"

Nikolai avoided her glare. "I was worried."

"I'd like to point out that we were lip-locked not long ago."

The instant the words left her mouth, the air in the kitchen thickened. Awareness pulsed between them, and Summer couldn't have looked away from him if she'd tried. Every part of her body ached for his touch.

"That was a mistake."

Summer shrugged. "Didn't feel like a mistake to me."

After two beats of pregnant silence, Nikolai shot to his feet. "I've got to go."

"Running away?" Summer said sweetly.

"It's the right thing to do."

Summer didn't agree, but she knew there was no point arguing with him. She shrugged. "Whatever." Summer watched him hobble from the kitchen. When he reached the door, she said, "I'll let you know if I need help with my investigation."

He whirled so quickly, it was a wonder he didn't catch her grin before she wiped her expression clean. His glare was dark, his eyes stormy as he snarled, "Over my dead body."

Chapter Five

"I think that went well," Summer remarked to Joe, Veronica's big-foot cat.

The slam of the door made them stare in that direction, then Joe returned to his grooming schedule. Summer shrugged and stood to clear off the half-eaten remains of their breakfast.

The phone rang just as she was drying her hands.

Summer smiled when she heard the familiar voice. "Hi, Dare. I enjoyed last night."

"I did too." His smoky voice slid smoothly down the phone lines like the best expensive brandy. "What are you doing today? I forgot to ask you last night."

Good timing, Summer thought. She wanted to start her investigation straight away. She checked her watch. "I've got a Tae Kwon Do lesson this morning, but apart from that I don't have anything planned."

"How does an afternoon at the beach sound and a barbecue afterward?"

"Sounds great."

"Good. My family has a bach at Maraetai Beach. You'll meet my two brothers and three sisters."

Summer grinned the second she heard the invitation to visit their holiday home. She couldn't have planned things better if she'd tried. Once she'd met Dare's family, she'd have a better idea of what to do next. "What time?"

"How does two sound? Good." He paused. "How about bringing an overnight bag just in case the barbecue runs late, hmm?"

"But—" The phone went dead before Summer finished. If Nikolai was right, she wasn't going to get involved any further with Dare. And she certainly wasn't going to sleep with the man. "Well, doggone it!" she muttered, making a face at the phone. "What am I going to do now? And how am I going to get past the big, bad SAS man?"

* * * * *

Sashay, with her nose in the air.

That's how she did it. Nervous tension bubbled in her tummy like a thermal mud pool, and laughter choked up her throat, desperate for freedom. But she made it to the car in one piece despite his black look.

"Does that man always glare like that?" Dare muttered in a low undertone as he seated her in the passenger seat of a black sports car.

"Afraid so," Summer said cheerfully. Now that she was inside the car, she felt marginally safer. "Just ignore him. I do."

The car started with a throaty purr.

Summer turned her attention to the soft, butter-colored upholstery and ignored everything else. "I've never driven in a convertible before. Does this car belong to you too?"

"Like it? It's new. I picked it up this morning. You're my very first passenger."

"I love it." She gestured at her old, dented car. "I'm obviously in the wrong business."

"Stick with me, sweetheart, and we'll go places." As he spoke, Dare reached out and squeezed her bare knee. "My family is looking forward to meeting you."

"I'm looking forward to meeting them too." And asking all sorts of questions. Her family might be overprotective, but they'd taught her a thing or two.

"So, have I kept my promise and kept you too busy to read your romances?"

Summer grinned at him as she tucked a strand of blue hair behind one ear. "I've read one." In the middle of the night, when she'd been trying to take her mind off Nikolai.

"How often do you get to that bookshop on High Street?" Dare asked.

Summer waved at Nikolai as they sped off. She imagined the look on his face, but refrained from glancing back. She didn't want to push him too far. "Once or twice a week. It's not far from the library. They stock a lot of my favorite authors."

"Romance," he teased with a sideward glance, as he paused at a give way sign.

"You're as bad as my brothers. I like reading romance, and I refuse to apologize for it."

"I don't get to the shop that often. I usually ring my orders through and get someone to pick them up for me."

"If you need anything picked up, just let me know. At least if I pick up your books, you won't end up with the wrong package." Summer smiled at Dare, while her mind worked busily. She thought she was doing well so far. And tomorrow she'd go through the pile of books she'd picked up from the library after her Tae Kwon Do class. She was bound to pick up a few hints on investigation from Stephanie Plum.

* * * * *

Nikolai couldn't believe it. No, that wasn't quite true. He believed Summer all right but after his threats, he'd thought she'd stay away from the clotheshorse. Obviously, he was losing his touch.

He was definitely losing his mind.

He headed for his kitchen at a lope and mentally thanked his Hitler-wannabe physiotherapist for pushing him. The knee was finally starting to feel as though it belonged to him again. Nikolai grabbed his mobile phone and his car keys then raced for his car. Two seconds later, he returned to snatch up a cap. He jammed it on his head and loped back outside.

Gravel spat as he reversed from his garage and shot down the road on the heels of Martin and Summer. The speedometer edged up. Nikolai jabbed a button on his mobile and held it to his ear while he negotiated a corner.

"Yo."

"Louie, it's Nik. Remember that guy I had you check up on?"

"Yeah."

"Do you remember if he has a beach house?" The beach was a safe bet. Summer had carried a beach towel in the top of that orange basket of hers, and she'd been wearing shorts. Nikolai swallowed. Brief shorts that had highlighted her long legs. He imagined them entwined around him—

"No beach house."

Damn. "What about his family?"

The clear sound of tapping computer keys filtered down the phone line. Nikolai was coming up to the motorway turnoff. He'd have to decide which way to go. "Hurry up," he muttered.

"Jeez, man, I heard that. I'm the one doing you a favor."

Chastened, Nikolai apologized. "Sorry." He slowed the car as he approached the turnoff. Still no sign of the black car. Which way should he go? They could have gone to any number of beaches around Auckland.

"The parents own a waterfront house at Maraetai."

"Yes!" Nikolai drove right past the motorway turnoff toward Papakura. "Where? What's the street number?"

Louie rattled off the details.

"Thanks, Lou. I owe you."

"Yeah. Don't think I won't call on it either."

Nikolai grinned as the phone clicked in his ear and he turned the car toward Clevedon and Maraetai beach.

* * * * *

Summer burrowed her bare feet into the sand and small, broken-up shells. She leaned back on her elbows, lazily grinning while the sun beat down from overhead. The sharp tang of coconut oil filled the air as Natasha, one of Dare's sisters, applied suntan lotion to her legs and arms.

"It's too bad Dare was called into work," Natasha complained, as she worked the lotion into her skin.

Summer shrugged. "It doesn't matter. The problems were unexpected. You saw how disappointed he was."

"But he's your boyfriend. Aren't you angry? I bet he didn't need to take my brothers and father with him too."

Summer idly surveyed the stream of people that passed them. "Dare and I are friends. We're not serious." Part of her was sorry she was alone and stuck with Dare's sister. There were some seriously good-looking bodies parading on this beach. Her gaze swept from the high-tide mark and back to the gently swishing waves surging and retreating from the beach. She adjusted her bikini top as her eyes came to a halt on the group of three men not far down the beach. Now that was some serious eye candy. Three bronzed bodies that came complete with the requisite muscles.

"You can't be just friends," Natasha said. "Dare's never brought a girl here before. Have you slept together?"

Summer's head jerked about in shock. "Natasha!"

"Sorry. I guess that was a bit personal."

Summer chuckled. Natasha didn't sound the slightest bit sorry. "Yes, it was. But here's your answer. We've only known each other for two weeks, and I'm only twenty-two. I'm way too young to get serious about a man." Her gaze swung back to the group of three men. They'd stood and were wandering down toward the water.

One wore a knee brace.

Summer bolted upright then grabbed for her flapping bikini top.

"What's wrong?" Natasha asked, jerking upright as well.

"Nothing." *That had better not be Nikolai.* Summer tied the strings of her bikini firmly in place and stood. After wrapping her sarong about her body like a suit of protective armor, she brushed the sand and shell fragments off her feet then thrust them into sandals. "I think that's someone from work. I'll just go and say hello."

"Where?" Natasha fastened her bikini top.

Summer pointed at the three men. "Down there, about to go into the water." She took two steps toward the water.

"They're going swimming. There's no point wearing your sarong and sandals."

Summer grimaced and stooped to remove her sandals. So, they'd all get an eyeful of her oversized curves. "Thanks." As she strode away, the man in the knee brace dived into the water. Summer let rip with a soft exclamation. It was definitely Nikolai. She'd recognize that butt anywhere.

"I'm coming too," Natasha declared from behind her.

Summer stiffened at the predatory interest in Natasha's voice. She didn't want anyone ogling Nikolai up close. "What will your brother say when he hears that I've been introducing you to older men?"

Natasha fell into step. "If Dare had his way, I'd leave the house wearing a yashmak."

The sheer feeling in Natasha's words ruffled Summer's conscience. Her brothers were the same—heavy-handed on the interrogation of any boy who'd dare turn up at the family home. She grinned in sympathy. "Dare's an overprotective brother?"

"Oh, yes. Let me live a little, even if it's only through you. And besides, you're only two years older than me."

"Come on then. I'll introduce you, but don't tell Dare. If you do, I'll deny everything."

"Great. Let's go in case Dare arrives back unexpectedly."

By the time they reached the water's edge, the three men were shoulder-deep in the sea.

"Looks like we're going to get wet," Summer said.

"Are you a good swimmer?"

Summer glanced out at the three men. They were out of her depth now and cutting through the water like champions. But she had expected nothing less from SAS members. "Not that good," she murmured. "How about taking a quick dip and we'll nab them when they come out of the water."

"Sounds good to me."

Summer waded further into the water. She gasped as the cool water struck her sun-warmed skin. "Eek! It's colder than I thought."

Natasha scooped up a handful of water and flicked it at Summer. "Don't be a baby."

"Take that!" Summer retaliated with gusto then fled for the deeper water.

Natasha swam strongly after her and seconds later, it was a full-on water fight. Summer laughed so hard she sank. A hand snaked about her waist, dragging her to the surface.

"Is this a private fight, ladies, or can anyone join?"

Louie and Jake trod water in front of her. That meant the arm around her waist belonged to Nikolai. Summer's pulse kicked up the pace. She blinked the water from her lashes and turned. Her bare legs brushed against his under the water and flames sprang to life inside Summer. She sucked in a hasty breath as she stared at him, recalling their kiss. The expression on his face and the way his gaze drifted down to her lips told Summer he remembered too.

"Are you Summer's friends?" Natasha asked.

The curiosity in Natasha's voice made Summer spring away from Nikolai as if she'd been stung by a bee. She tried to stand up then went under the water before Nikolai hauled her back to the surface. Summer came up spluttering. "Ah." Heat grew in her cheeks and she rushed into speech. "This is Louie and Jake." She pointed to the two grinning men then gestured at the man holding her against his chest. "This is my neighbor, Nikolai."

"Hmm," Natasha said.

She packed a lot of meaning into that one soft sound. The heat in Summer's cheeks soared to a new high, and she couldn't meet Natasha's gaze. "I think I'll go in now," she muttered. "I'm a bit cold."

Natasha tossed her head. "I'm going to swim out further." She smiled at Jake then gave Louie the same treatment—a flash of white teeth and fluttering eyelashes. "Care for a race, boys?" Then she dived through a wave and raced off without waiting for an answer.

Louie and Jake grinned at each other and took off with whoops and white water, leaving Summer and Nikolai alone.

Summer stared after them while every atom in her body sizzled, aware of Nikolai's arm under her breasts, holding her afloat in the water. "You're meant to babysit me, not act as a guard dog."

"I'm the one that needs a guard," Nikolai growled right next to her ear.

His breath feathered across her cheek, and she shivered, wanting nothing more than to turn in his arms, draw his head down and kiss him.

"Summer, don't."

She turned at the warning note in his voice. "I'm not doing anything." His intense gaze made her stomach soar then swoop until she felt as though she was on an out-of-control roller coaster ride.

A wave rocked their bodies together. Her breasts flirted with his bare chest and she gasped at the lightning bolt of sensation. Summer looked up and met the answering fire in Nikolai's eyes. Then, as she watched, his gaze iced over.

"We can't do this," he said. "You don't know me. The things I've done."

As he spoke, he loosened his grip on her arms and pushed her away.

Summer bristled. "You don't know me, either. And you can't make my decisions for me. Why won't anyone let me make my own mistakes?" Much to her disgust, the end of her sentence came out on a wobble. Confrontation. She wasn't very good at it, which was why she was running away from the problem with her family. Deep down, she knew it. Sooner or later, she'd have to tell her parents and her brothers that she needed to live her life on her own terms. Without babysitters! Her mother would cry, she just knew it. Already, she felt the lash of guilt before she'd voiced a word.

"I promised Henry."

"Yeah, I know." Summer started for the shore and the splashing behind indicated Nikolai was getting out too. Summer waded through the water as if a stingray chased on her heels. She loved her parents and her brothers, and she knew they loved her, but they had to let her go. She just wished she could take her own advice and push Nikolai away, and mean it.

Once she reached the sand, she paused and turned around. The strange thing though, was the way she consistently stuck up for herself with Nikolai. It felt good. Right. Maybe it was the enforced break from her family. "Will you walk with me along the beach?"

Caution chased surprise over his face. "All right." He fell into step with her.

"Do you have proof about Dare's family yet?"

"No, it's still all rumor."

"Then please back off and stop following me. Dare's taken me to three different restaurants and today to the beach to meet his family. I haven't seen drugs or anything remotely illegal." Summer paused then exhaled. "You realize that by playing the heavy-handed parent you're making me choose sides."

"I'd noticed you're stubborn."

Summer snorted. "Not usually. It's a new thing since I arrived in Auckland. It must be the water. Usually I let everyone ride roughshod over me."

Once they reached the wooden wharf, they turned and headed back in the direction they'd come.

"So we're agreed," Summer said, breaking the silence that had fallen between them. "You'll trust me to look after myself without interfering? And I promise to let you know if I have a problem? You'll go back to the original plan of watching from afar — getting a visual?" Her one quick darting look at him intercepted a fierce frown.

"I don't think that's —"

"You can't watch me twenty-four hours a day," she snapped, without a single squeak in evidence. "You have to sleep sometime."

Chapter Six

Nikolai stared at Summer, taking in the stubborn jut of her chin, the flash in her blue eyes. Without thinking, he reached out to sweep a lock of damp blue hair off her face. Silky smooth skin slid beneath his fingers, tempting him to explore more. His gaze slid down, past her neck. Lingered.

Nikolai exhaled slowly. He wanted her—in every possible way. He admitted it, despite fighting with every fiber of his being. Perhaps he should introduce Summer to Laura, his ex. That would light a fire under her—she'd be off like the hounds of hell when she heard Laura list his many faults as a husband, as a man. She'd never speak to him again.

"So, we're agreed?" Summer said, her voice low, strained.

Nikolai searched her face, saw the same physical awareness burning in her open gaze and groaned softly. Hell, who ever said life was fair?

"Look, Summer. If Henry were here, he'd tell you to give Martin the shove. I think you're playing with trouble, but I'll back off as long as you promise not to investigate Martin on your own. If you go out with him, make sure it's in a public place. Please, promise me that." Nikolai kept the lie smooth, as smooth as her soft skin, told it in an even tone and looked her in the eye the whole time. When she finally nodded, he felt like a pile of dog turd. Eventually, she'd find out he'd lied, and she'd never look at him in the same way again.

The idea should have made him happy.

Summer stood on tiptoe and brushed a kiss across his cheek. "Thanks," she whispered.

"Hey, Summer!" Natasha bounced up and down as she hailed them. Nikolai noticed the sly grins on his friends' faces as they stood at the girl's side.

"Mum said Dare's definitely not coming back. Feel like going to the movies?" she asked. "Nikolai, you'll come with us? Jake and Louie said they'd like to go."

Nikolai waited for Summer to decide.

"Sure," she said slowly. "Nikolai?"

"Sounds good to me, as long as we don't have to go to some weepy chick-flick."

* * * * *

After the movie, Nikolai gave her a ride home. In the dark, intimate confines of his car, Summer took the coward's route and pretended to go to sleep. It wasn't that the evening hadn't gone well, because it had. No, she was in full-out panic because during the course of the evening, she'd discovered — admitted — she'd fallen for Nikolai. She huffed silently. Talk about a bolt from the heavens.

She'd fallen for a clone of her brothers — a bossy take-charge kind of man who liked to tell her what to do. And true to type, Nikolai had tried to veto her friendship with Dare, making him out to be second cousin to an axe murderer. Summer's mouth firmed as she thought of the past. She needed to use two hands to count the number of boyfriends her brothers had sent running for cover.

The question was — what did she do now?

So far, she'd enjoyed her independence, and she wasn't remotely tempted to give it up for something that might be love or might not. Maybe she'd ignore the attraction and search for another male — one who would let her express her opinions and listen to her instead of reducing every word to clipped orders.

"Summer, are you awake?"

"Huh?"

"We're home."

Summer opened her eyes and sat upright. So they were. She'd been so deep in thought she hadn't noticed. She turned to Nikolai. "Thanks for the ride home."

"I'll walk you to the door."

Summer sucked in a deep breath then let it ease out. *Pick your fights.* "Thanks." She scrambled from the car with her straw basket and fumbled for her house keys. They were right at the bottom of the basket, of course. Feeling the weight of his stare, she fumbled, and the keys dropped to the ground with a metallic rattle.

"Let me," he murmured. He picked them up and shoved the key in the lock. "Hell, Summer. You didn't lock the door."

"Yes, I did. Don't you remember? You were there."

He cursed. "Stay there. Don't move." Then he slid through the open door into the darkness.

Summer ignored the order and stepped inside after him.

"Don't you ever listen to what I say?" he demanded, materializing from the dark shadows on her right.

"When you ask instead of ordering, I might consider."

"There wasn't time to pretty it up," he snapped.

"But—"

"Quiet." Nikolai shoved her behind him.

Summer heard a noise too. She snapped her mouth shut, freezing like the marble statue of Peter Pan out in the garden. The tenseness left Nikolai's body, and he turned, dragging her close enough to his side so he could whisper in her ear.

"Sounds like they've gone out the window. You can come with me, but for God's sake, if I tell you to run, make sure you do. Can you do that?"

Astonishment made her blink, but she didn't let it show in her voice. "Yes. I understand." Her heart thudded as adrenaline built inside.

"Come on then." Nikolai edged through the darkness, moving with stealth and confidence.

Summer attempted to follow as best she could. Even though she was familiar with the surroundings, the lack of light threw off her judgment of distances. Not Nikolai. He never faltered.

In her uncle's den, Nikolai stopped abruptly. "They've gone. Turn on the light."

Summer flicked the switch and blinked in the sudden bright glare. The cords of the wooden Venetian blinds rattled against the sill, disturbed by the stiff southerly blowing in from outside. When she looked closer, she noticed the muddy footprint on the sill.

Summer sighed. "Should I phone the police or check to see if anything is missing first?"

"I wouldn't worry too much about missing items," Nikolai muttered.

The strange note in his voice made her jerk to attention. She wrinkled her brow. "What are you talking about?"

He indicated the packets of white powder sitting on the top of her uncle's desk.

"Are they what—?"

Sirens sounded in the distance, loud and insistent.

"Yep, I'd take that bet," he said, leaning against the wall. "I take it those packages aren't yours?"

Summer inched toward the desk, eyeing the packets as though they might pounce. Curious, she reached out to touch.

"Don't." Nikolai moved so quickly she blinked. "You don't want to leave your fingerprints."

Her head pounded in time with the sirens. She stared wordlessly at Nikolai as a car pulled up outside. The siren shut down then there was blessed quietness, not a sound except the pounding of her heart and Nikolai's slow, controlled breathing.

A fist hammered on the door.

Nikolai dropped the arm from her shoulder. "I'll get it."

"No. Let me," Summer said. She turned for the door then paused. "You're not going to do anything stupid?"

Nikolai's mouth twisted. "No point. The cops know it's here."

"How? I don't understand. This is like a bad movie," Summer muttered.

A bark of laughter sounded seconds before a fist pounded on the door again. "Somehow, sweetheart, I think it's gonna get worse."

How? Summer thought as she strode for the door. Her mother would have a cow when she heard, and Summer was in no doubt that she would hear one way or the other. She heard masculine voices outside, a discussion about whether to knock the door down. "I'm coming," she snapped. She yanked the door open before they took further action. "Yes?"

Blue and red lights flashed on top of the unmarked police vehicle. Two men in plain clothes stood on the doorstep. Summer should have felt intimidated, but Nikolai's presence in the house gave her confidence. "Can I help you?"

"Police," one of the men said. They both held up identification for Summer to scan.

"Can I do something to help you?" she repeated, standing in the middle of the doorway. "It is rather late."

"We've had a tip-off about one of our investigations. Can we come in?"

Summer frowned as the older of the two policemen stepped toward her. She stood her ground. "Don't you need a warrant or something?"

Nikolai appeared behind her. "Let them in, Summer."

Wordlessly, she stepped back to allow the officers to enter the house.

"I think you'll find what you're looking for in the study," Nikolai said.

"Who are you?" the younger policeman asked.

"Nikolai Tarei." As he spoke, he moved closer and curved his arm around her waist, drawing her against his side. When she opened her mouth to speak, he tightened his grip, and Summer slammed her mouth shut. Inwardly, she fumed. Once again, Nikolai was taking charge.

"We have a few questions for you."

"Come through to the kitchen," Nikolai said.

Summer wanted to protest that she was capable of dealing with the policemen. She glared her annoyance at Nikolai, but he merely shook his head and propelled her into the kitchen. One of the policemen followed them into the kitchen while the other stepped into her uncle's study.

"Can you tell us what this is all about please?" Summer asked after subsiding into a chair. Her voice held clear impatience.

The policeman ignored her prompting. "Your name?"

"Summer Williams."

"Do you own this house, Mr. Tarei?"

"My uncle owns this house," Summer replied before Nikolai could answer. "Nikolai lives next door."

The second policeman entered the kitchen. He held the packets of white powder in his right hand. Summer noticed straightaway that he wore gloves and held the packets by the corners.

"Do these belong to you, Miss Williams?"

Summer leaned back in her chair. "No."

"Do you have any idea how they came to be on the desk then?"

Summer glanced at Nikolai, and at his imperceptible nod, she answered the question. "Nikolai and I have been out all day. We returned about fifteen minutes ago. The front door was unlocked, and when we came inside we both heard noises. By the time we investigated whoever was inside had left via the study window. If you look, you'll see a footprint on the windowsill."

"Hmm." The older policeman scratched the stubble on his chin. "I'd like you to accompany us to the station."

* * * * *

"I didn't expect them to keep us there all night," Summer muttered. "For a while there, I thought they were going to lock us up."

Nikolai shrugged as an unmarked blue sedan pulled up beside them. "This looks like our ride home now."

He spoke to the driver, then opened the back door for Summer to get in. Nikolai slid in beside her and the car pulled away. On the short drive home, neither of them spoke.

"Looks like you have company, Summer."

Summer jerked upright, a flush pooling in her cheeks when she realized she'd gone to sleep and used Nikolai as a pillow. Good grief. She hoped she hadn't dribbled on his shirt. She wiped her eyes with the back of her hands and surreptitiously checked her mouth and chin for dampness. "Sorry?"

"Martin's here."

Summer's head jerked about. She gasped, then turned back to stare at Nikolai. "What do I tell him?"

"I'd stick to the truth," Nikolai said in an undertone.

"At least I'll be able to prove that he has nothing to do with crime."

"Maybe."

The car pulled up alongside Dare's convertible. After thanking the driver, they climbed out.

"Hi, Dare." Summer smiled. "Have you been waiting long?"

Dare's look held antagonism as he glared at Nikolai, and Summer knew she had to get rid of Nikolai before things turned ugly.

"Thanks for the help, Nikolai. I'll see you later." She backed up her words with a wave, then took Dare's arm and dragged him toward the front door. Luckily, Nikolai seemed to trust her to deal with the situation on her own.

"Where have you been?" Dare demanded in a low, furious voice.

Summer unlocked the door then stood back for him to enter. She refused to argue in front of Nikolai. Summer knew he was watching, sensing his gaze even though her back was to him. A tingle sprang to life inside her, and it had nothing to do with Dare's arrival.

Summer forced another smile. "I could do with a cup of coffee. Come on through to the kitchen, and I'll explain everything. It's been a rough night."

Five minutes later, the scent of freshly ground coffee beans filled the air and the water had started dripping through the filter.

"You know that Natasha and I went to the pictures last night?" she asked.

"Yes."

"When Nikolai dropped me off here, someone was inside the house. Whoever it was left several packets of cocaine and called the cops to alert them."

"Cocaine?" Dare stared at her in astonishment.

And the reaction was genuine. Summer would swear to it. "It wasn't very good quality, but definitely cocaine. Lucky for me, the culprit left a boot print on the windowsill and none of the packets had my fingerprints on them, either inside or out. But the police still took me in for questioning. I've been there all night."

"And the police don't have any idea who called them?"

Summer glanced at the coffeemaker and wished it would hurry up. "No. They think the call was made on a cell phone — probably one of those prepaid ones that are difficult to trace."

"What was your next-door neighbor doing with you? Why didn't you call me?"

There had been a time, not long ago, when Summer would have felt thrilled to have two men pay attention to her. And without either of her two older brothers chasing them away. "I didn't call you because I thought you were busy."

"But you called him."

He sounded like a sulky child. Male egos. She could do without them. "The police took him in for questioning too because he was still here."

"I don't like the way he hangs around. Or the way he looks at you. He probably called the cops."

Summer suppressed a snappish comeback. "He's my uncle's friend. I suspect my uncle asked him to watch out for me. I can't be rude. The coffee's ready. Black, isn't it?"

"Yeah." Dare paced the length of the kitchen. "Thanks," he added as an afterthought. He stopped then turned to stride back across the tiled floor.

"Coffee's ready." Summer plonked the mug down on the wooden table then muttered under her breath when her undue force made coffee splash over the maroon tablecloth. She grabbed a cloth to wipe up the spill then sat to drink her own.

Dare paused mid-pace and whirled to face her. The intense frown on his face made her stare. As she watched, he strode past the table, past his waiting coffee. He was leaving? Or was he merely doing an extra large lap?

Summer swiveled in her chair. Her mouth dropped open when he kept going through the open door. "Dare, what about your coffee? Dare!"

He halted and turned to face her. "Something's come up. I have to go."

"Right now? Without drinking your coffee?"

"Sorry."

The apology lacked in the sincere department. Summer leapt to her feet. "What's come up?"

A flash of irritation crossed his face. His full mouth firmed to a line as he checked his watch. "I need to go to work. I'll ring you later."

Talk about a pat on the head. Summer sank back to her chair. What had happened to make him run off that way? She replayed the last quarter of an hour in her mind and came up blank. One moment he'd been acting the jealous boyfriend, then the next he was in full business mode. Then another thought occurred.

What if Nikolai was right about Dare? Did Dare know more than he was letting on about the drugs they'd found in Uncle Henry's study?

Chapter Seven

The puzzle regarding Dare's sudden defection niggled at Summer for the rest of the morning, so much so that she had difficulty concentrating on the Sunday paper. She half expected him to call yet heard nothing.

By two o'clock, she gave up waiting and grabbed up the car keys for her Mazda and her exercise gear. If she hurried, she'd make the Tae Kwon Do class, and she needed groceries. She'd get those on the way home. And if Dare rang while she was out, too bad.

Her car started with the usual bad-tempered splutters. Summer muttered a lot before she and the car came to terms and traveled sedately toward Papakura. The traffic became heavier the closer she came to the motorway turnoff. People heading home after the weekend away, she surmised, a flicker of loneliness making her homesick for friends and family. She slowed at the intersection then indicated a right turn onto a quiet road that would get her to her class on time and avoid most of the traffic.

While she drove down the hedge-lined road, Summer puzzled over Dare's weird behavior. A screech of tires behind her made her glance in her rear-vision mirror. Another vehicle was close behind and rapidly closing the distance.

She gasped.

Fear made her mouth dry. The reflection of a four-wheel drive vehicle filled her mirror—black with lots of silver chrome in the front. Summer pressed her foot down on the accelerator. Tires shrieked and her aging car shuddered, protesting the sudden demand for speed. The black monster continued to stalk her. Every two seconds, like a magnet seeking metal, her gaze was drawn to her rear-vision mirror. A maniac! That's what the driver was. Summer gripped the steering wheel, her heart galloping in outright panic. If anything, he'd sped up.

"Idiot," she gasped out between clenched teeth. Strong, colorful curses danced through her head. Her hands tightened on the steering wheel, while sweat broke out on her forehead, her hands—all over her body.

A witness. She needed a witness. She prayed for a car to come from the other direction. It didn't happen. Instead, the roaring behind grew louder, more frightening. More threatening. Summer glanced in the mirror again. She caught a glimpse of white teeth and lips curled up in a wolfish smile. A crash sounded. Her car shot forward with the impact. Summer's body snapped toward the windscreen then jerked to a halt when the seat belt jammed. The air exploded from her lungs. She groaned. The four-wheel drive slammed into her bumper for a second time. Metal ground against metal in a horrible, expensive grating.

Summer's car shunted off the road, flying over a low bank into a ditch. The branches of the roadside hedge scraped across the window and the paintwork, sounding like fingernails on a blackboard. Her car plowed into the hedge, blocking the sun. Her engine cut out. She heard the roar of the four-wheel drive as it slowed, then hurtled away. Behind the hedge, an animal bleated in fright, then all was quiet.

With trembling hands, Summer tried to release her seat belt. A shaft of pain shot across her chest. A soft moan escaped. She had to get out of the car. What if it caught on fire? Or what if that idiot returned? He'd rammed her car on purpose. He'd wanted to injure her.

Summer reached for the seat belt release again and on her third try the button went down, freeing the seat belt. Once that was done, the belt quit digging into her chest. Summer let out a sigh of relief. A splash of blood dropped to her hand. She needed to... What did she need to do? It was nighttime, wasn't it? She'd go to sleep.

The plaintive moo of a cow jerked her eyes open. Somewhere in the distance, a dog barked. Summer looked around her and realized she was in her car. That's right. She needed to get out. She struggled with the door. It opened a fraction then stopped. Outside the car, the hedge shook.

Jammed. She'd have to try the passenger door. Summer reached over. An arrow of pain darted through her upper body while inside her head, someone played a drum solo. Summer gritted her teeth and kept pushing the door. Without warning, it dropped open. A blast of fresh air blew into the car, caressing her hot cheeks.

Summer sucked in a painful breath and crawled from the driver's seat to the passenger side. The gear stick jabbed into her thigh while the drum soloist worked up into a crashing finale. She winced, and wiped a hand across her face. It came away covered with blood.

Behind her, she heard a vehicle. She froze, her heart leaping into her throat. The driver had returned. God, what was she going to do?

"You there! What the devil do you think you are doing? I heard you speeding. No wonder you drove off the road. Stupid idiot. Don't you watch the road safety ads on television? Probably been drinking," the voice finished in disgust.

This didn't sound like the driver—not the way he was haranguing her. Summer crawled out of the car and dropped into the long grass. Water seeped into her clothes while the stiff breeze tore at her hair. Summer shivered.

"You there! Are you all right?"

Was she all right? Summer considered the question.

"Look at you," the man said in disgust. He stomped closer, and when Summer looked up her vision was filled with a pair of red and black gumboots. She tried to raise her head further to see his face but didn't get any further than the patched knees of his faded woolen trousers before the pain kicked in.

"If you've caused Mabel to go into premature labor, I'm gonna sue. Don't think I won't either, missy." The boots kept coming until they were three inches from her nose, and she could have touched them. "Huh! Should have known. You're one of those young punks with weird-colored hair and metal pins in places that I'm sure the good Lord doesn't approve of. You're bleeding." He sighed loudly. "Suppose I'll have to use that newfangled phone thing my daughter gave me for emergencies."

The man squatted beside her, his knees creaking loudly. "Hope you know how to use this thing 'cause my memory is a bit hazy on the instructions. I'll ring for an ambulance, but I can't wait. I've got to check Mabel."

"I'm fine," Summer muttered, trying to lift her head to survey the road for a body. She hadn't run anyone over. She hadn't. "Just ring Nik—" No! That wasn't a good idea. She struggled to sit but ended up in an undignified sprawl. The elderly man pulled a cell phone from his pocket and eyed it doubtfully. He held it away from him then stabbed at a button. A satisfied grunt emerged. After pushing more buttons and more grunting, he spoke. "Lisa, I need you to ring for an ambulance."

Summer heard the panicked squawk from where she was.

"Not for me, Lisa," the man shouted. "Some fool girl's driven off the road. Right near Mabel's house. I don't know. Better ring the cops too. If Mabel's hurt I want to sue."

The man shoved the phone back in his pocket, glanced at her then stood with another round of creaking joints. "Can you stand?" he demanded, his voice gruff.

Summer nodded then immediately wished she hadn't. The man with drums was still present in her head, her nod inducing him to drum louder. She bit her bottom lip and pushed upward. She made it to her feet but wavered like a sapling in a strong wind. The man's hands shot out to steady her, strong and sure despite his age.

"Thanks," she mumbled, battling both dizziness and the urge to throw up over the man's gumboots.

In the distance, the faint cry of sirens sounded.

"Good. They'll be here soon. Bleeding looks to have stopped. Lean against the car." The man led her toward her car. He glanced down the road, clear impatience showing in his lined face. He vibrated with worry.

Summer tried to focus on the road. "I can't see...Mabel. Go check. She might need the ambulance."

The man's head whipped around to stare at Summer. "The vet maybe, but not the ambulance. Mabel's my angora goat."

A goat? A flash of white and the incessant screech of sirens told Summer that help was at hand. Alice in Wonderland. All she needed was a pink rabbit to go with the goat, and she'd fit right in at the tea party. A mechanic... A tow company. She shuddered inwardly at the thought of repairs and the resulting bill. When would they turn off that infernal racket? Her right hand crept up to touch her throbbing temple.

"Over here," the old man hollered.

Summer moaned.

A lady in a white shirt and dark-colored trousers inserted herself in front of the elderly man. "Where does it hurt, love?"

"Head," Summer muttered. Lord, did it hurt.

"What about your eyes? How many fingers am I holding up?"

Summer squinted through narrowed eyes. The fingers wavered in front of her eyes, changing from four to two and back again. In the end, she guessed. "Three?"

"Concussion," the woman murmured to a second man. "Come on, love. We'll get you to a hospital."

"But what about Mabel?" Summer demanded, looking wildly about, her heart thudding with panic. She must have hit Mabel. That man had said so. "Is she hurt?"

"Was someone else in the car? Where are they?"

From behind her, a small cough sounded. The two ambulance attendees looked past her.

"Mabel's my goat," the man said. "Her house is the other side of the hedge. And if she's injured, I'm suing." His words were punctuated by a plaintive bleat from the other side of the hedge.

Oh, yeah. A goat. Mabel was a goat. He'd said that before. Thank goodness. Summer slumped, suddenly aware of every aching bone and muscle. A shiver danced through her body. Another mournful bleat scraped through her pounding head. Summer bit back a groan. Man, she'd really stuffed up this time. When her mother heard about this accident, she'd yank every parental rein at her disposal. Summer would find herself back in Eketahuna quicker than Superman could change into his fancy duds.

The elderly man stomped into Summer's vision. "Mabel doesn't sound too good."

Perhaps this man was related to her mother?

"Sir, we need to get this girl to hospital. What's your name, love? Can we get the police to contact your family?"

"Summer." Funny, she'd swear there were cartoon birds flying about inside her head. If she listened hard enough, she could hear their frantic tweeting.

"Summer, your family?"

The woman's last question finally registered. Family. No way. She'd give Nikolai's number. He'd help.

Nikolai.

Summer grimaced. Lately, she turned to Nikolai with all her problems. She was coming to rely on him. A sharp pain in her lungs reminded her to breathe. In fact, old Nikolai was like a handy-dandy crutch. Panic started to unfurl deep inside like a ball of her mother's yarn. Was she a person who needed a crutch?

The wail of another siren cut through the tentative chirp of birds and the buzz of a bee seeking nectar from the wildflowers.

Mabel bleated indignantly on the other side of the hedge. A car pulled to a stop, sending a billow of dust sailing through the air. Summer sneezed then held her aching head. At the sound of footsteps, she opened her eyes. Her gaze met with shiny black shoes and crisply pressed navy trousers.

"You!" a masculine voice said. "We've just let you out of custody. How can you be in trouble again already?"

"There! She's a criminal. What did I tell you?" the elderly man cried in a triumphant voice.

"You can talk to her later. We need to get Summer to hospital," the female attendant cut in.

Summer wanted to strenuously deny everything. All allegations. She was the innocent one here. Why did no one believe her? She allowed the woman to propel her to the ambulance and subsided onto a soft mattress with a relieved sigh. She had important things to worry about. Somehow, she had managed to find an enemy who was becoming bolder in their methods. Summer finally admitted she was way out of her depth in dealing with this. Her journey to find herself and to assert her independence was fraught with problems. She needed help, and the obvious person was Nikolai.

Outside the ambulance, the two policemen huddled together, talking in low voices. The one who had interrogated her this morning stepped inside the ambulance.

"Looks like someone rear-ended you."

Summer attempted to nod then groaned. "Yes," she gritted out past the swooping cartoon birds.

"Are you coming with us or staying here?" the female ambulance officer demanded.

"I'll stay. The evidence we've found changes everything. This accident looks deliberate." The detective stared at Summer, an assessing look on his jaded, seen-it-all face. "Lady, you have an enemy, and he means business."

* * * * *

Nikolai eyed the lack of lights in the house next door for the third time in as many minutes. His gut churned relentlessly as he checked his watch. Nine o'clock. Something was wrong. Every single one of his senses screamed it. The Mazda wasn't parked out front either.

That was even more alarming.

The throaty purr of a car drew Nikolai's attention. The clotheshorse. Summer must be with him. Although he didn't like the idea of Summer spending time with the man, the tense set left his shoulders. His gut, however, continued to burn, and he reached for a tube of antacids.

Martin climbed out of his convertible and went to the front door. After a brisk knock on the door, he stood back and waited expectantly. Nikolai hesitated, wondering whether to go out and interrogate the man or wait.

The continued uneasiness inside him and his promise to Henry made the decision for him. That he'd begun to care about Summer in a sexual way, he shoved aside.

Nikolai slid out the open window and loped around to the front of Henry's house. He watched the man for a few seconds, hoping to pick up on the situation without the need of questions. When the man knocked for a second time on the wooden door, Nikolai knew something had happened to Summer.

He stepped out of the shadows so Martin could see him. "Martin."

"*You.*"

Nikolai felt a smirk curl across his lips. Like a dog sizing up the enemy, his grin widened to show teeth.

"Is Summer with you?"

Nikolai slouched against the trellis near the front door. Despite his relaxed posture, every muscle was primed to spring at the slightest hint of provocation. "I was gonna ask the same thing. I haven't talked to her since this morning."

"But she knew I was coming back. We were having dinner."

"Her car's gone," Nikolai said, straightening and prowling closer to Martin. The man looked worried and that made Nikolai's insides burn with renewed vigor. "She left early afternoon."

Martin cursed under his breath. For a long drawn out second they traded a stare.

Martin's face turned an Incredible Hulk green. The man knew something, and he was damned well going to share even if Nikolai had to beat it out of the man. Nikolai pounced, grabbing two fistfuls of linen shirt. "If something's happened to Summer because of you…" His glare concluded the sentence, and he took immense satisfaction from the way Martin inched away as far as he could, given Nikolai's grip on his person.

"Have you tried to ring Summer on her cell phone?" Martin asked.

Pique rippled through Nikolai. Hell, she hadn't given him the number. "Nope. Have you?"

"A couple of times. It rings but she doesn't answer. I've left a message, but she hasn't rung back."

Nikolai let the man go. "Give me your phone."

Martin stepped out of Nikolai's range before he dug in the rear pocket of his designer jeans. He pulled out a phone not much bigger than a cigarette packet. "It's on speed dial four."

Speed dial four. Why didn't the man just rub his face in it? Nikolai took the miniature phone and stabbed the speed dial. He held the phone to his ear and hoped like hell Summer would answer. Four rings. Five rings…

"Hello."

"Who is this?" Nikolai demanded. "Where's Summer?"

The person on the other end wasn't cooperative. "Who is this?"

"Nikolai Tarei. Summer's neighbor," Nikolai gritted out. Damn this man had better have answers.

"Detective Matthews."

Fear sliced through Nikolai with the suddenness of guerilla fire. "Where's Summer?" He listened to the detective at the other end of the phone, his grip tightening on the phone until white showed on his knuckles. "Yeah. Okay." Nikolai hit the end button and handed the phone back to Martin. "Summer's in the hospital. Someone rear-ended her vehicle and fled the scene." He didn't add that the detective had sounded worried even though the man had tried to hide it. Nikolai took a deep breath, but it did little to dispel his own rising fear.

"Hospital? What's she doing there?" Dare asked.

Martin appeared uneasy, glancing at his watch every few minutes. Nikolai wondered why. "An accident. Someone ran her off the road. They're keeping her in overnight. You coming to the hospital?" Nikolai hated to ask but knew Summer would probably want to see the man.

Dare checked his expensive wristwatch again. "I can't. I have an important meeting in half an hour. That's why I've been trying to ring Summer—to cancel our dinner date. Look, tell her I'm sorry and that I'll check in on her later tonight."

"All right." Nikolai watched the man rush off to his car, but instead of driving off, the man made a call on his cell phone. Weird. Martin wasn't acting as if he was in a hurry. He didn't seem worried about Summer either. If anything, he looked pissed. Something or someone had rattled his cage.

Nikolai's thoughts turned back to Summer, and he hurried inside to collect his car keys. The cushy babysitting number Henry had handed him was turning into the assignment from hell. Summer was in danger right up to her pretty little neck, and if he wasn't careful, he was going to fail in his assignment.

Chapter Eight

Nikolai stood at the door of the hospital room, his gaze on the still form in the single bed. His heart jumped and stuck halfway up his throat, his pulse hammering as if he'd just finished training maneuvers. Summer looked so pale, so defenseless in the hospital bed, her blue-streaked hair a bright contrast to the wan face and the white pillowcase. A cold sweat beaded his brow. Hell, if anything happened to her he'd never forgive himself. This wasn't a mere job, a favor to Henry any longer. Somehow, somewhere along the line, Summer had wormed her way into his affections with her smart mouth and sassiness. Nikolai shook himself and stepped closer to the bed. He must have made a sound because Summer's eyes popped open.

"Hi," she whispered.

"Are…" Nikolai paused to clear the lump from his throat. "Are you okay?"

Summer nodded but winced slightly, enough to let him know she needed to stay right where she was in the hospital.

Nikolai grabbed a chair from the adjacent cubicle and set it next to Summer. "Are you up to telling me what happened?"

"I was driving to my Tae Kwon Do class. The traffic was heavier than normal so I took one of the back roads. A vehicle raced up behind, rear-ended me then drove off."

"Bastard." Anger flared and pumped through his veins. Nikolai didn't like the picture that was developing. Murky and disjointed as it was, it spelled danger for Summer. It was obvious someone wanted to hurt her. But that wasn't going to happen, not on his watch. Nikolai's jaw tensed—even if he had to watch her 24/7.

The need to touch her, to reassure himself that she breathed was a fire in his blood. After battling the need for long tension-filled seconds, he finally gave in and ran his fingers across the smooth skin of her brow. It wasn't enough. He had a desperate need to haul her into his arms and hold her, body aligned to body. A sexual charge jolted him, tightening his balls and jerking his cock. Instantly, disgust flew through his mind. Summer was hurt, yet he couldn't get past the sexual heat that licked through his veins whenever he was in the same room, breathing the same air as her. Hell, he wasn't sure whether to kiss her senseless or ream her out for being so reckless.

"I think it was on purpose. When I went off the road, he slowed then took off."

Bastard. Nikolai looked forward to plowing his fist into the driver's gut as soon as he caught up to him. He had to get rid of the angst riding him somehow. "Did you get a good look at him?"

Summer sighed. "Not really. Not enough to pick him out from a group of people."

"Number plate?" Nikolai snapped out.

"It was covered with mud."

A nurse bustled into the room, her soft-soled shoes squeaking on the hard floor. "How are you feeling? Still have a headache?"

"Yeah." Summer sounded rueful, and Nikolai noticed she refrained from nodding this time.

"How long before she can go home?" he asked the nurse.

"Tomorrow morning," the nurse answered with a cheerful grin. "Keeping her overnight is just a precaution. Your wife will be fine, Mr. Williams."

"Thank you." Nikolai caught Summer's hand and laced their fingers together, ignoring the soft choked sound that came from her.

"There was a phone call at the desk for you earlier. Your brother. He said he'll be by later to visit," the nurse said.

Summer's hand tightened within his, and her mouth opened to deny the possibility. Nikolai sent her a silent warning with an imperceptible shake of his head.

"Thanks," he said to the nurse. Nikolai waited until the squeak of her shoes faded into the distance before he voiced his suspicions. "Did you get someone to contact your family?"

"No. I asked the detective to ring you."

"It took him long enough," Nikolai muttered.

"He apologized for that. Your cell phone was switched off, and then he was called out on another case and forgot. He was really embarrassed. And I couldn't ring anyone because my phone was left in the car. The detective found it." She grinned. "Like I said—embarrassed. I think that's why he made a special trip to drop it off. Anyhow, I didn't ask him to ring my family. If they get wind of me being in the hospital they'll arrive *en masse* and ship me back to Eketahuna before I have time to blink." Summer clutched at his arm with a hint of desperation in her blue eyes. "Please don't contact them. You heard what the nurse said. I'm all right."

"If that wasn't your brother on the phone then we have a problem." Nikolai thought rapidly. There was only one solution. He needed to take her home, but first he'd check with the medical staff.

Nikolai stood. He passed the call button to Summer. "I'm going to find a doctor. If anyone comes in here and you don't like the look of them, press on the call button. Don't let up until someone answers. I'll be back as quickly as I can."

Nikolai returned in under ten minutes, his gut twisting with uneasiness the whole time he was away from Summer. When he strode into the hospital room, he found Summer asleep, her hand clutched around the call button. He considered telling her the clotheshorse intended to drop by to see her but decided to ignore his conscience. He'd keep her away from the man until he knew exactly what was going on and where the danger was coming from.

"What am I gonna do with you?" he muttered, shaking his head, the anger that had flared earlier dying when he saw her pale, tired face.

Her eyelid flickered. "Nikolai?"

"Yeah, sweetheart. Come on, let's get you dressed, and we'll split this joint."

"We're going?" Summer sounded fractionally more alert.

"Yeah. Under the circumstances, the doctor said I can take you home." He tugged the thin sheet away and helped Summer stand. No point filling her in on the rest of their conversation.

"Stay in the front," Summer mumbled.

Her disgruntled tone brought a grin. "Scared?" he taunted.

"Cautious." Summer wobbled a little.

Nikolai held her firmly. "I'll close my eyes." Not that he meant a word. He was a red-blooded male. Of course, he'd peek if she gave him the opportunity.

She wavered again, and Nikolai took control. He deftly undid the tapes that laced the hospital gown at the back and tugged it down her arms. She wore high-cut, pale blue panties beneath and nothing else. Nikolai paused, his gaze on her luscious breasts.

"You're beautiful," he murmured with a trace of awe. Coral-colored nipples were puckered as if begging for his touch. Nikolai swallowed before he remembered the need for urgency. They needed to leave before Summer's so-called brother turned up. Wordlessly, he held out a T-shirt for Summer to tug on. Once she was safely covered, he handed her the pair of jeans and steadied her while she stepped into them.

Nikolai shrugged out of his leather jacket and held it for Summer to slip her arms into. "It's cold out," he said when she hesitated. He curled his arm around her waist, and they walked from the room.

Despite the need to get Summer home and into bed, Nikolai took the precaution of driving in a roundabout route to make sure they didn't pick up any followers. Thirty minutes later, Nikolai drove into his garage and lowered the door using his remote control.

By the time Nikolai carried a sleeping Summer inside, stripped her to the sexy panties and placed her in his bed, all hints of temper had dispersed, leaving outright fear. Summer's reckless behavior of jumping in before she thought out the consequences had landed her hip-deep in trouble. If he wasn't careful, it would get her killed. Nikolai brushed tendrils of blue-streaked hair from her face. His gut twisted with tenderness at the childlike innocence he saw while an ironic smile curled his lips. He couldn't wait to see the expression on her face when she woke to find him in the same bed. Difficult to guess what her reaction would be. It could be outright horror or it could be a totally different reaction. His body tightened enough that he didn't have to second-guess his thoughts. He was bloody sick of fighting the sexual thing between them.

Nikolai gritted his teeth and ripped a black T-shirt over his head. He couldn't afford to relax his guard even if he gave into the lure of the woman-child. Summer was his responsibility and this time he intended to prove everyone wrong, despite the fact he'd never asked for the job in the first place.

His hands went to the button closure on his jeans. He hesitated, then shrugged and removed them, tossing the denims on the floor. Summer wanted grown-up, then that's what she'd get. This adult male slept naked and since she was the guest, she'd have to abide by house rules. Nikolai snorted at that piece of brilliance. Hell. And he thought she pushed the boundaries. Seemed he was ready to do some shoving of his own.

* * * * *

Summer woke slowly, cocooned in warmth and sublimely comfortable, apart from something digging into her back. Half awake, she stretched slowly and tried to wriggle away from the sharp, prodding object in her lower back. A masculine groan froze Summer on the spot. Her heart leapt while her brain processed the available information. Warm. Male. Hard object. Holy heck! She hadn't. She didn't. Who?

Summer turned rapidly and backed away from the warmth, clutching the sheet to her naked breasts.

"You awake?" Nikolai asked, his voice low and gritty.

He looked sleepy, sexy and dangerous as hell to every single one of her resolutions to stay away from big, bad SAS men. Yep, temptation personified.

Summer peeled her tongue off the roof of her mouth. She swallowed even as her gaze traced the dark stubble on his jaw and then across the broad shoulders. Naked shoulders. She searched her mind for answers and came up empty. Just her luck. She'd finally managed to corral a sexy man, there wasn't a parent or brother in sight, and she remembered zilch about the experience.

Zilch. Zip. Nada.

"Are you okay?" Nikolai propped himself up on his elbow and scrutinized her face.

Summer felt heat surge across her face. Inwardly, she tested her body. Nothing ached. Nothing hurt. She still had her panties on, but that didn't necessarily mean anything. She didn't feel the slightest difference. She should feel something. Shouldn't she?

"Did we...ah...do anything I should know about?"

Nikolai's eyes narrowed then a slow grin spread across his lips. "Was it good for you too, sweetheart?"

"Don't you know?" Summer retorted.

The grin transformed into a full-out chuckle. "Nothing happened."

Summer couldn't help the disappointment that surged through her body. It tinged her voice too, and she glanced away from his humor-filled face, chagrined by his lack of action. Here she had a man in the same bed, and he couldn't bear to touch her.

"Not yet."

The husky tone drew her gaze, but it was the seductive grin that held her still. "Not...not yet?" Her words were scarcely louder than a whisper, and they seemed to hang in the air between them.

Nikolai's gaze dropped to her breasts. "I thought we might explore a few possibilities."

Summer's jaw dropped. "Possibilities?"

"Is there an echo in here?"

"You're not making any sense. I'm confused."

"That makes two of us," he muttered, pouncing at the same time.

Summer found herself flat on her back, staring up at Nikolai. "What are you doing?"

"I don't know." His grin was slow and very personal. "When I find out, I'll let you know."

"Reassuring," she whispered. The hot look in his dark eyes made her breasts throb unbearably.

He combed his fingers through her hair, gently removing snarls from her curls. "Do you have a headache?"

"No. Is that my way out?" she murmured, feeling unaccountably nervous after seeing the intent in him. Her heart beat so fast she was sure he'd notice. The sweet ache in her breasts intensified, and she writhed uneasily, curious and suddenly nervous.

Nikolai traced the shape of her mouth with his forefinger. "That mouth of yours is full of sass. One day it's going to get you in trouble." He dipped his head and replaced his finger with his mouth.

Summer gasped, feeling as though the ground had been pulled from under her feet. But not Nikolai. He took total control of her mouth, angling and aligning their mouths for deeper contact. Summer clutched at his shoulders, and let him kiss her, part of her surprised and astonished in the reality.

Nikolai was kissing her of his own free will. What was wrong with this picture?

He lifted his head and smoothed the back of his hand across one cheek. "What's wrong?"

"I'm not sure. You tell me."

"You're looking a little confused."

Summer frowned. Although she found Nikolai attractive — very attractive — she wasn't entirely sure that the two of them together was a good thing. In some cases, one plus one didn't equal two. She sucked in a deep breath and met his brown eyes full on. "That's because I'm feeling confused. What's happened that's changed your mind about us?"

Nikolai toyed with one of her blue curls. The man seemed fascinated by her blue hair. "Someone is after you. You could have died yesterday."

Yesterday seemed hazy. Dreamlike. "Oh, yeah. The goat."

"The scum ball that ran you off the road," Nikolai said in a hard voice. "It made me realize we were wasting time. We want each other. So we should act on it."

Summer darted a gaze past his right shoulder then stared at Nikolai. "Who are you, masked man?" she demanded. "What have you done with the big, bad SAS man?"

"He's still here," Nikolai growled. "And he's fed up with talk."

"Oh, an action man," Summer purred.

Nikolai bent to kiss her again, his hands gliding beneath the sheet that covered her. "I could always put you over my knee."

A quiver rocked her. "I must be sick," she muttered. "That actually sounds like fun."

Nikolai drew in a sharp breath. "Enough." He took her lips in a masterful kiss that left her in no doubt of his impatience with talk. The sheet disappeared from between them and suddenly skin touched skin.

Summer forgot about talk. Especially since his bare chest flattened her breasts. He traced the shape of her lips with his tongue then teased them apart. Summer's heart thudded with an erratic beat. Her hands curled around his upper arms, her fingers flexing against his biceps. She made a shy foray with her tongue, probing the cavern of his mouth, learning his taste and texture.

Nikolai pulled away and stared down at her. "I shouldn't be doing this, Summer, but so help me, I don't think I can stop." His voice was low, smoky and a trifle unsure, but his eyes blazed full of heat.

"I want this, Nikolai. I'm not a child. I know what I'm doing."

"Sure as hell glad one of us does."

If he started spouting about their age differences, she was going to commit murder. Summer thought frantically and came up with one possible solution. It wasn't her best but she'd go with it. She pushed against his shoulders until he moved off her.

He flopped over on his back and stared up at the ceiling. "You don't have to shove—"

Summer launched her body across the bed and pinned him in place. "Don't move an inch," she snarled.

For an instant he looked nonplussed, then a sexy grin crawled across his face, making his eyes twinkle with pure devilment. "Sweetheart, I'm all yours. Do your worst."

A snort built at the back of her throat. Now why didn't she believe that? The man couldn't help himself. He'd have to take control at some stage. Her lids lowered to hide the burst of excited emotion that tore through her body. She might not have much experience when it came to sex, but she wasn't a librarian for nothing. She, Summer Williams, was hell on wheels when it came to research and intended to put every bit of her knowledge to use.

Sucking in a breath, her gut and all other necessary parts, she stood and rounded the bed. Nikolai followed her movements avidly. She could feel his gaze scanning her breasts, her waist and hips. Everywhere his gaze touched, her skin tingled. A light-headed sensation flooded her mind — part fear, part exhilaration — sort of how she imagined a person felt standing on the edge of a bungee platform. If she added hunger to the pot, along with curiosity and good old-fashioned lust, then she had the makings of a successful affair. All she needed to do was a little mixing and folding of the ingredients.

Summer stooped close, giving him a good view of her breasts. The sharp intake of his breath gave her confidence a boost. There were two people in this game. At the same time as she flashed her boobs in his face, she tugged at the cotton sheet that covered him. Feeling like a kid at Christmastime, she peeled back the cotton sheet and excitement flooded her, drying her mouth as inch by inch his body was revealed.

She mentally added tight abs, muscled and strong plus slim hips to the set of broad shoulders and the muscular, almost hairless chest she could already see and visualize without any problem. The sheet snagged a little at this point, and Summer felt a flood of heat collect in her cheeks. Somehow, seeing the male penis in books was different than seeing the real thing.

A soft choking noise dragged her gaze from the tented sheet at his groin to the glint in his eyes. His mouth twitched as though he was trying to choke back a laugh.

"Your wish is my command, sweetheart."

She'd have to be both blind and deaf to miss the overt challenge. *Your wish is my command.* Huh! Summer intended to give him command all right. She forced a sly smile to her mouth even though the effort brought a renewed surge of color to her cheeks. Then, recalling something she'd read in *Miranda* magazine, she let her tongue snake out and slowly and carefully licked her lips, making sure he had an excellent view of the whole procedure.

To her immense satisfaction, the laughter vanished, replaced by alertness. His hands clenched beneath his head, his face tightened and even better, she noticed a tic throb to life in his jaw.

Right, now she had his attention, she'd continue with her exploration. Her heart thudded as her gaze returned to the tented sheet at his groin. As she watched, it twitched. A soft groan from the other end of the bed fueled her courage, but even so, her hand trembled as she lifted the sheet from his lower body and let it drift to the floor.

The man was all muscle and smooth, lightly tanned skin, but it was his...*his cock*, she thought, determined not to act old-maidish at the first hurdle that snared her attention. Long and thick, it jutted out and upward. Summer glanced at Nikolai and saw he watched her, no doubt waiting for her to bolt.

That wasn't going to happen.

She wanted to touch him so badly. Her breasts tingled, the tips feeling tight and achy while her panties were damp. Summer sat on the edge of the bed, right next to his hipbone. The position was awkward so she crawled onto the bed and wantonly straddled his legs. Under her fascinated gaze, his cock jerked and seemed to grow even larger. Longer. As if hypnotized, she reached with her hand, caressing the warm length of him. Her palm curled around him as she explored. Warm—yes, she'd discovered that. Smooth yet with an underlying strength. The cliché of satin over steel fit perfectly, and Summer could see why the expression was used so often. Not exactly attractive to the eye but definitely fascinating, she decided.

She ran her thumb along the length of him then caressed the smooth, swollen head. A deep red, almost purple color with a tiny slit at the end. As she smoothed her thumb across the slit, a bead of liquid appeared. Summer ran her thumb over the glistening end, and Nikolai jerked, a low hum of need issuing from deep in his throat.

Okay, so she hadn't killed him. Yet.

Summer absently worked her hand the length of his erection while she pondered what to do next. An article in *Miranda* magazine popped into her mind. Oral sex. The thought didn't horrify her—in fact, it sounded interesting. Summer bent closer and stroked her tongue along his length. The soft groan from Nikolai and the jerk of his hips made her smile. Power. She had the ability to bring the big, bad SAS man to his knees. She repeated the move, breathing deeply. He smelled faintly of soap and tasted a little salty and musky. She licked around the swollen head of his cock and lapped across the slit. Another bead of liquid appeared and she licked it up. Then she opened her mouth and took the tip of his erection inside, swirling her tongue around him as though he were an ice cream.

"Summer," Nikolai whispered hoarsely.

Using one hand, she scraped her hair back from her face and glanced up at him. The deep emotion she saw in his eyes sent her pulse skittering. The knowledge that she'd brought that look to his face made the small victory all the sweeter. She lapped around the head of his cock again, loving the taste and the small sounds he made at the back of his throat. His hips jerked upward, pushing him deeper into her mouth before he drew back and away.

Summer stared at him in surprise. He'd seemed to enjoy what she was doing. Why was he stopping? "Why?" she whispered.

"Not for your first time, Summer. It is your first time?"

She nodded, unable to take her eyes from his face, his mouth. She felt as though she was balanced on a tightrope with the object of her desire inches away. A sweet ache pulsed in her lower belly, the harbinger of more to come.

"I should be shot." Nikolai brushed his hands over his face then centered his attention on her. "I want your pleasure too," he murmured. "Not just mine."

Summer licked suddenly dry lips. Had she been too forward? Too eager? "So, what do you want to do?"

"Let's start with Lovemaking 101." A gentle smile took the sting from his words. "And the first thing we should do is even the odds. I'm feeling a little underdressed." His eyes concentrated on the silky blue fabric that screened her from his sight. "What do you say?"

His words wound around her heart and gripped so tightly she could barely think let alone answer. Her hands skimmed down to her hips, and she pushed her fingers under the elastic band.

"Let me," he said, moving so quickly that she didn't have time to think of all the reasons why showing her naked body in broad daylight was bad, let alone utter them. He tugged the panties down her legs then lifted her off him to complete the process. Seconds later, she found herself flat on her back with Nikolai looming over her. Gone was the sullen SAS man who looked after her under protest. Gone was the teasing male who'd suggested they start with the basics.

"You're so beautiful," he said in a low voice she had to strain to hear. "I don't know why you picked me, but I'm not giving you another chance to get away."

"I don't want to get away," Summer said. "I want...you."

Nikolai stroked one of his hands the length of her body, from her collarbone, over one quivering breast and lower, across her belly to come to a stop at heart-shaped pubic hair. He glanced up. "Now this is a surprise." His head dipped and he ran his tongue around the outside of the small heart.

Summer felt his touch clear to her toes. The throb in her belly centralized, and she stirred restlessly, needing his touch. Heck, she'd start begging soon. And from the glint in his eyes, the man knew it. Was probably waiting for the words to spill from her mouth.

"I touched you," she pointed out, not too happy with the breathy sound of her voice.

"Yes." He splayed her legs and settled between them, his gaze on her nether regions.

Summer swallowed. Her pussy. Instantly, the heat intensified there. To her mortification, liquid gushed from her, trickling down the inside of one thigh. She squeezed her eyes shut. She'd never, ever become this hot from masturbating. Already, she felt as though she'd burst from her skin, and he'd scarcely touched her. Damn, she might beg yet.

"So pretty." Nikolai's fingers traced around her heart then drifted lower still to her aching center. He brushed his thumb over her clit, just enough to give her a buzz. The sensation that shot through her was half pleasure, half pain.

"More. Harder. I need you to touch me." The words rushed past her lips, and she waited for him to act the smug male.

It didn't happen.

Nikolai smoothed his thumb across her clit again and pushed one finger into her tight channel. His finger eased emptiness inside that Summer hadn't realized she had.

"That would feel so much better if it was you," she said.

"Last time I checked, the finger belonged to me."

Cursed color flooded her cheeks and seeped even lower to tingle through her breasts. "I mean *you*. Your cock," she added with a trace of defiance.

He gave a bark of laughter. "Still trying to call the shots, sweetheart? This is my turn. We'll do things my way." He slid a second finger inside her, pushing them as deep as he could.

Summer quivered at the sense of fullness, squeezed her eyes shut and concentrated on every sensation. The squelch as his fingers forged inside her then retreated. The shimmer that swept her body with each cruise of a finger across her clit. The thud of her heart. But most of all, she savored the feeling of closeness, of sharing something intensely personal with Nikolai.

A different sensation across her clit made her eyes fly open. Nikolai's head was bent as he tongued her clit, teasing the small nub then retreating so she balanced on a pinnacle. His fingers slowly pumped in and out while he continued to tease. Summer lifted her hips trying to maintain pressure on her aching clit. The feeling was too much. It wasn't enough. She wanted...she wanted...

Just then, Nikolai looked up and met her gaze. He lapped his tongue around her clit, the bundles of nerves jumping while he maintained eye contact. Summer couldn't have looked away if she tried. His pupils were huge. Black. Full of heat and promise. With each pass of his tongue, she throbbed with sensation. He picked up the pace, alternately licking her clit and filling her with his fingers. The ache intensified until it became painful. Each lap of his tongue made it worse. Made it better. Summer swallowed and bit her bottom lip, trying not to cry out. Making love felt so much better with Nikolai. So much better. More fulfilling.

Another slow foray of his tongue deepened the feeling. Her entire lower body prickled and throbbed. Her hips jerked sharply upward. Nikolai grasped one hip, holding her still. One soft lap of his tongue across her sensitized clitoris sent her over the edge. She shuddered deeply, her clit pulsing rapidly, sending spasms of pure pleasure shooting the length of her body. Her pussy clasped around Nikolai's fingers, gripping tightly. Slowly, Summer floated back into her body.

Nikolai grinned up at her, and moved up the bed to kiss her. She tasted herself on his breath and something else that was uniquely Nikolai—wild and dangerous and intense. Their tongues twirled together in a lazy dance then Nikolai pulled away slightly. He fingered a nipple, and automatically Summer arched her back, moving into his touch.

"You're so responsive," he breathed. He rained a trail of kisses from the corner of her mouth, down her neck and across her collarbone. When his mouth latched onto a nipple, Summer's heart skipped a beat. The tug of his mouth caused a corresponding tug, a clench of her womb.

Summer clasped his head to her breast, her fingers tangling in his curly black hair. "That feels great," she murmured.

Nikolai pulled away, letting go of her nipple slowly to gaze up at her with sleepy eyes. "There's more yet," he promised. "And it will be even better."

Summer's heart flip-flopped, and she couldn't help the blazing smile that curved her lips. "More?"

"Oh, yeah." Nikolai tugged on a lock of her hair, the small pain making her frown. He covered her mouth with his, feeding from her lips and stoking the fire deep inside her to greater heights.

Nikolai cupped a breast and tucked a hand under her butt, aligning their bodies together. His penis fit between her legs, fueling longing in Summer.

"I want you so bad," Nikolai murmured. "Are you sure you want me? It's not too late to change your mind."

"Too much talk," Summer protested. "More action required."

Nikolai clutched her tightly against his larger frame, squeezing the air from her lungs. "Don't say I never gave you the opportunity," he said in a fierce tone.

He left her then, leaving Summer gazing at him in bewilderment. But when he opened the top drawer of his bedside table, enlightenment followed in the guise of a small foil packet.

Summer gulped. She'd read the articles in *Miranda* magazine, but in the heat of the moment, she'd forgotten. Not Nikolai. He ripped the foil packet open with his teeth.

"Can I do it? Put the condom on for you?"

Nikolai groaned. "Not this time, sweetheart. I'm too close. One touch and I'll lose it." He smoothed the rubber on with an expertise that Summer could only admire. "I want to come inside you."

Oh, boy. Grown-up stuff. Summer wanted that too.

He trailed a hand across her belly and journeyed downward to teasingly circle her clit. A frown crossed his face, and he glanced up at her. "This might hurt. Talk to me. Tell me what you're feeling."

Real grown-up stuff. Nikolai's clever fingers skated across her clit again then parted her folds and pressed into her channel. Juices moistened his way. Summer heard the embarrassing squelch and winced.

"Don't. It turns me on knowing that you're wet for me, that you want me so much." His large frame shuddered as he uttered the words, and he pulled his finger from her, replacing it with the blunt tip of his cock. He shuddered again. "I'll take this slow, even if it kills me."

Summer's breath caught as he pushed slowly inside her, stretching untried muscles until she felt unpleasantly full. Then he pulled out. She clutched at his tight buttocks, only relaxing when he pushed into her again. A little further this time.

"You're so tight," he murmured, surging and retreating, pushing deeper each time.

A twinge of pain took her by surprise. A cry escaped, and Nikolai stilled, seated deep inside her womb. The sense of fullness was weird, yet she liked it. He kissed her, and after searching her face, he continued with his strokes and kisses. His tongue plunged into her mouth with the same slow surge and retreat as his cock. Each easy stroke of his cock massaged her clit. Summer picked up the rhythm, moving with him in countermoves. Gradually, Nikolai increased his speed, cupping a butt cheek in each hand to lift her higher and angle the strokes.

Summer felt the familiar hum of arousal streak from her clit. She groaned and swallowed, directing his strokes with insistent hands on his backside. She was close. So close. "Nikolai," she breathed, reaching, searching for more. Suddenly she was there. Heat scorched her body, streaking along her length. Ripples of fulfillment shot through her body for long seconds after. It was like a signal to Nikolai. He stroked harder, faster. Quicker. Her pussy clenched tight around his cock with neverending ripples. Nikolai gasped, his hips thrusting in quick, frantic strokes. He shuddered and clasped her tight, his heart pounding against her ribs.

When his breathing finally returned to something resembling normal, he eased from her body then folded her into his arms as if she were the most precious object. The big, bad SAS man held her, running his hands across her sweaty back, his body heat searing her chest, making Summer feel safe, and valued. Making Summer feel loved.

Chapter Nine

Nikolai held Summer tight and savored the feel of her plastered the length of his body. He couldn't regret making love to her, even though he knew Henry wouldn't see things the same way. Nikolai's mouth twisted in a rueful grimace. He didn't especially look forward to meeting her family, reacquainting himself with her brothers. Good blokes to have on the same side, he remembered from a previous mission when his team had combined with another unit. The two Williams brothers were a force to be reckoned with. He shrugged inwardly, knowing he wouldn't change things even if he could. The only way to keep Summer safe was to stay at her side.

"Whatz the time?" Summer mumbled against his chest.

Nikolai glanced across at the bedside cabinet. "Just gone eight."

Summer bounded upright so quickly she almost fell off the bed. "I'm going to be late for work. Mrs. Ferguson will have a cow."

"You're not going to work today," Nikolai said.

"But I—"

"I'll ring Mrs. Ferguson. What's the number?" He climbed from the bed and grabbed his jeans off the floor. Seconds later he held up a cell phone, his finger poised to dial.

"This will be good," Summer muttered. "Does it have speaker phone? I can't wait to hear Mrs. Ferguson get the better of you."

Nikolai loved the way Summer said what she thought and stood up to him. Laura had acted a little frightened of him, watching him as though he were a lit fuse. A throwback to her childhood, he presumed, since he'd never hit a woman in his life. He hadn't realized how much Laura's quiet anxiety had bugged him until he'd come face-to-face with Summer's feistiness.

"No speaker phone," he said. "You'll have to listen to a one-sided conversation." Someone picked up the phone on the other end and he asked for Mrs. Ferguson. A minute later, he hung up. "There," he said. "What did I tell you?" He hid a smirk at her distinct eye roll. Nikolai glanced at the clock again and aimed for casual as he sat on the bed beside Summer. Or as casual as a man could be with a raging hard-on. "We have time for breakfast or time to sleep some more. Your call."

Dark brows shot upward, and her breasts jiggled when she made a sudden move. Nikolai would have been half dead if he hadn't appreciated the sight.

"Would there be sleep involved?" she asked in a throaty drawl.

"That would depend on you." A grin stalked his lips although he tried to keep it low-key and under control. He didn't want to frighten her off, but hoped like hell she wanted a repeat performance as much as he did.

Summer pursed her lips while her blue eyes twinkled. "Actually, I have a few ideas of how we could spend that time."

"Yeah?" The naughty twinkle in her eyes hiked his pulse rate. This was the woman who had been a virgin until a little under an hour ago. Call him a macho pig, but he was meant to be the one with the ideas. The wry thought made him shake his head. Luckily, he hadn't verbalized that one. Summer had already shown she had definite ideas about being allocated the little woman slot.

"I'd like to try some different positions. For a start."

Nikolai gaped momentarily before snapping his mouth shut. Hell, he'd created a monster. "Sounds interesting," he said cautiously. "What did you have in mind?"

"Everything," she said simply. "Everything you want to teach me."

Nikolai swallowed. He had to. Everything covered an awful lot of ground. He closed the distance between them. "Are you sure you feel okay? No headache?"

"I'm more than all right." Summer leaned back against a pillow, stretching her body the length of the mattress like a cat.

Nikolai's grin sprang free. Unlike some women he'd been with, she didn't seem worried about her body being on display. She wasn't cowering under the sheet, moaning about big hips, the wrong size breasts or a large butt. He liked that.

"What are you grinning about?" she demanded, her lips curved in a sultry pout. The mischievous glint remained. "Going through your repertoire of positions?"

A snort escaped. *Positions.* What would she come out with next? He advanced on her, intending to crowd her, to make her aware of him. And to fill her mind so full of him, she wouldn't keep trying to call the shots.

"What do you know about positions?"

"I'm a librarian. I'm good at research. There's missionary, which we've done, doggy-style, ride—"

Nikolai lowered his head. Only one surefire way of shutting her up. His lips closed over hers just as she let loose a giggle. It was like kissing a glass of champagne. He'd never particularly liked the girly drink. On Summer, it tasted classy and made him hotter than he'd ever felt before with another woman. Their lips slid together, tasting, sipping until the laughter disappeared. Sexual energy arced between them.

Amazing. Bloody amazing, Nikolai thought. He let his tongue flicker into her mouth, exploring the moist warmth beyond. His cock twitched insistently, aching for possession. God, he wanted to sink into her warmth any way he could. He didn't care about position. Like a Neanderthal, he just wanted in. Immediate satisfaction. Nikolai pulled away from her mouth and kissed a trail down her neck, exploring the curve of her chin, the delicate skin by her ear where a pulse beat madly. He scraped his teeth lightly over the jumping pulse, and she moaned.

"That feels amazing," she murmured in a low voice. "I have the urge to tell you to bite harder, to mark me." Summer lifted her head then, her blue eyes full of wonder and smoky promise that pushed his heartbeat into a gallop. "Except Mrs. Ferguson does neck check every Monday morning."

"I thought you worked in a library?"

"Yeah. Mrs. Ferguson is big into leading by example. Hickeys don't set a good example to our younger customers. Hickeys are directly responsible for teenage pregnancy."

Pregnancy. For one frozen millisecond, Nikolai pictured Summer swollen with his child. And once the idea took root in his mind, it was difficult to shake. He breathed deep then brutally pushed aside the vision. He'd been a father once, and a damned fine job he'd made of that. Soldiers had no right thinking about parenthood when they couldn't be home to raise their children and keep them safe.

A soft touch on his cheek jerked him back to Summer. "Where were you?"

"Just trying to decide which position."

"And?" Summer's eyes twinkled naughtily. "Go on. Don't keep me in suspense."

A bark of laughter escaped Nikolai as he grabbed Summer and rolled her on top of him. "We'll start slow with you on top."

"I always liked riding." Summer's cheeky grin as she straddled his hips brought awe to the surface. She made everything fun, and it was a new experience for him. Almost as though he were the pupil and she the teacher.

"Come up here," Nikolai murmured. Perhaps it was time to enjoy the fun, embrace it. He patted the bed at chest level. "So I can see better."

"That's not the business end," Summer retorted, not moving an inch.

"I'm the teacher here." His mouth quirked. Man, she cracked him up. "Why don't you follow instructions like a good soldier?"

"I don't do orders."

"No, but aren't you curious?" Of course, she was. The inquisitive spark in her eyes glowed true and clear for him to see. "Come up here. Please."

Summer moved at the pace of a geriatric snail. Intense anticipation roared through Nikolai. The urgent need to claim her pulsed through his mind, but he wanted to prolong the loving, and make it mind-blowing for both of them.

"There. Stop there," Nikolai said. His voice came out hoarse and tight. Summer still straddled him and, stretched as she was, she gave him the perfect view. Her dark pubic hair was trimmed into the sexy heart while the rest of her was bare and smooth under his questing eyes. "You're pretty. Plump and ripe for my touch." As he spoke, he strummed a finger across her labia and parted the plump folds. Using his hands, he urged her closer and blew softly on her swollen clitoris.

Summer swayed. A small mew escaped. Nikolai glanced up, his gaze savoring her ripe breasts and pillowy curves before he saw her eyes. They were squeezed tightly shut. He blew again, and her body jerked. So responsive. Nikolai drew one finger the length of her smooth pussy, ending with a slow circle around her clit. Her juices moistened his finger as he repeated the process.

"Touch me," Summer pleaded in a breathless voice. "No teasing."

Nikolai smiled inwardly. Teasing was half the fun, especially with a woman as hot as Summer. "Tell me what you want." Nikolai smiled up at her. "Be precise so I don't get it wrong."

Summer sucked in a harsh breath. Her lovely breasts lifted then settled, her nipples tight and needy, reminding him he had to explore her a little more.

"Okay." Summer sounded breathless but determined. "I want you to touch my clit with your tongue. I want you to lick me until I'm hot and can't bear it any more. Then I want you to put your cock inside me. I want you to thrust hard and fast while I ride you. I want you to make me come."

A quick grin replaced the niggling doubt inside him. He'd been right. Nothing fazed her. She wasn't all talk about wanting to meet on equal terms. She really wanted a man who challenged her and was man enough to accept any challenges she issued. Nikolai felt his balls tighten painfully. He hoped he was capable enough to keep up with her demands.

"Is that all?" he asked.

"For starters," she said primly.

"You got all this from research?" Nikolai brushed his thumb across her clit, reveling in her sigh, her musky scent.

"Yeah."

Man, he couldn't wait to hear what else she had in mind. "Move a little closer," he whispered. He positioned her level with his mouth and breathed deep. She smelled musky of sex and citrus, and tasted better. Going slow and easy, he parted her folds and raked his tongue along her cleft, then teased her clit with a much lighter pressure. She shuddered and gave a soft moan that tugged at his cock. He felt his penis lengthen while his heart thundered. Nikolai listened to his body and increased the pace. Instead of teasing, he alternatively licked and lapped at her engorged flesh. Summer was so wet for him. And a vocal lover.

"More. Harder. I need you inside me."

Nikolai gave her the steady thrust of his finger while he continued to lap and nibble around the edge of her clit, feeding on her juices, and urging her higher and higher.

"Oh, Nikolai. I'm so close. Stop. It's too much."

He didn't think she meant that so he kept on pushing her higher, thrusting two and then three fingers deep inside her cunt while he licked and sucked some more, slowing now to tease because he loved the way she moaned, her hips jerking, silently pleading for a deeper possession.

"No more!" Summer wrenched away, her chest rising and falling rapidly as though she'd run a race. She ran a hand the length of his cock, her thumb smoothing across the drop of precum at the end. "I want to come with you inside me. I want to feel your cock stretching me."

"Condom," Nikolai muttered. Damn, she unmanned him with her honesty. His gaze wandered the curves of her rounded ass as she bent to retrieve a foil packet from his bedside cabinet. Tempted, he ran his hand across one smooth butt cheek then down the crack between, down her perineum until his fingers touched her moist pussy. Her intense shudder filled him with anticipation for the weeks ahead, the adventure in store.

Summer tugged the foil packet open and pulled the latex out, handing it to him. "You do it."

"Don't you know — ?"

"I know how to do it. Done it before," she said with a grin. "Banana."

A banana. *Hell's teeth.* And she called that experience? Bemused, Nikolai rolled the condom on with a trembling hand and waited for her next move.

"Haven't done this next step before," she said cheerfully. "I figure you'll tell me if I don't do it right."

Her honesty was gonna kill him. Nikolai helped her guide his cock inside her pussy then waited for her to impale herself. She did — inch by tortuous inch until he shook like a green boy, so close to climax that he was afraid to move. He took refuge in talk, trying to distract himself from the raw sensation that stalked his body searching for a way out.

"Nothing we do together is wrong, or has a right or wrong way," he muttered through gritted teeth.

Summer moved the last fraction of an inch until she was fully impaled. She rocked her body in an experimental move. "I feel so full that it almost hurts. But it's a good pain," she added. "What do I do now?"

Nikolai almost laughed. She asked for instruction now? Hell, if she did any better he'd internally combust. "Just move. Any way that feels good to you."

She lifted then sank down. Her eyes drifted shut while her breasts bobbed in front of his face. "That feels sooo good." She repeated the move and added a swivel of her hips. Her breath hissed out. "Good."

Nikolai reached for a breast when it moved close to his face again. Her eyes flew open as he shaped the globe with his callused fingers then drew her pouting nipple into his mouth and sucked hard.

"Bite me," she murmured, rising until her nipple almost released from his mouth, then returning.

The fire in his loins blazed. Higher. Harder. Deeper. With each lazy rock of her hips. Nikolai bit down on her nipple, giving her enough teeth to send signals through her body, but not hard enough to break any skin. Her entire body shook while her sweet pussy clasped him tighter. He bit down a little harder and pinched her other nipple with his hand. Her cunt tightened around his cock. Nikolai groaned, his hips jerking, moving in counterpoint to her slow rocking. Nikolai let go of her breasts and grabbed hold of Summer's hips.

"Close?" he murmured.

"Mmmm." Summer arched her back, grinding her clit against the base of his cock.

Nikolai smoothed a finger across her clit, and she exploded around him, her pussy squeezing him rhythmically.

"Nikolai." Summer threw back her head and groaned.

He thrust upward. Once. Twice. Hard and fast while her cunt grabbed at him. Orgasm burst through him, an explosion of heat that seemed to go on and on as he spurted his seed.

They fell on the bed together, Summer aligned along his body. Nikolai held her tight, their bodies still joined. His eyes closed and he drifted into sleep.

* * * * *

Insistent thumping on Nikolai's front door pulled him awake. For an instant, he had no idea where he was, and then Summer's soft sigh clued him in. He moved her carefully off his chest and dealt with the condom that still cloaked his semi-limp cock.

"Not the smartest thing to go to sleep like that," he muttered as thoughts of his seed leaking from the condom filled his mind. Better not happen again.

Whoever was at his door started to lean on the doorbell. He grabbed up his jeans, thrust his legs into them and yanked up. He hurried down the passage leading to the front door and dragged up the zipper before he opened the door.

Jake and Louie stood on the other side.

"I should have known," he groused, glaring at his mates. "What do you want?"

"Looks like we caught Nik at a bad time," Jake said.

"Can we come in?" Louie asked.

"No," Nikolai said flatly.

Louie peered past Nikolai and the partially closed door. "Do you have a guest?"

"Yes."

"A man of few words," Jake mused. "We want details."

"None of your bloody business. What do you want?"

"Who do you have in your bed? I didn't think you let women into your house since Laura." Louie grinned hard enough that Nikolai was tempted to hit him.

"Back off," Nikolai muttered.

"I wonder if it's the babe," Jake said.

"Henry's niece?" Louie asked.

"Cut it out," Nikolai snarled. "Summer is here but not for the reasons you think," he muttered when they both grinned like loons. "Someone tried to run Summer off the road yesterday. Then they rang the hospital and said they'd be in to visit. They told the nurse they were related to Summer. No one else knew she was there except the cops and Martin. Someone planted drugs in Henry's house then informed the cops. I tell you Summer is here for her protection, no other reason."

His friends sobered, and then suddenly Louie's grin took flight again. "You know, Nik, I almost believe you." He leaned close and whispered, "But the babe looks as though she's had more than a sleep. In fact, if I was being crude, I'd say she'd had a good f—" The air exploded from his lungs, encouraged by Nikolai's fist applied to his stomach. He danced out of range to complete his sentence. "Fuck."

"No one asked you," Nikolai snapped. He wanted to slam the door in his friends' faces, but the soft footsteps behind told him Summer had made an appearance and had most likely seen their visitors. The footsteps moved closer. Nikolai smelled his soap as she stopped beside him. Desire kicked him in the gut when he glanced at Summer. Damp curls framed her face while her lips were red and swollen. Damn. He'd wanted to share a shower. The first woman he'd ever met who took quick showers and he missed it. His gaze wandered her body, noting she'd also taken the time to raid his wardrobe. The long navy blue T-shirt plus the pair of black boxer shorts looked damned fine.

Taking advantage of his distraction, Louie pushed past him into the house, and ran a quick hand across Summer's cheek. "Nik said someone tried to hurt you."

Nikolai suddenly felt very possessive. If Louie didn't step away, he'd be the hurt one. He growled under his breath, but of course, Louie didn't back off.

Jake stepped inside his hallway too, taking Nikolai unawares and forcing him to take a step backward. His friend slung his arm around Summer's shoulders. "You okay, cupcake?"

"I'll make coffee," Nikolai muttered. No one took the slightest notice. With a last glare at Louie and Jake, Nikolai stomped into the kitchen.

Eventually, they all ended up in the kitchen, sitting around Nikolai's wooden table and nursing cups of black coffee—black being mandatory since the milk was off. Jake and Louie looked comfortable, as though they had settled in for the duration. They chatted away with Summer and generally made themselves at home.

"Is there a reason for this visit?" Nikolai asked, doing his best to keep his voice calm. Level. It didn't come off. He sounded plain testy and pissed.

"Captain wants us to go in this afternoon," Louie said, his gaze skimming across Summer in silent warning.

"So, why are you here?" Nikolai snapped. "I'm on sick leave."

"Captain said he wanted you in on the mission too."

Nikolai glanced across at Summer and saw she was watching him. A faint smile twitched at her lips. And it made him wish his friends to Outer Siberia. The need to claim her lips leapt inside him, but the last thing he wanted was an audience, especially spectators who were likely to critique his performance.

Summer stroked her fingers across his forearm. Nikolai barely suppressed the shiver of awareness that raced through him. Damn, he had it bad. He was sick—definitely too ill to go on a mission. But no, that wasn't good either. *Remember Henry.*

The smile widened as though she read his confused thoughts. "You don't need to worry about me. I'll be fine."

"As far as I know, it's only a strategy meeting," Louie said. "We'll only be gone a few hours."

"No problem. What can happen in a few hours?" Summer said.

Nikolai snorted. "Where you're concerned—quite a bit." She'd lived in Auckland for a few days short of a month and so far had hooked up with a gangster, had a break-in, been taken in for questioning by the police and someone had run her off the road. And that was just for starters. Nikolai didn't intend to add losing her virginity to an older man to the list—not when he was trying to convince himself that sex didn't count in this situation since it was consensual.

"I'm not a child."

"No one said you were." Nikolai glanced away from Summer to see Louie and Jake observing them closely. "How long? Two hours? Three? Okay. You've got my number. You can ring if you need us."

* * * * *

Summer watched the three men leave with something like relief. The testosterone in the kitchen had been so thick she'd thought about getting up to open the window. It was the same when her brothers were at home with their friends. One on one was fine, but if you had a herd of the big he-men, then things turned ugly. Especially if you were unlucky enough to be related to some of them. Summer shut the front door and wandered back into Nikolai's kitchen. The room was functional and basic with no feminine frills. The gray bench, the color of her father's goslings, which her mother muttered about tossing into the soup pot, and the teal blue cupboard units were newly installed. Nikolai had tiled the floor with tiles a shade lighter than the bench. The wooden table in the middle of the tiled floor still needed sanding down and varnishing. Add a few plants and a blind or some curtains and the place wouldn't look too bad.

From the little her uncle had told her about Nikolai, he'd purchased this house some time ago but had only started on renovations recently while he was on sick leave. Nikolai's bedroom and the kitchen were completed, while the other rooms were stripped back to basics, waiting for a coat of paint and some tender loving care. Summer wrinkled her nose at the sharp scent of paint. It was worse in this part of the house. Despite breathing in slow, shallow pants, the paint was affecting her breathing. Her chest tightened enough that she knew she'd have to go home to find her inhaler.

Summer collected the clothes she'd worn the previous day along with her handbag and keys. She peered out the windows for a long time, checking for anything that looked remotely suspicious. Living with SAS brothers and an uncle had taught her a thing or two—not to mention the *Heroine's Handbook* she'd found on the library shelves. Positive the coast was free and clear of anything dangerous, she let herself out of Nikolai's house, navigated the missing boards on his deck and ducked through the gate in the boundary fence.

The door was locked when she tried it and nothing seemed out of place. Summer fished her keys from her bag, unlocked the door and stepped inside, flicking the safety chain on once she'd stepped into the foyer. First stop—her bedroom and an inhaler. The thought of an asthma attack hurried her along. Summer grabbed an inhaler off her dresser, took a quick puff then headed back to the kitchen.

A small red light flickered on the answering machine. Guilt stabbed Summer for an instant as she reached for the play button. She knew Nikolai wouldn't approve of her being here alone, but then he wouldn't want her to have an asthma attack either. Nah, no problem. She had a cast-iron excuse if—when—he started to holler.

Summer listened to the messages. Two calls that consisted totally of heavy breathing. Charming. Then Dare's voice floated into the kitchen. "Summer, it's Dare here. I wondered how you were. I rang the hospital but they said you'd signed out. I'm glad you're feeling better. I presume you're at work, so I'll ring you later this afternoon. Perhaps we could get together for dinner?"

Dare's message was the last one. Summer pressed the erase button then checked her watch. Maybe she should go to dinner with Dare and let him know she couldn't go out with him again.

A frown wrinkled her brow at the thought. She'd slept with Nikolai and enjoyed it, but were they actually together?

Hard to say. Summer pulled a rueful face when confusion poured through her. But the truth stood out. If she wanted to go further along the relationship road with Nikolai, she needed to talk to Dare. She was strictly a one-man-at-a-time kinda girl.

Decision made, she started to dial Dare's number then stopped and replaced the phone. It wasn't difficult to imagine Nikolai's reaction if she went out to dinner with Dare tonight. Besides, she rather liked the idea of exploring more positions, once she'd looked up the relevant article in *Miranda* magazine. Summer picked up the phone again. She'd suggest lunch and arrive back before Nikolai returned. What the big, bad SAS man didn't know wouldn't hurt him. Or her.

Chapter Ten

"Summer, how are you?" Dare rose from behind his desk and came around to greet her. Dressed in a smart charcoal gray suit with a black shirt and black and gray tie, he looked handsome and successful. But he wasn't Nikolai.

"I'm fine." she smiled, and wondered how to avoid a kiss without making a big issue of it. Dare aimed for her lips and in the end, she turned her head so his kiss landed on her cheek.

Dare grasped both her hands in his and stood back to study her, seemingly unperturbed by her action. "I've tried ringing. Your mobile was switched off. I wasn't sure if you were going to work or not."

"I slept in this morning." Summer felt the crawl of heat in her cheeks and knew she needed to change the subject fast. "Thanks for meeting me for lunch. I'm not a good invalid. Got bored with my own company." Summer found herself thinking about Nikolai's assertions—about Dare and his family being involved in illegal activities. If criminal propensity was written on his face, she couldn't see it. Dare appeared the same as he always seemed to her. Sophisticated. Attractive. Sexy.

Dare cleared his throat. "Do I need to wipe my face?"

Summer blinked then rapidly fixed a smile to her lips. Could she be any less subtle?

Amusement glittered in his eyes. "If there's lipstick on my face, it came from my mother. She popped in to see me about an hour ago."

Summer imagined her parents meeting Dare, and knew that although her mother was no pushover, she'd like Dare. Her father might take a little longer to warm to a man going out with his daughter. Ditto her brothers.

"Sorry," Summer said, aware she was woolgathering yet again. "Are you ready to go?"

"I'll let the restaurant staff know I'm going out then we're all set." He paused by the door to his office to smile at her. After tucking a curl behind her ear, he leisurely kissed her, taking Summer by surprise.

When they parted, Summer felt breathless. Her pulse throbbed faster than it had mere seconds ago. There had to be something wrong with her. She'd spent the morning in bed with Nikolai, enjoyed everything they'd done together and wanted to repeat the experience, yet she'd enjoyed kissing Dare. Go figure. She'd have to give the matter some rapid thought because her family wouldn't approve of her stringing along two men. Heck, she didn't approve! Especially since the object of the luncheon exercise was to end the budding relationship.

"You look beautiful," Dare murmured, his eyes skimming her body.

Summer had dressed carefully for the meeting, needing to bolster her nerves. Maybe she should have settled for the casual jeans and shirt instead of her favorite black skirt and the cream knit top that clung to her breasts. Too late now.

"Thanks." Summer nibbled her bottom lip as she tried to think of the right words to put a halt to their romantic liaison but remain friends. Not a single word came to mind.

Dare hustled her from his office with a warm hand at her waist. "I thought we'd have lunch at the Sky Tower today."

"Really?" Call her shallow, but she'd wanted to see what the penis-shaped tower looked like from the top. There hadn't been the time or opportunity so far. "That sounds great."

Minutes later, they were inside a cab heading for the Sky Tower.

"What are you doing for the rest of the day?" Dare asked.

"I'm not sure. I might stop by the bookstore on the way home. I want to see if my special order is in." She also intended to explore an adult shop and the different sex toys available, although she wasn't about to tell Dare that. An arc of energy buzzed from breast tips to her pussy at the thought of trying out toys and exploring her sexuality further with the help of Nikolai. The naughty thought solved Summer's dilemma. Yes, she'd enjoyed Dare's kisses, but she hadn't once thought of him and sex toys in the same sentence. She'd let this thing with Nikolai run its course, whatever that might be, and take each day as it arrived. Summer found herself wriggling about on the backseat while her heart jumped in acute anticipation.

Dare took possession of her hand, a small and private smile playing on his lips. "Were you a hyperactive child?"

"Not as bad as my brothers."

"Hmm. I think I'd like to meet them."

Summer didn't think so. "I liked your family," she said, changing the subject.

"I was sorry about being called away on business." Dare picked up her hand and pressed a moist kiss on her wrist right where her palm ended and her arm began. It tickled, making her uncomfortably aware of her body and the way her knit top clung to her breasts.

The cab pulled up outside Sky Tower. *Thank goodness*, Summer thought. He'd have to let her go. The man hadn't acted so touchy-feely on previous dates. Yes, he'd kissed her but he hadn't acted so obvious. What was going on here? Whatever it was, his actions were doing her head and giving her pulse a hell of a roller coaster ride.

Dare climbed from the cab, helped Summer out, then paid the driver.

Summer checked her watch, aware of the ticking clock stashed at the back of her mind and the continued confusion inside.

Dare took her arm, holding her close to his side, and whisked her into the Sky Hotel. Then they were in the lift speeding to the top of the tower before she knew it.

"Wow, that was quick." Summer yanked her hand from Dare's warm grasp to clutch at her stomach. "I think I left my tummy on the ground floor," she said with a rueful smile. At least she'd managed to regain possession of her hand.

They stepped from the lift and walked straight into the restaurant.

"Is this the revolving restaurant?" Summer peered out the closest window in awe. Auckland harbor stretched out in front of her with the dormant island volcano of Rangitoto in the foreground. Boats of all shapes and sizes dotted the blue water. It was no wonder people called it the city of sails. To her left was a marina of yachts while to her right a huge passenger ship disgorged tourists for their Auckland stopover. She turned to Dare. "Thank you for bringing me. The view is breathtaking."

A pleased smile softened his mouth. "I thought you'd enjoy it here. Once we get to our table, I'll point out some of the sights for you."

They were seated and had drinks in front of them before Summer had time to blink. She picked up her tall glass of orange juice and took a quick sip to wash away the dry cotton nerves in her mouth.

Dare consulted the menu and ordered for both of them without bothering to check her preferences.

"How do you know what I wanted to eat?" Summer asked, not bothering to hide the tartness in her voice. He'd done this before.

"I don't have much time. It speeds things up if I order."

The man was a control freak in all facets of his life as she was learning. Each date underlined the annoying habit a bit more.

"Would you like to go out to dinner tonight?" he asked, ignoring her protest in typical fashion.

"I'm sorry," Summer said evenly.

"I'll drop in and see you on the way home."

Summer stared. Bottle Top Bay was a little out of his way.

"Not tonight," she said.

"I won't stay long. Just long enough to reassure myself that you're okay."

His words made her nervous. Was he going to turn out to be one of those weird stalkers? A man she couldn't get rid of? Summer's stomach flipped with an attack of sudden nerves. It was easy to imagine her family's reaction. And Nikolai's. Summer sucked in a deep breath.

"I think we should slow things down between us. I'm not ready for anything serious. I'm too young." Summer cringed inwardly at the words. She'd never thought she'd admit to youth, not when she fought so hard for independence.

"Can you see the marina down there?" Dare asked.

Summer's mouth dropped. Was that it? That had been English coming from her mouth, and not a foreign language. "Yes," she muttered.

"We keep our boat there. You'll have to come out with us one weekend."

"Us?" Crooks used boats to run drugs, didn't they?

"My brothers and I. We use the boat mainly, but sometimes my sisters or parents come out."

"Where do you go?"

"We visit the islands around the Hauraki Gulf or sometimes go further afield."

Summer's mind was stuck on drugs, and crime and Nikolai. But mostly Nikolai at the moment, because she knew how furious he'd be when he found out who she was with.

"What do you say?"

"I… Maybe," Summer said finally.

The meals arrived—a large steak and a selection of vegetables. Summer would have preferred the portabella mushrooms and rice, but picked at the vegetables.

Dare kept up a steady stream of conversation, talking about the movies they should see and the restaurants he wanted to check out with her in attendance.

"I need some time to study," Summer said. "And I have to work several late nights now that I've settled in."

"We'll work around your commitments," Dare said.

His words stumped Summer. This situation wasn't covered in *Miranda* magazine. She'd tried the nice approach, the polite approach. Tried blunt too. What part of *not interested* didn't the man understand? She placed her knife and fork across the center of her plate and dropped her napkin on top.

"Good. You're finished." Dare stood and strode over to the desk to pay for the meal, leaving Summer gaping after him yet again.

In the lift, he took her arm and stood close despite them being the only occupants. One of the ingredients in his sophisticated aftershave didn't agree with her, tickling at the back of her nose. A sneeze burst from Summer. Dare stepped back, giving her room to breathe.

"Excuse me," she said. "There's something in your aftershave that doesn't agree with me." Okay, that was blunt.

Dare steered her from the lift, up the ramp and outside. A cab appeared magically beside them and they climbed inside.

"Parnell Road, please," he told the driver.

When they arrived back at Dare's restaurant, Dare gave Summer some money.

"That's to pay for your cab fare home. You still going to the bookshop first?"

Summer nodded dumbly.

Dare leaned inside and kissed her on the mouth, then rattled the address off to the driver and stood back. At the last moment, he knocked on the window. Summer wound it down.

"Sorry I haven't been very good company today. My mind is on business, I'm afraid." He slipped two more fifties out of his wallet and handed them to Summer. "My order is in. Can you pick it up for me? I'll collect it when we go out to dinner tonight." Dare bent to give her another quick kiss then waved and strode away.

Summer stared after his rapidly retreating form. What was all that about?

"Are you ready to go now?" the cabby asked.

"Yes, thank you." Summer settled back to puzzle out Dare's behavior. No matter what way she looked at it, Summer came up with the same thought. Weird. Extremely weird.

Ten minutes later, she entered the bookshop. *Miranda* magazine was in. Several of the romances she'd ordered were in, and so was Dare's package. She paid for them all, caught another cab and headed for home.

* * * * *

"Where the hell have you been?"

The masculine holler scared three myna birds from their quest for food in Uncle Henry's garden. Summer watched them take off with indignant squawks and tried to control the spurt of panic that made her stomach do nervous flips. Nikolai stood on his section, glaring across the wooden fence at her. She aimed for calm as she stooped to pull a pair of wet jeans from the laundry basket.

"Doing the laundry." Although she would have thought that was pretty obvious given she was hanging it on the line to dry.

Nikolai stomped out of sight before reappearing on Uncle Henry's side of the fence, looking as if he was fighting for control of his temper. "You were meant to stay inside my house. For safety reasons. Remember?"

"The paint smell was affecting my breathing."

"You didn't have a problem last night. Or this morning."

If Summer had thought she was attracted to Dare and was in danger of becoming a two-man woman, then one look at

Nikolai cured her of the misapprehension. Nikolai, bossy gene and all, was her man of the month. For as long as he wanted her.

The big, bad SAS man scowled. Summer felt heat bloom in her face and lower down in her body. The air charged between them. Sexual sparks. Full of possibilities.

"No problem at all." Oh, my. Her voice—it sounded like a sultry screen siren. All throaty and flirty. Turned-on.

Nikolai stepped closer until warmth jumped from his body to hers. Her nipples tightened against the cotton cups of her bra. Then he closed the remaining distance between them and her pointy nipples flattened against his chest. Summer's breath whooshed from her lungs and nothing replaced the air. She felt breathless, excited, and it had nothing to do with asthma.

He glanced down at her, his blunt finger traced over her bottom lip. His dark eyes glittered. "So, where have you been?"

Summer opened her mouth to speak and his finger popped right between her lips. Acting on instinct, she sucked lightly and rolled her tongue across the tip of his finger. A low groan erupted from Nikolai. His eyes fluttered shut, a pained look on his face. Then his eyes opened again. Heat, dark and stormy, surged between them.

"Hey, man! I thought you were only going to take five minutes."

"Go away," Nikolai growled without turning.

Summer let go of his finger, but couldn't take her eyes away from Nikolai. What she wanted more than anything at this moment was to rip his clothes off and touch him all over. Of course, he'd need to do some touching too.

"Hell, Louie and I wouldn't want to miss the show," Jake said.

Louie chuckled with real amusement, and Summer saw the waggle of his dark brows. "Yeah, not when you're about to rip each other's clothes off. Things were getting mighty interesting."

Nikolai's broad chest rose and fell with a harsh breath. "Later," he whispered. "We'll finish this later tonight. I have to go out for a few hours." His hands tangled in her hair, and he lowered his head as if he were about to kiss her. "Please lock the door when we leave. With you inside," he added.

"Okay. I'll be at Uncle Henry's house. The paint really is bothering me."

Nikolai nodded, and despite the audience, he lowered his head until their mouths touched. Bold lips stole her breath, and his tongue surged into her mouth then retreated and returned. Summer wrapped her arms around his neck and held on tight. Finally, he lifted his head. "Stay safe," he murmured.

Summer nodded solemnly then stood on tiptoe to whisper in his ear. "I visited an adult shop today."

Nikolai's hands closed over her shoulders. "A sex shop?" he gritted out.

Louie whistled long and low. "Did you hear that, Jake? A sex shop. Sounds like our Nik is in for some fun."

"Out the front," Nikolai snapped. "Wait for me there."

The two men went but not without big grins and banter between them.

Nikolai waited until they'd walked past the rose garden and disappeared around the corner of the house. He took her face between his hands. "What am I going to do with you?" A slow smile spread from his eyes down to his mouth. "Should I be worried?"

"About the toys I bought?"

His forehead wrinkled in a quick frown. "Yeah."

Silent laughter bubbled up inside Summer as she thought of the vibrator, the selection of condoms, including glow-in-the-dark green, and the set of pleasure balls. "Nothing too radical."

"That," said Nikolai, "is what I'm afraid of. I'm thinking your radical and my radical are miles apart."

An impatient honk sounded as one of Nikolai's friends leaned on the horn.

Nikolai leaned close, flicking his fingers over her distended nipples hard enough that she jumped. "Don't start playtime without me."

Even though Summer was aware of the jut of his cock, his smoky voice would have given him away. She flashed a grin. "Don't be late, big boy."

"Big boy," Nikolai muttered. His words came close to an undignified splutter. "One of these days, I'm gonna smack your luscious backside."

"So you keep saying." Summer chortled, enjoying the novelty of sexual banter. "I look forward to it."

"Humph!" Nikolai said, but he kissed her before he strode off to join his friends.

* * * * *

The rest of the afternoon passed quickly enough since Summer caught up with chores and watered Uncle Henry's rose gardens.

The phone rang around six-thirty.

"Summer, I'm sorry. Something's come up, and I can't make our dinner date," Dare said.

"But I—" Summer inhaled sharply. She'd told the man they weren't going out again. Her breath huffed out again. "Thanks for letting me know."

"I've got to go," Dare said. "I'll ring you."

The phone thudded down. A frisson of unease skidded down her backbone. Dare Martin was a successful businessman. The man wasn't stupid, so why was he acting obtuse? Summer hated to admit it, but it seemed Nikolai might be right in his warnings about Dare.

Summer replaced the phone and wandered over to check out the contents of the fridge. Nothing looked inspiring. She slammed the door shut and reached for the kettle.

Two minutes later, Summer sat outside on the deck with a cup of peppermint tea at her side and her parcel of new books.

Summer reached into the paper carry bag and pulled out a thick book first. *Fly-Fishing in New Zealand*. It was exactly the same book that she'd received by mistake earlier in the month. Summer opened the pages at random, flicking past illustrations of fish and feathery hooks. Why would Dare buy two copies of the same book? And even stranger, from what she'd seen, Dare preferred the cut and thrust of the business world. He never walked when he could ride. The thought of Dare in the great outdoors up to his waist in cold water boggled her mind.

Chapter Eleven

Nikolai hadn't arrived home by midnight. Disappointed, but trying hard to contain it, Summer put down her book and switched off the bedside lamp.

The house creaked and groaned, but they were comforting sounds, and she drifted closer to sleep. The abrupt rattle of the wooden window frame jerked Summer rigid. Her skin crawled. Her eyes flipped open. The window frame protested as it was lifted up to the fullest extent.

Summer tensed, ready to run or at least try to defend herself. She slid her legs from under the quilt and prepared to leap from the bed the second the floorboards creaked. Summer glanced over her shoulder. A large form blotted out any hint of the moon as they fitted their shoulders through the window. She'd locked all the doors just as Nikolai had instructed, and she was positive she'd locked the window as well. But she hadn't double-checked.

A sharp creak broke the agonizing silence. Terror clamped around her heart, and everything moved in slow motion. The figure stepped toward the bed.

Summer stared in fascinated horror. He was undoing his trousers! "Is that you, Nikolai?"

"Who else would it be?" a masculine voice demanded. "I'd better not find any other blokes coming in that window."

Summer flicked on the bedside light. Her hands planted on her hips. "You scared the shit out of me. Why didn't you ring the doorbell? Like a normal person."

"Checking the security."

In the dim light cast by the lamp, Summer caught the smirk on his face. Suspicion narrowed her eyes. "You've been drinking!" *The louse.* And to think she'd worried a little about him not being home. She made a point of not looking at his bare chest—the well-muscled chest and the set of wide shoulders that tapered down to a narrow waist with not a trace of excess padding. *She* would not weaken despite the temptation. Summer had a point to prove. She was no commodity to be taken for granted.

The grin widened to broad. "Not enough that I can't get it up."

He wouldn't be getting anything up anywhere at the rate he was going. Summer sniffed, turned her back in a pointed manner and crawled back into bed. She tugged the covers up to her chin. "Turn off the light on your way out."

"Oh, no. No, sweetheart." Nikolai's hands went back to the zipper on his jeans. It rasped downward, and Summer closed her eyes. Clothing rustled before silence reigned.

Summer strained to hear. Bother. She shouldn't have closed her eyes. All her senses were registering way off the Richter scale. Her imagination. Just thinking about running her hands down his golden flanks, across his broad chest, made her temperature rise. Thinking about his cock and the way it had felt pounding inside her, pushed her even higher.

All of a sudden, the mattress depressed. Summer's eyes popped open and came face-to-groin. His cock was fully erect, the head a deep plum red. As he'd said, primed and ready for action.

"You couldn't ring?" Summer squeaked. It was difficult to remain calm and dignified with a one-eyed snake staring you straight in the face.

Nikolai slid under the quilt, stretched out and pulled their bodies flush. "The meeting went late."

"You can't take me for granted, expecting me to wait for you."

"You didn't wait for me today." His brown eyes bore into her as though searching for truth. Summer held his eyes, but felt like a mouse being baited by a cocksure cat. But lucky for her, she'd learned a thing or two from watching *Tom and Jerry* cartoons.

"I'm not a quick f...flip for you to use whenever the timing fits your schedule."

His dark brows danced up and down, but he didn't crack a smile. "Flip?"

Habit made Summer sneak a look over her shoulder. *All clear.* She turned back to Nikolai. "My mother trained us well. Four letter words starting with f and ending with k are banned in our house. She has an endless supply of soap bars and a strong arm to go with it. Ask my brothers if you don't believe me."

A slow, sexy smile crawled across his mouth. Summer's heart pumped out an extra beat. Oh, my. The man needed a license for that smile.

"I'll make sure I guard my mouth when I meet your parents." His hand cruised across her ribs and settled on her hipbone.

Okay. Now he'd confused her when she'd thought she'd had him pegged. In truth, she hadn't thought much past the six-month visit to Auckland. Summer assumed—her family assumed—she'd go home to Eketahuna when the library course ended.

Nikolai's hand fondled her bottom. "You going to show me your toys? Or do you want to save them for another time when there's more time?"

"More time?"

"Jake and Louie are picking me up at six tomorrow morning. We have to go out of town for a couple of days."

Disappointment surged through Summer, and she must have made a sound because Nikolai's hands came up to cup her head. He pressed his lips to her forehead before moving far enough that he could see her face.

"I'm not exactly happy about it myself. I don't like to leave you on your own with the weird things that have been happening around here."

Warmth replaced the disappointment inside Summer. "I'll be fine. I followed your stringent security instructions to the letter." *Apart from going out to see Dare*, she thought with a trace of guilt. But she'd kept up her guard the whole time.

"Jake said you could go and stay with his sister."

"No, I promised Uncle Henry I'd look after his house and his precious roses. I'll be all right here."

"You are so much like Henry, it's scary," Nikolai muttered.

"You wouldn't be in bed, naked, with Henry." The shudder that swept his body brewed a giggle. It bubbled from Summer suddenly, lightening the subdued mood that had fallen between them at the talk of her safety.

"Hell, no! Henry was my boss. A mate. The picture… Hell, that's downright disgusting."

A *Tom and Jerry* moment. How to distract a male in one easy lesson. Summer felt like blowing on her finger and ceremoniously marking an imaginary scorecard. She resisted.

"How are you feeling? The lump on your head has gone down."

"That was sneaky."

"I'm not in the military for nothing."

"Don't remind me," Summer muttered.

"You tired?"

"Not really."

"Good." Nikolai rolled without warning, taking her with him. Summer ended up lying on top of his hard body, his erection trapped between them.

"New position?" she asked, the sultry film-star voice making a return appearance.

"We have time to experiment."

"How about sex outside? That sounds like fun." Summer licked her lips and watched Nikolai closely the whole time.

"Baggage." Nikolai slapped her on the rump.

Summer froze. The slap and resulting sting on her butt should have fueled anger. Instead, her pussy tingled pleasantly. A spurt of juices moistened between her legs. The need to kiss him, to taste him became more important than banter. She lowered her head and covered his quirking lips with hers. A hint of whiskey, smoky and suggestive of peat, tickled her taste buds. She took the kiss deeper, swirling their tongues together and exploring the softness of his inner cheek, the contrasting hardness of his teeth. A quick punch of heat tightened her nipples, making them ache for his mouth and the corresponding tug lower in her clit. While their mouths mated, Nikolai's hands slid in a long, luxurious stroke down her back, ending on her butt cheeks. He palmed them with his hands then slid a finger down the crack between, skimming across nerve endings and her cleft. Summer groaned softly at the back of her throat.

"You like that?" he whispered.

Words failed her so she nodded, her heart beating with acute anticipation. Nikolai moved again, exhibiting raw strength as he lifted and rolled her smoothly beneath him. He grinned down at her. "Then you'll probably like this too. Warm up before we do some riding."

Whatever. It all sounded good to Summer, and the clever fingers running over her body felt even better.

He slid one leg between hers and bent to press wet kisses across her aching breasts. Summer explored his body too, running her hands over bulging muscles and his smooth back, but at the back of her mind she waited for him to close his mouth over her breasts. She craved the sweet ache as his lips circled her nipple. The fierce tug. And the faint bite of teeth. Her nails dug into his back as he continued to tease, kissing around the edge of her nipple, coming close but not close enough.

"Nikolai?" she whispered.

"Yeah?"

"Open your mouth."

He grinned up at her, managing to look tousled and sexy as hell. "Like this?" he teased, opening his mouth then shutting it abruptly.

"No, not like that," Summer said in a cross voice. Frustrated, she decided to spell out her needs. To tell him what she wanted and how she wanted it. "Open your mouth exactly like this and leave it open."

Humor glinted in his dark eyes. "Dangerous if there are mosquitoes around." But he opened his mouth and waited.

Summer moved quickly, shoving her nipple in his mouth. Nikolai didn't move a muscle.

"You can shut your mouth now," she muttered.

Nikolai laughed, and her nipple popped from his mouth. Damp from saliva, her nipple seemed to glisten. The humor left him and without being bidden, he took her in his mouth again. Soft suction speared a bolt of lust through her body. Summer panted. They hadn't gotten anywhere near the good stuff and already she felt as though she balanced on the pinnacle, ready to topple into climax. She wondered if that made her easy, then shoved the thought away for later. Nikolai moved his leg, widening her legs. Cool air contrasted with the warmth of her pussy as he swept the covers aside. He mouthed her nipple a little more roughly, and she felt a spurt of her juices. Summer stirred restlessly, needing more, needing the emptiness inside filled by Nikolai. Only Nikolai. But Nikolai seemed determined to tease her to breaking point and make her plead.

He released her nipple and laid a string of kisses across her quivering belly. Then lower. Her breath caught...waiting until her lungs burned.

"Better breathe, sweetheart. Don't want to explain your faint to the hospital."

Summer gasped, both with indignation and the desperate need for air.

Then he parted her folds. His gaze traveled slowly across her feminine flesh. Summer trembled so much on edge, she was positive a butterfly touch on her clit would push her over into orgasm.

"So pretty," he murmured in a voice that spelled trouble. She knew it. He was going to tease her more, push her further. Summer opened her mouth to complain, but then a trace of sensation drifted along her cleft. Her hips jerked upward while her heart slammed against her ribs.

"So quick to respond." He glanced up at her then, devilment on his face. "Are you sure you haven't spent the evening playing with these toys I've been hearing about?"

Summer's head thrashed from side to side, the pillow throwing out the scent of lavender. It was meant to calm, but Summer was too far gone for the benefits of aromatherapy. "No, I wanted to wait for you," she murmured.

"Then maybe we should play."

A snort escaped Summer. "That's what I've been trying to tell you."

"Ah, but you didn't say the words. I'm not a mind reader." Laughter shaded his voice. She wanted to deck him. She wanted to scream. Most of all she wanted to climax.

"Just as I'd always suspected," Summer said, propping herself up on her elbows to glare down at him. "You big, bad SAS types only do orders. Fine. This is your objective. An orgasm for me." She patted her breastbone. "Do your worst."

Nikolai chuckled long and loud, each successive gasp and breath of air puffing out of his lungs and hitting her achy clit. If she'd thought he was into torture before she knew better now. The man had barely started. Finally, his laughter subsided. He gave a lopsided salute. "Aye-aye, ma'am. My pleasure, ma'am."

"Well, hurry up, soldier," Summer growled. Outwardly, she sounded bossy but calm and in control. Inside, she was anything but. Her skin temperature felt off the scale and hot enough to melt a knob of butter. She imagined butter running over her belly, dripping down... Nikolai licking. Chocolate sounded better, with her tongue doing the chasing over smooth, bulging muscles. A whimper escaped before she could catch it.

Nikolai spread her legs wider, then paused to study her face quizzically. "Fantasizing, sweetheart?"

"Because you're not going fast enough," she purred back.

"Tell me about this fantasy or else I'll take things even slower." His finger dipped into her vagina, it rotated then he removed his finger and popped it in his mouth to clean. He removed it with a soft smacking sound. "You're wet," he murmured wickedly. "I know you're ready to take me, but some self-control and restraint on your part will make it even better."

"You're a sadist."

"A connoisseur," he corrected. He slid his hands between her butt and the cotton sheet and lifted her to his mouth. "I intend to sip and savor," he whispered in a husky voice. "Enjoy the entrée before the main course." Each warm breath blasted against her inflamed flesh. Summer trembled, her heart beating so loudly it was difficult to hear his bold, sensual words.

"God, Nikolai!" His rough words wrapped her in sensation. Tingling from head to toe, she shuddered. Her eyes slid closed, enclosing her in a private world of sensation. Pure feeling. Acute expectation.

"Open your eyes. I want to see the expression in your beautiful eyes when you come." A finger stroked down her cleft but didn't venture near her clitoris.

Summer tried to follow his instructions—orders—but her lids felt weighted and too heavy to lift.

The stroking stopped. "Summer."

Yep, definitely orders. Since when had control passed over to him? Her lids struggled to half-mast.

Nikolai replaced his finger with the tip of his tongue. A delicate flutter at the mouth of her pussy, then a slow thrust and retreat. Summer gave up the fight and let her eyes drift shut. Instantly the sensation of his tongue flickering against her flesh ceased. A deep-seated throb pierced her languor. Her eyes shot open. Nikolai made a hum of approval and licked the length of her weeping cleft, stopping just short of her clit. The throb repeated, radiating outward from her clit. At the next stroke of his tongue, she jerked her hips and his tongue lashed her clitoris. A soft, prickling heat rushed the length of her body, but this time she remembered and fought to keep her eyes open, her gaze locked on Nikolai's intent face. Rosy color streaked down her face and across her breasts.

Sexual hunger stabbed at her mind, her body. All over. "Again, Nikolai. *Please.*"

His soft chuckle brought another shiver. His finger stroked again, but this time instead of stopping, his digit continued its journey and feathered over her needy clit. A jagged sensation streaked the length of her body. Summer arched into his touch, aching for more, for total, body-pulsing ecstasy.

"Greedy little thing," he mused.

"Not little," Summer panted.

"Notice you're not denying the greedy," Nikolai drawled, doing another pass with his finger.

Bother the man. Not only was he teasing now, he was pushing her higher. "Damn straight," she gritted out.

The third pass of his finger made tingles spring to life. They spread outward from her clit in a soft wave. She bit her bottom lip, preparing to fly, but the tingles dissolved, along with another tingling roll like the end of a wave on its journey to the shore. Disappointment bopped her over the head and brought a frown to the surface. Heck, was that it? Summer relaxed in Nikolai's hold, her gaze remaining locked to his.

"At last," he muttered in a guttural voice. "Surrender."

Before she could react, he lifted her higher and sealed his mouth around her clit. A gentle flick of his tongue against her swollen core brought the fizzing anticipation back to the fore. Her hips jerked as he flailed her clitoris. Once. Twice. Three times. Summer exploded with a wallop of heat, shards of sensation rocketing to every pleasure point in her body.

Gradually, she came to her body again. She'd kept her eyes on Nikolai the whole time, but only now did she register the fiery heat and promise in his eyes.

"Tell me you have condoms," he said in a hoarse voice.

Summer batted her eyelids at him. "If I were a teaser, I'd say no, but I wouldn't do that sort of thing to you."

"Only because you want me to fuck you," he muttered, a tide of red highlighting his cheekbones.

Summer nodded thoughtfully, and manfully hid her smirk. "Yes, there is that. Top drawer, in the cellophane bag."

Nikolai lowered her hips to the mattress then bounded off the bed. He yanked the wooden drawer open, rifled through the bag, and pulled out the unopened box Summer had purchased that afternoon. He turned to her with a frown, totally unconscious of his body in a way that Summer really admired. From this angle, his cock appeared huge. Pre-cum glistened on the tip, and just like that, Summer was hot, achy and desperate for his touch.

"Hurry," she urged.

His brows shot up toward his hairline. "Glow-in-the-dark, Summer?"

"Yeah."

"Neon green?"

"It was a toss up between glow-in-the-dark, chocolate flavored or raised dots for great stimulation."

"What happened to normal, everyday condoms?"

"They left along with your sense of adventure?"

Nikolai ripped open the packet and pulled out a foil-covered square. For a few seconds, he stared at the bright green package. Then he glared at her. "You tell anyone about this, I'll deny it."

"I wouldn't dare," Summer deadpanned.

Nikolai barred a set of white teeth in a low growl, but Summer saw the humor lurking beneath. Physically, the man was much bigger than her but his size didn't inspire fear. "On your stomach," he ordered. "Up on all fours."

"Oh! A new position."

"Yeah, the spanking position," Nikolai drawled. "Because I sure as hell haven't met any woman who needs a spanking more than you."

"I've heard across the man's knees is better."

Nikolai groaned and shook his head. "If you don't shut up, I'm gonna gag you as well."

"Tie me up? Oh, I like the sound of that!" Summer cooed.

The foil wrapper crackled as he tore it open. A snort escaped, and Summer noticed another imperceptible shake of his head. "They're the color of an ogre," he muttered.

An imp rattled Summer's cage. "Is that what you call it?" She stared fixedly at his cock, taking delight in the twitch she witnessed. "Ogre."

"Your mother didn't wash your mouth out nearly enough."

"Enough that I don't like the taste of soap."

Nikolai rolled the condom on and prowled to the edge of the bed.

Summer flicked off the bedside lamp. She stared at his erection, a long, thick batten that glowed soft, neon green. "They work!"

The disapproving snort of a man pushed almost to the limits bounced off her bedroom walls. Summer grinned and decided to act the submissive. Just for the moment. She shifted onto her side and then moved to her knees, still smirking.

Nikolai cupped the round globes of her buttocks, his thumbs skirting close to the entrance of her vagina. Juices surged at his touch, and the laughter left her, a groan trembling at her lips instead.

"This is gonna be hard and quick," Nikolai muttered.

Summer felt cool air on her labia, her clit, as he parted her folds. His cock nudged at her opening, then he surged fast and deep all the way into her womb. Shock at the sudden filling stole her breath. Wide and thick, he stretched her almost painfully. A good pain. His balls slapped against her backside as he pulled out then thrust deep again. Fast. Hard. Quick.

The scent of their arousal filled the air. A rough growl vibrated in his chest. Flesh smacked against flesh. The familiar tingle commenced as his cock thrust high and deep, scraping across her sensitive core. Summer teetered on the edge of climax, her heart thundering. Nikolai's hands curled around the dip of her waist then moved higher to palm heavy breasts. He pinched a nipple, his fingers biting. Summer gasped. He tugged and her womb contracted.

"That's it, baby," he murmured. Nikolai tugged her distended nipple a second time, and she exploded into a series of intense spasms. He slammed into her then stilled, his breathing hoarse, his chest rising and falling rapidly against her sweaty back.

Summer twitched her butt, slowly rocking back against Nikolai. Sated and sleepy, the pleasure continued to hum through her veins like golden syrup. She'd missed a lot before Nikolai.

Nikolai drew a deep breath. When he'd entered via the window, he hadn't bothered drawing the curtains and a stream of moonlight pierced the shadowed corners of the room. His gaze traced the sweet dip of her waist, the rounded ass cheeks, and guilt surfaced. He'd made a mistake fucking Summer. She was too young, and everything, every relationship he'd had in the past had turned to murky custard. The fact remained—he sucked at relationships, but even knowing that, he wasn't sure he could walk away. Not now.

* * * * *

She'd forgotten to tell Nikolai about the fishing book. She'd meant to. Summer skipped a couple of steps and came to a stop by the kettle. Her hands grabbed at the marbled bench top. A breath whooshed from her. With a pained grimace on her face, she did a quick series of breathing exercises. Gradually, she straightened and gave an embarrassed laugh. Thank goodness, that breathing hitch had happened while she'd been alone. Summer went through the automatic motions of making tea and mused over the situation. Nikolai's fault for distracting her this morning. It wasn't as though she fired on all cylinders in the mornings anyway. But this morning she'd been semi-awake when Nikolai had yanked the covers off the bed. Summer grinned as she recalled the wolfish expression on the man's face, how rough and rumpled he'd looked. Her heart pounded anew just remembering. Chocolate-coated sex on a stick. The man had picked her up and carried her to the shower where he'd proceeded to wash her whole body with a washcloth and the Brazil nut shower gel she kept in the shower. Once he'd washed her, he'd briskly washed himself then pulled on a neon, glow-in-the-dark condom. Summer squirmed, shifting from one foot to the other. The kettle whistled and switched off. Summer reached for the kettle and picked it up. Her hand shook as she guided the wobbly kettle back to the bench. Deep breaths. Summer breathed deeply, seeking control of her wayward emotions. Sex. And Nikolai. She seemed to dwell on them a lot these days. A shiver worked down her body, ending in an intense ache in her core. Arousal soaked her panties despite making love with Nikolai before he'd left. She had to get a grip. But Nikolai hadn't helped. He'd dared her. Summer didn't like to back down from a dare.

In the shower, he'd turned her around so her back was to him. He'd placed her hands on the white tiled wall then crowded her from behind. The water had spilled over them, warm and steamy, and scented with Brazil nut. Then he'd entered her from behind, and Summer had thought she might expire on the spot.

Her pulse jumped enough that she knew it wasn't safe to pick up the kettle yet. Her clit tingled as she remembered, as she relived the quick thrusts that had gone deep into her womb. Nikolai filling her, surrounding her with his strength, propelling her into a climax that shuddered through her body for long seconds afterward. Then he'd withdrawn, slapped her on the ass and turned her around for a possessive kiss.

But it hadn't ended there. He'd washed her again then shut off the shower. In the steamy intimacy of the bathroom, he'd dried her then disappeared into her bedroom. Seconds later he'd returned with one of the toys she'd purchased in the adult shop on K Road. The set of pleasure balls. With an intent look in his eyes, he'd pulled them from the packet then slowly inserted them into her pussy. Summer shifted from foot to foot. Her core contracted suddenly. Nikolai had instructed her to think of him during the day. How could she not?

Every step she took made the weighted balls vibrate inside. The sheer naughtiness factor turned her on just as much as the pulsing movement of the balls.

Summer picked up the kettle again and successfully poured a cup of tea this time. She perched on the edge of a wooden chair and took a sip.

Back to the book. She'd placed it in her straw basket, ready to take to work and drop for Dare at the restaurant. A frown puckered her smooth brow as she stared at the paper bag that contained the duplicate book. What if Nikolai was right? What if Dare was using her for some ulterior motive?

Summer thought about that indigestible fact for a few moments longer. Then an idea occurred, simplicity itself.

She could always exchange the book for another of the same—that was assuming she could find another. After twisting the idea in every possible direction, it sounded even better. The reckless rebel inside Summer rejoiced at the thought of doing something constructive. This was a simple plan to prove or disprove Nikolai's theory about the Martin family. And Dare.

The perfect plan.

And it would work.

Summer wrapped her hands around her cup and figuratively congratulated herself on her cleverness. She was pretty sure that in a week or two she'd be able to rub Nikolai's nose in the fact. The big, bad SAS man would have to eat crow.

Chapter Twelve

The hairs at her nape prickled without mercy. Summer's whole body pulsed with uneasiness. The desire to spin around and demand whoever was following her to piss off hammered through her brain, finding an outlet in clenched fists. But she didn't have SAS brothers for nothing. She'd learned a thing or two about subtlety. A snort escaped. Well, they were subtle and canny when it came to their work. Ditto Nikolai. Just thinking about Nikolai made her hips sway a fraction more than normal and the pleasure balls seemed to vibrate a bit harder inside her womb.

Summer paused to survey the contents of a large department store. Instead of looking at the clothes, she scanned the reflections. Nothing out of the ordinary. But that didn't mean no one was there. She trusted her instincts. Perhaps she should tell Nikolai. Except he was sure to start yelling and ram a few "I told you so's into the conversation. Of course, when he started yelling she could always try distraction.

After scanning the colorful swimsuits in the window, and the reflections of the passersby in the street, she carried on, heading for one of the three secondhand bookshops she sometimes frequented.

The bookshop was small, the shelves crammed to overflowing with books of all shapes and sizes. The bell on the door tinkled when she pushed it open. Summer took a deep breath, the book lover in her enjoying the dry, musty scent that permeated the shop. Heaven. She made her way between the shelves, rapidly searching for the section on hobbies and fishing. Not a single book on fly-fishing. Disappointment punched her gut. She nibbled her bottom lip, considering her options. It wouldn't do to order one since she was time-challenged. The thin, elderly man behind the counter wasn't a good option either, since she didn't want anyone remembering her asking for the book. She'd have to try the second shop on her visiting list.

Twenty minutes later, she rushed inside. Luckily, she was a frequent visitor so was familiar with the layout of the cavern-like shop. Summer checked her watch. Heck, she was going to be late back from lunch. Mrs. Ferguson would have two cows. She did that. A lot. The shelf space allocated to fishing took up a whole section of shelving in the narrow shop. She scanned the titles but almost missed the fly-fishing book in her haste. Her stomach lurched. *It was here.* Her hand closed around the book, and she pulled it off the shelf. Her heart thudded erratically. The point of no return. If she bought the book, then she was committing to the plan.

* * * * *

"Earth to Nik. Earth to Nik." Louie clicked his fingers right in front of Nikolai's nose.

Nikolai blinked back to the present, away from black thoughts of Laura and the baby. Nightmares tangled with the future and Summer. "Huh?"

Jake peered closely. "He looks tired."

"Perhaps he didn't sleep well." Louie smirked at Jake. "Wonder how Summer slept?"

"Leave Summer out of this," Nikolai growled.

"You didn't stay *out* of Summer."

A wave of fury swept Nikolai. He had his hands fisted in Jake's shirt before either of his mates could blink.

"Whoa." Jake held up both hands in surrender but didn't try to fight his way from Nikolai's determined grip. "Joke."

Louie placed a heavy hand on Nikolai's tense shoulder. "Let him go, Nik."

Nikolai unclenched his hands and shoved Jake away from him. A fist-sized circle of wrinkles remained on Jake's shirt.

"Sorry, man. Bad joke."

Nikolai didn't want to discuss Summer with Jake and Louie. "Time to get back to the rest of the men." Hell, he was kicking himself as it was. He didn't need his mates' help to fuel his betrayal and helplessness. Nikolai turned and strode back to the assault course, leaving Jake and Louie to fall in behind.

What the fuck was he going to do? He'd betrayed Henry's trust, taken Summer's virginity, and he continued to compound the bitch of a mistake. He couldn't keep his hands off Summer. But the worst part was the way his mind wandered to the future—a rosy dream of togetherness with the woman. Nikolai bit back a curse. He'd once dreamed of a future, a family with Laura, and look what had happened. While he'd been away on missions, Laura had got bored, felt neglected. So she'd gone out on the town, made friends, got in with a bad crowd. A crowd that treated drugs like candy. Bittersweet memories poured over him as he recalled the moment he and Laura had discovered her pregnancy. Their child would have been almost five, ready to start school. A lump of emotion clogged up his throat. Nikolai blinked rapidly and called upon every bit of control inside. He had a mission to complete. Now wasn't the time to dwell on what might have been.

* * * * *

She'd done it. Exchanged the books. Nerves pushed a shiver through her body as the cab drove up Parnell Road. Summer stared out the window at the rush hour traffic, the scurrying office workers heading home and the mature trees in the Domain. Please, please let her pull off the switch without making Dare suspicious. The cab pulled up outside the restaurant. She paid the driver and dawdled inside. Even the pleasure balls vibrating inside her pussy didn't quell the skip and jump of nerves. If she wasn't careful, she'd give herself away.

A wave of chatter greeted her as she pushed through the double doors that led to the bar and restaurant. One of the men standing in the group at the bar gave a long whistle. "Over here, sweet cheeks." His gaze roved up and down her body, taking in her short black skirt and figure-hugging pale blue top.

Summer ignored him, too wound up to flirt. Her heels clicked as she maneuvered through the crowd waiting to enter. *A bit like machine gun fire*, she thought fancifully.

Summer stepped up to the reception desk when the large group of people waiting disappeared into a private function room.

"Is Dare busy?"

"Afraid so, Summer," the receptionist said.

Summer nodded and tried to look disappointed, but in actual fact, everything was going according to plan. "Can I leave a package for him? I promised him I'd drop it off as soon as I had time to pick it up." She handed the book over and was glad when another group of diners arrived behind her. "Looks like you're busy so I'll leave you to it." Summer lifted a hand in farewell.

"Bye, Summer. I'll make sure Dare gets his package."

Outside on the pavement, she took a deep breath and held on to the nearest streetlamp, swaying on unsteady legs. Had she done the right thing? Summer sighed, unsure if she'd made the granddaddy of mistakes or not. But at least if Dare made a fuss about the book, she'd know something was up. She let go of the lamppost and looked around for a cab. The prickly sensation of being watched had started up again. The sooner she got home, the better. The pleasure balls had her so hot it was a wonder she hadn't burned from the inside out.

* * * * *

Nikolai pulled up outside his house after another long, full-on day. His knee ached like hell, letting him know he'd pushed too hard during the last two days. He needed a shower. Bad. He stunk like the bottom of a sewer pit after running the obstacle course through mud and God knows what else. But at least they were prepared for the mission. It was good to be involved in a mission again, even if it was only as part of the strategic planning team.

Nikolai clambered out of his car with all the grace of a three-legged giraffe. Bloody good thing none of the top brass were witness. He didn't think he could stand being stood down on medical grounds. Too much time to think about other parts of his life.

Laura and the baby.

Summer.

Nikolai unlocked the door and dragged his weary body inside. With the house being locked up all day, the scent of paint almost knocked him over. And that sent his thoughts winging to Summer. Nikolai's jaw firmed. He'd come to a decision. He had to stop seeing her in any capacity, except as a neighbor. Horizontal dancing was a no-go.

Nikolai scrubbed his hands over the stubble on his face. His smell offended him, but hell, he needed a drink before a shower. He hobbled into the kitchen, opened a window, then jerked open the pantry and pulled out a bottle of whiskey. Irish whiskey that was too good to scull like he intended. Nikolai grabbed a glass and the bottle, and made it as far as the table before the jagged shard of pain made him bite off a cussword. He sank into a chair and slumped, riding out the waves of pain. Shit, he'd been okay this morning. He hoped like hell this pain settled by the morning in time for another go-round.

The peaty scent of the whiskey rose as he splashed it into the glass. Nikolai sighed, and leaned back in the wooden chair, knowing he needed to take it easy on the alcohol despite the driving need inside to bury the painful memories of the past that kept biting today. He took a sip and let the whiskey burn down his throat in a slow trickle.

Outside, darkness approached despite the extra hour of light granted by daylight savings. The faint call of a seabird drifted on the breeze. A soft creak made Nikolai's hand clench around the glass. Shit. He watched as Summer closed the small gate that bordered the two properties, then skip across the lawn. Even though he knew he'd have to blow her off, his heart skipped a beat. No way would she make this easy for him. He knew it at gut level.

"Pooh! It stinks of paint in here," Summer yelled from the front door.

"Wait until you come in here and get a whiff of me."

"Eew! I heard that." Summer grinned, but kept her distance. "What have you been doing?"

"Training with the men for a mission."

"What about your knee?"

"My knee is fine," Nikolai snapped. Hell, maybe if he said it enough it might come true. As if he didn't have enough worry bones to gnaw on.

"Good." Summer seemed unperturbed by his uncertain temper. Nikolai wondered how she'd react when he told her they couldn't be together anymore. Their relationship was a mistake—a slip of judgment on his part.

He hoped like hell she didn't cry. The way he was feeling, he might just break out and howl with her. He took another sip of whiskey and savored the burn as it slid down his throat.

"Are you going to have a shower? I could scrub your back."

"I thought the paint bothered you," Nikolai growled.

"It does, but I came prepared." She dug inside a pocket and brandished an inhaler for him to see.

Fuck, she wasn't gonna make it easy for him. Nikolai stared at the dregs of amber liquid inside his glass. Maybe he should lay out the truth for her, tell her why he was such bad relationship material. His gut twisted at the thought of laying his emotions down for her to trample on. From experience, that's what women did. After they'd gutted a man first.

"Henry won't approve of us."

Summer straightened from her sprawl against the doorframe. Her blue eyes narrowed. "Uncle Henry isn't here. And even if he was, it's none of his business. I'm legal."

"He asked me to look after you, not to drag you off to bed and fuck you all ways to Sunday." Nikolai let the grit hang out in his voice, made himself sound tough. Inside, he felt as though he was dying.

"My mother isn't here. You can say that word, you know. I have heard it before."

"Summer." He wanted to shake her. He wanted to kiss her. But he wasn't fool enough to touch her.

"I'm going out to a nightclub on Friday night. The new one — Raven Too. You — "

Nikolai cursed. He slammed his glass down on the table hard enough to make Summer jump.

"Who are you going with?" he demanded. Jealousy, pure and simple, poured out along with his words. Man, was that a giveaway or what?

Summer pulled a face. "With some of the girls from work. There's a group of us going."

"It's not safe." He'd heard about the Raven Too. All sorts of kinky things went on there. Jake and Louie had picked up a couple of woman there… "You're not going unless I go too."

"And are you going as my boyfriend or my chaperone?" Summer asked, her tone sharp enough that he knew he'd pushed a hot button.

"Dammit, this isn't funny. I'm bad news," Nikolai muttered.

"So you keep saying," Summer sniped back. She advanced on the table and Nikolai, and jerked out a chair. Then she sat and looked at him in clear expectation. "Tell me. Let me judge."

"Why? It won't change anything."

Obviously not the best time to tell him about exchanging the books, or the distinct feeling she'd had of someone following her for most of the day. Summer took a shallow breath and ended up with a lungful of paint fumes. She stood abruptly and dragged her chair over to the open window before sitting again. "So tell me about this bad thing you've done. Do a proper job and scare me off." Her tone was mocking but inside, panic jumped around like a kangaroo she'd seen on a family visit to Australia. She really liked Nikolai, and despite his bossy gene, they were good together. Given time, she might even cure him of the malignant gene.

Anguish crossed his face briefly before his expression blanked. He snatched the bottle of whiskey and poured some into his glass. Then he glanced at her with chocolate brown eyes full of pain and tortured memories. "Want some?"

"Sure, why not?" She jumped up to get a glass from the cupboard he pointed at. He poured half an inch into her glass, and Summer returned to her seat to wait for him to speak. He glanced at her with his dark eyes again, hesitated, then his broad chest rose and fell, and he looked away.

"I was married before," he said, concentrating on his glass.

Summer's breath stalled in her throat. He was older. Of course, he'd had relationships with other women. But it hurt, dammit.

"Laura and I married young."

Bother. Now the woman had a name. Summer bet she was slim, blonde and beautiful. Everything that she wasn't.

"We married too young. Neither of us… We shouldn't have married. But Laura had problems with her old man. He was a drunk, and he used to bash anyone he could get his hands on. Marrying seemed like the best solution. I mean, we'd known each other since we were kids. We went together through high school." He paused, seeming deep in thought.

Summer's mind raced ahead. What had happened to Laura? Why weren't they together now? Questions pounded her mind while she waited impatiently for Nikolai to speak again. "And?" she finally prompted.

"The marriage didn't work out."

Duh! Summer wanted to grab him by the shoulders and give him a good shake. Now was not the time to turn taciturn. "Why didn't it work out?" Ugh, this was worse than trying to worm information from her older brothers.

"We married too young. I was away a lot for work. Laura was bored."

"Why didn't she get a job? It wasn't your fault she had too much time on her hands."

Nikolai's head jerked up. He stared at her as though she'd suddenly sprouted another head. "Is that what you would have done?" His tone was harsh, his face tormented like a man in the grip of deep emotions.

His words confused Summer. Wasn't a job the obvious solution? Or volunteer work? Or some sort of hobby? It's what she would have done in the same situation. The world was full of new things to learn, new things to experience, like the bungee off the top of the Sky Tower in central Auckland, which Summer had booked, along with some of the girls at the library. Next week was D-day, and she was already scared spitless. But fear wasn't going to stop her grabbing a new experience.

"Boredom and the need for change was one of the reasons I jumped at the chance to do the library course in Auckland. Eketahuna is a small town with not much going on. Everyone knows me there."

Nikolai's mouth twisted with sudden humor. "You mean you can't get up to much mischief there."

"True. That and the fact that most of the eligible males my age are too frightened of my brothers to ask me out." Summer scrutinized Nikolai. He seemed a little calmer now, not so introspective, but that didn't mean she was going to let him off the hook. He owed her an explanation. And once she had it, she intended to entice him into bed. Actually, make that shower first and bed second, she amended silently. The man didn't smell pretty.

"Laura was bored. She met up with some old school friends while I was away on a mission. She wrote and told me about it. I was pleased because she sounded so much happier. It made things easier when I managed a few weeks at home." Nikolai paused again and seemed to drift off.

"Nikolai," Summer said, reaching over to squeeze his arm. "Tell me, before I'm too old and gray to sympathize."

Nikolai speared her with a narrow-eyed glare. "The group she hooked up with was into drugs. Anything they could get. Ecstasy. P. Among others."

"I'm sorry, Nikolai." Summer squeezed his biceps again in a show of sympathy. "But you can't blame yourself because Laura took drugs. We all have freedom of choice."

"But I left her alone. I thought she'd kicked the habit. She'd gone to rehab and come out clean. We were expecting our first child."

A lump the size of a golf ball choked up Summer's throat. She swallowed several times, but her throat remained tight and tears of sympathy prickled at the back of her eyes. A child. That made Laura more real. An image that was harder to fight. "What happened?"

"I'd gone off on a mission. Communication back home was difficult. I'd talked to Laura on the phone a couple of times, and she sounded happy. The mission was extended. Something happened to Laura. I'm not sure what exactly, but she started on the drugs again. The police told me her system was full of P. She drove off a ravine on the way home."

Despite squeezing her eyes shut, a tear escaped and trickled down her cheek.

"Don't cry, dammit," Nikolai snarled. "I know I stuffed up. I should never have left her alone. Now you know why any sort of relationship between us is impossible. I have a demanding job. I can't guarantee I'd be here for you when you needed me."

Summer swiped at the tears on her face with the back of her hand. Resentment burned in her gut. Who'd asked him to baby sit her anyway? Everyone kept forgetting she was an adult, and it was time they remembered. She jerked upright, standing rigidly to attention. "I don't need a babysitter. What I need, what I want, is a lover. I thought that's what you were. Obviously, I was wrong." She stormed to the door and took great pleasure in slamming the door on the way out.

Chapter Thirteen

The door slammed so hard, Nikolai could have sworn the house trembled. He'd got his way. He'd driven Summer off. So why didn't he feel good about returning to the friends-and-neighbor slot? Because he— Damn! He was not even going to think about entering into emotional territory. That's what tripped him up every bloody time. No point repeating mistakes.

Nikolai hauled his body off the chair and limped to the kitchen doorway. His progress down the passage to his bedroom was slow and laborious, his boots leaving a trail of dried mud as witness to his journey. He'd clean it up tomorrow when he had more energy. The reality of not being able to tackle the assault course tomorrow, in his present condition, danced into prominence, but he shied away from it and continued his journey to his bedroom. Once there, he dropped to the bed with a pained groan to remove his boots. More caked mud dropped onto the gleaming wooden floor he'd rescued from under a layer of brown carpet.

His mind wandered back to Summer, and the look on her face right before she'd left. He'd hurt her just as he'd hurt Laura by being away from home so often. He loved his job and wasn't trained for anything else.

"Get over it, Tarei," he growled as he yanked off his shirt then struggled from his army fatigue trousers. The deed was done. Summer and he were no longer an item, and that was the way he wanted it.

* * * * *

Summer hadn't spoken to Nikolai for three days. She'd got up at the ring of the alarm clock each morning, dragged her weary body from bed and gone off to work. The workday had passed like the slow trickle of syrup on a winter's day. She'd tried to keep busy but still her mind wandered back to Nikolai, and the pleasure they'd experienced together. Her mouth firmed as she watched the big, bad SAS man limp from his house and climb into a battered sedan driven by his mate Jake. Stubborn, infuriating male. She glared through the closed window, confident in the knowledge he wouldn't know she watched. The limp had returned. He shouldn't be trying to work. Not if he didn't want to end up like that permanently. The scar that sliced past his kneecap signified the extent of the damage. The man needed a keeper. A babysitter, she thought with dry wit.

Summer grabbed a packet of breakfast cereal and poured the mix of bran flakes and dried fruit into a bowl. After sloshing milk on top, she shoveled it down, keeping one eye on the clock on the stove. It wouldn't do to be late, not with Mrs. Ferguson conducting a staff meeting at nine.

Ten minutes later, Summer rushed out the door and locked it before heading for her Mazda. It was good to have the old girl back from the garage. Summer checked her watch, let out a yelp and ran the remaining distance to her car. Luck was with her as the traffic was lighter than normal on the run up the motorway to central Auckland. She rushed into the staff meeting room at two minutes to the hour.

"Just made it," her friend Angel said.

Summer slid into the empty chair beside her and tried to look as though she'd been there for ten minutes.

"Give up," Angel said. "Your cheeks are scarlet, your hair has gone all wispy with funny, sticky-uppy bits and you're breathing like a dragon about to put out a fire."

"Charming," Summer muttered. "With friends like you—"

"Have you heard about the...?"

Summer listened with half an ear, as she sometimes did with Angel. Although she liked the girl and found her fun to work with, she was a bit of a gossip. Which was why Summer hadn't mentioned Nikolai to her friend. She didn't want her personal life all over the library.

"*Summer.*" Angel shook her vigorously by the shoulder, digging in her lilac-tipped nails in the process. "The murder at the book shop. Have you heard about it?"

Summer shot to attention. "Murder?" The bottom seemed to drop out of her stomach, and a fine tremor shook the hand that rested on the desktop. She snatched it off the wooden surface and stuck it in her lap out of sight. A bookshop? Thoughts screamed through her mind fast as boy-racers and their cars on a Friday night. *Well?* she felt like demanding. Perhaps she should grab Angel by the shoulders and shake briskly to jiggle the information loose. "Where?" she demanded finally, a sharp edge to her voice.

Rapid footsteps in the passage outside the meeting room heralded Mrs. Ferguson's arrival. She bustled into the room, casting an eagle eye over her charges. "Good, everyone's here. We have a lot to get through."

"Which bookshop?" Summer mouthed urgently at Angel.

"Summer Williams!" Mrs. Ferguson's voice cut across the hushed silence. "Organize your social life during your lunch hour."

"Sorry, Mrs. Ferguson," Summer said, working at maintaining a calm face. Difficult when worry, fear and outright panic crashed around inside. What had she done?

"Firstly, I'd like to talk about the training courses…"

Summer tuned her boss out while her mind danced around the subject of murder. Although Angel hadn't confirmed the whom, Summer didn't believe in coincidences. Not when she'd swapped the books. Lord, what was she going to do. Panic swarmed through her stomach like a malignant virus. Her lungs tightened so much it felt as though she was pushing weights off her chest with each breath. She bent to fumble through her handbag for her inhaler and took a quick, furtive puff.

"Summer!"

Summer jerked upward and hit her head on the corner of the wooden table as she straightened in her chair. Pain lanced through her head, and she bit back a groan. Bother. Another knock to the noggin. Just the thing for clear thinking.

"What are you doing, Summer?"

Mrs. Ferguson glared at her across the top of her rimless glasses.

Summer bit her lip, while tears smarted at the corners of her eyes. Her fingers delicately probed the tender spot. Great. Definitely another lump on her head to match the previous one. "I'm sorry. My asthma is giving me trouble. I needed to use my inhaler."

The harsh expression on Mrs. Ferguson's face faded to concern. "Do you need to leave the room for a few minutes?"

"I think I'll be okay," Summer murmured. "I'm sorry for interrupting."

Mrs. Ferguson continued, and Summer tried to concentrate. But it was difficult when guilt poured through her mind. She couldn't help but wonder if it the murder was because of the book swap she'd done a few days ago.

* * * * *

Summer hadn't made a conscious decision to tell Nikolai, but she found herself looking for him while watering Uncle Henry's roses. She aimed the hose at the base of Tom Thumb, Uncle Henry's favorite, and tried to quell the ever-present anxiety. The weird thing was that Dare hadn't rung, asking about the book. If he'd found something wrong with the book, wouldn't he have contacted her? Apart from a hurried phone call, canceling a dinner date, she hadn't heard from him. The book hadn't been mentioned. After soaking the roses for way too long, Nikolai still hadn't arrived home. Summer weeded the garden, a chore she hated, then mowed the lawn and still the big, bad SAS man hadn't returned. Darkness crept over the landscape, cloaking the trees and paddocks with the same gray.

Birds fell silent and the cars that passed on the country road had their headlights on.

Still no Nikolai.

Summer wandered inside and flicked on a light. She toed off her red canvas shoes and headed for the kitchen. Halfway along the passage, she paused then turned back to lock the door. Summer pocketed the key and retraced her footsteps.

The strident ring of the phone pulled her from deep thoughts of murder.

"Hello."

"Hello, Summer."

"Who is this?" Summer didn't recognize the voice. The hoarse whisper brought a rash of goose bumps. The fact that the man on the other end knew her name sent terror skittering on the heels of the goose bumps.

"Watch your back, girlie."

Anger came to her rescue. "Who is this? If you don't stop, I'll —"

The phone thumped down on the other end, leaving Summer talking to herself. Swallowing, she replaced the phone. There had been several heavy breathing calls but this was the first time her caller had spoken.

Summer glanced out the kitchen window. What if Nikolai wasn't coming home tonight?

Although she was tired of being told what to do by her family and Nikolai, there was the odd time when being looked after felt right. This was one of them.

Even confiding her fears would help. She picked up the newspaper she'd purchased during her lunch hour. Not that it had given many details.

Man Found Dead in Book Shop.

The owner of the Pen and Quill bookshop was found in the early hours of Wednesday morning. Police suspect theft was the motive, and are chasing up several leads.

Summer dropped the *Herald* back onto the bench top with a sigh. Theft, they said. But what if it hadn't been theft? What if murder was the motive, and the culprits had made it look like theft to throw the police off the trail?

The faint sound of a car pierced her troubled mind. She ran for the window. The car slowed, its headlights piercing the darkness and highlighting the hedge that ran the length of the roadside boundary. It wasn't Nikolai. Summer stilled, her heart pumping. Then she realized with the light on in the kitchen and the curtains and blinds wide open, anyone would be able to see inside. Ducking out of sight, she leapt for the light switch and flipped it off. It took precious seconds for her eyes to adjust to the dark, and by the time she reached the window, the headlights were no longer visible. The car was gone.

Or was it?

Her stomach knotted at the thought, her imagination conjuring dragons and monsters lurking in the dark. She peered out into the dark front garden and scrutinized the whole area. Nothing. But that didn't mean a thing. Uncle Henry had so many bushes and hedges in his flourishing garden. Anyone with nefarious purposes could hide and skulk close to the house without detection.

A sharp creak sounded.

Shit. Had she shut the gate between the property boundaries when she'd knocked on Nikolai's door earlier? Or had someone else left the catch unfastened? Summer licked her lips as she tried to remember. The sound repeated. A ghostly rat-tat-tat. Summer clasped and unclasped sweaty palms. Overactive imagination. That's what it was. Voices drifted on the air then a car started. Light flooded the area behind the hedge and it bled through the greenery on to her side, casting huge black shadows. The car drove off down the road leaving silence. The driver had probably stopped to answer his cell phone or for some equally innocent reason.

Summer expelled a held breath. Telling herself to quit being a drama queen, she made her way to her bedroom and started preparations for bed. She was about to climb into bed when she decided it would be a good idea to have the portable phone at her bedside. She switched on the passage light and when she saw it was clear, ran into the kitchen, scooped up the phone and tore back to bed.

"Get a grip, Summer," she muttered in disgust. The sound of her voice didn't comfort. It just made her realize how isolated and alone she was.

The phone rang again. Summer started. A gasp escaped before she could bite it back. The sharp peal of the phone continued. She'd have to answer it in case it was Uncle Henry. Her hand trembled when she reached for the portable. Summer stabbed the answer button and held it to her ear.

"Hello."

"That you, Mariah?" The deep masculine voice sent ripples of apprehension writhing through her body.

Summer jerked upright in bed. "I think you have the wrong number."

"Don't think so. It's right here on the telephone booth. Mariah Twining will jump-start your day."

"No, I—"

"How much you charge for extras? You do extras dontcha?"

Summer hung up. Almost immediately, the phone rang again. Summer hesitated, then cut the caller off and left the phone off the hook. Uncle Henry had rung a few nights ago, right after she'd walked out on Nikolai. It was improbable he'd call again in the same week.

Summer lay down again. She closed her eyes and tried to ignore the empty sound of the night. Suddenly, she jerked awake. Man, she must have dropped off. The crick in her neck told her she'd fallen asleep with her neck at a weird angle. Tension seeped through her, the silence in her dark room broken only by the tick of her alarm clock. She strained her ears, searching for anything out of the ordinary in case she'd missed it the first time. When nothing sounded out of place, she fumbled for the bedside lamp and squinted, trying to focus on the face of her watch in the blaze of light. Almost one in the morning. Surely, Nikolai would be home by now.

She reached for the phone then jerked her hand back. Ringing him was admitting that she'd landed herself in a mess.

"Stop being stupid. You can't carry on like this."

Biting her lip, she reached for the phone and punched the speed dial button for Nikolai.

"Yeah?"

Summer let out a sigh of relief. "It's me. Summer."

"What is it?" He sounded alert and ready for whatever action was necessary. A good man to have in her corner.

"Can… Could you come over?" The last of her words rushed out so quickly they tangled on her tongue. Asking for help sent a quiver of anxiety through her too. What if he turned around and told her uncle? Uncle Henry would feel obliged to ring her parents. It would be like a chain reaction if she didn't handle things with speed and decisiveness.

"Now?"

"Yes, please," she whispered.

"Make coffee. I'll be there in five." The phone crashed down on his end.

Summer pulled a face and saluted with her free hand. "Yes, sir!" She placed the phone on the bedside table and decided to dress. The idea of meeting the big, bad SAS man in her nightie made her feel weird, even though he'd seen her already. Summer pulled on a pair of old, faded jeans and a T-shirt before hurrying down the hall. She'd barely filled the kettle and plugged it in when a knock sounded on the door.

"What is it?" Nikolai demanded, pushing past her.

Summer stared at him wordlessly, her body responding to his nearness even more now that she knew what it felt like to touch his skin and run her fingers across his muscles. His dark hair lay loose and touched his shoulders. A wild jumble of damp curls that made her palms itch to touch. His jeans hugged his hips, his muscular thighs and no doubt his butt if he'd taken the time to do a twirl. He hadn't bothered to put on a shirt, and his hairless chest rose and fell with each breath.

"If you've finished undressing me, maybe you could get to the point," he muttered.

Nothing about his face looked soft. Instead, he appeared the warrior he was with not a hint of softness or emotion about him.

Summer wondered if she'd made a mistake. Maybe she should have called home.

"Summer, I don't have all day to do this. I haven't slept for hours. Please spit out whatever you need to say then I can get some sleep. Did you make coffee?"

"I haven't quite finished. The jug's boiled by now." Summer shut the front door and walked past Nikolai, careful not to touch him as she passed.

As she led the way to the kitchen, she felt his gaze. A tingle of excitement sprang to life inside. Lord, she'd missed him. She'd tried to tell herself she could get by without him, but the truth—the truth was she wanted to jump his bones. More than that, she wanted an exclusive relationship with him. But that wasn't going to happen, not when he insisted on living in the shadow of the past.

In the kitchen, Summer found the jar of instant coffee and measured a heaped spoonful into a mug. All the time, she was aware of his enigmatic gaze, his scent of raw male and soap, and the sounds he made as he settled onto a stool at the breakfast bar.

Summer hesitated. Where to start? At the beginning, she decided.

"I met Dare because somehow I received his book special order instead of mine." Okay, that was good. Nikolai hadn't reacted one jot.

"That's how you met the clotheshorse?" His brow wrinkled as she placed the mug of coffee in front of him. "How did you know they were his books?"

"The order had a card inside. I went to the address, and that's when I met him. We exchanged packages and went from there."

A low growl vibrated in the air between them. "And?"

"Maybe this isn't such a good idea."

"Summer." Nikolai placed his mug on the table with a soft clunk. He stood and prowled toward her.

Summer found herself backing up until the kitchen cabinets blocked further retreat. Seconds later, Nikolai's hands thumped either side of her, effectively caging her in place. She swallowed.

"Spit out whatever your problem is, Summer. I don't have time for games."

"Since I go to the bookshop quite often, I've picked up the odd package for Dare. Last week, I brought Dare's books home. We were going to go out for dinner, but Dare had to cancel at the last minute."

Nikolai's jaw clenched. "I thought I told you the man was bad news."

Her mood veered sharply to anger. "Look, this is hard enough as it is without you saying 'I told you so'."

He gave a clipped nod, but didn't move his large body so much as an inch. Having his bulk so close made her nervous. Actually, that wasn't quite the truth. He made her think of sex, sweaty bodies sliding together in a sensual dance. Her body. His body. Summer swallowed convulsively and felt the inevitable heat swamp her face. She hurried into speech to hide her unease at his proximity.

"I don't know why, but I opened the package. It was exactly the same copy of the very first book. A book on fly-fishing."

"Fly-fishing." Nikolai showed his opinion with a sharp snort. "Hard to believe the clotheshorse likes standing up to his waist in icy mountain water."

Summer agreed but didn't bother to comment. "It made me think. I couldn't believe Dare would buy a book for one of his brothers or his father. They didn't strike me as fishermen either. The more I thought about it, the weirder it seemed. So, I found another book exactly the same and replaced it, and yesterday the owner of the bookshop was found murdered in his shop," Summer finished in a rush.

"You did what?" Nikolai's tempered voice was worse than a bellow.

"I exchanged the books," she whispered. "I think it's my fault the man was murdered."

"Fuck." Nikolai moved without warning, stalking across the kitchen floor with a distinct hitch in his stride. "What did you do with the book?"

"It's in my room."

"You'd better get it."

"But there's nothing different about it. I've checked."

"Let me look. Another set of eyes."

Nikolai watched the sway of Summer's hips when she hurried away to get the book. The urgent need to throw her over his shoulder and lock her away somewhere safe pounded through him. The situation she'd described stunk to high heavens. Summer appeared minutes later with the book and handed it to him. *Fly-Fishing in New Zealand*. He checked the book and opened it. Nothing about it seemed out of the ordinary yet like Summer, his gut screamed there was something odd about Dare Martin and fishing. Buying two books about fly-fishing that were exactly the same raised blood-red flags. He placed it on the table between them and noticed Summer stared at it as though it were one of New Zealand's native wetas, poised to leap on her and nip. "What do you know about the murder?"

"There wasn't much in the *Herald*." Summer stood, picked up a paper off the kitchen counter, and after scanning the first few pages, handed it to him.

Nikolai read it then glanced at Summer. Her face was pale with a fine dusting of freckles visible on the bridge of her nose and cheeks. His gut twisted. She was intelligent enough to know she was in danger. He knew it too. Now what the hell did they do about it?

"You can't stay here alone." Nikolai captured her face in his hand and gently forced her to meet his gaze. "I know you value your independence, but it's too dangerous for you here on your own. If Dare's involved, and we have to assume he is, he'll be eliminating every possibility. You'll be on that list, Summer."

He saw her swallow once and then again. "I know. Nikolai, what am I going to do?" The underlying terror in her voice tugged at him. Responsibility sat uneasily on his shoulders as he shuffled through possible plans of attack. Hell, what if he stuffed up again? Nikolai shoved the thought aside, knowing it was dangerous. He'd do what he did on a mission, what he was trained to do — plan objective. Carry out objective.

"I think Jake's cousin is based at Auckland Central. I'll start things rolling. I want you to pack a bag. You'll have to stay with me." And he'd have to try to keep his hands to himself. Nikolai glanced at Summer, his cock sitting up with clear expectation, pressing against his zipper until he had to make a clandestine move for comfort. Yeah, no problem — as long as she reverted to her sack dresses he'd have no problems at all.

"Nikolai, I know it makes sense not to stay here, but I can't stay at your house."

"Why not?" The rejection stung. "Don't you trust me?"

Summer came to him then and before he could blink, plopped on his lap. His arms came around her automatically. It was like coming home — her flowery scent, her soft feminine curves, her ass rubbing against his militant cock. Nikolai closed his eyes briefly and fought to remember the dangerous situation

Summer was in. She needed a friend right now, not a lover. *But couldn't he be both?* a traitorous voice whispered.

"My asthma is acting up lately. I don't want to risk the paint smell setting off an attack. I don't want to be more vulnerable than I need to."

"Okay. Pack a bag. We'll go to Jake's and cadge a room there."

"What about the book?"

Nikolai picked it up. "I'll take it with us. I'll wait for you then grab a few things from my place."

Summer nodded, and climbed off his knee. Nikolai wanted to protest her leaving; he wanted to grab her back. But he did neither. His mission was to keep her safe. Full stop.

Chapter Fourteen

Jake's house was in Red Hill, a fifteen-minute drive away. Nikolai drove his four-wheel drive vehicle via a circuitous route, which took an extra ten minutes, but by the time they arrived, he was positive no one had followed them.

The porch light was on when they pulled up, and the front door flew open. A sleepy looking Jake ushered them inside then locked the door after them.

"Thanks," Nikolai said.

"No problem, man. Spare room is through there. You know where everything is. I'm going back to bed." Jake yawned, scratched his bare chest and wandered off, disappearing down a dark passageway.

"Come on. I'll show you the spare room." Nikolai flipped on a light and ushered Summer into a double room. The bed dominated the room, diverting his worries from crime bosses to a more direct problem—keeping his hands to himself. Nikolai stopped in the doorway, unwilling to step further into the room.

"Bathroom and toilet are right next door." Nikolai scanned her pale face and knew she needed sleep. "If you don't need anything else, I'll leave you to get some sleep."

"Nikolai." Her soft voice froze him to the spot. "I don't want to sleep alone. Please stay with me."

If she'd flirted or tried to seduce him, Nikolai wouldn't have had any trouble saying no. He was used to knocking aside military groupies. But the unwilling plea in her voice drew him back into the room. "I'll stay with you until you go to sleep."

Summer bit her bottom lip then rushed into speech. "The bed's big enough for both of us. Stay."

Hell, it was what he wanted wasn't it? To watch over her. He could do it easily here in the same room. "Just sleep. Nothing else," he said, spelling it out while inside he railed at the impossibility of a relationship between them.

Summer nodded then unzipped her overnight bag and pulled out an oversized T-shirt. She turned her back, stripped rapidly and tugged the pale blue T-shirt over her head. When she pulled back the bed covers, Nikolai was still staring.

He jerked from his reverie, and immediately another problem presented itself. He hadn't packed anything to sleep in. His eyes zapped to Summer.

"I know I'm safe with you, Nikolai. You've made it very clear you don't want a relationship with me, but I thought we were friends. I've seen your body before. I don't want anything other than friendly comfort." Her gorgeous mouth twisted. "I won't push in where I'm not wanted."

Summer climbed beneath the covers and turned her back to him as though she didn't care whether he stayed or left.

God, he wanted to stay even though he knew it wasn't wise. Nikolai consciously relaxed his tense shoulders and took his weight off his aching knee. His inability to protect the ones he loved lay at the root of his confusion. He acknowledged that. His hands went to the button fly on his jeans. Then he yanked his shirt over his head and discarded it. Seconds later, his shoes and the rest of his clothes joined his T-shirt on the floor, and he flicked off the light then slid into bed.

"Thanks."

The soft whisper warmed him and steeled his willpower. Summer needed comfort and protection. He could try to give that to the best of his ability. Nikolai moved closer to Summer until he was almost touching her. Gradually the tautness dissolved from his muscles. Summer's slow, deep breaths told him she'd dropped off to sleep. The best thing for her, he decided. He'd noticed earlier she'd lost weight, although she still looked damned fine to him. Knowing they were safe tonight, at least, he closed his eyes and let sleep take him.

Nikolai jerked awake suddenly. His heart slammed in an adrenaline rush before he calmed enough to realize he'd drifted into nightmare material. The vision of Laura floated through his mind again without warning, followed by one of the young soldier who'd lost his life on the same mission in which he'd injured his knee. Both glared at him through reproachful eyes. A bad omen? Nikolai wasn't sure, but he knew he wouldn't rest easy until Dare Martin was behind bars, and Summer was home in Eketahuna, safe in the care of her family. Yeah. He'd rest much easier once the only responsibility he had was for himself.

* * * * *

Warm water bubbled around Summer's bare shoulders. In a flax bush over to her right, a pair of tuis squabbled over the nectar from a spear-like flower head. A third tui flew in to join them and a noisy fight ensued. Gradually, one bird emerged the victor and peace reigned again as it fed. Jake's garden, at the rear of his house, was a private haven and exactly what she needed at the moment.

Summer stretched, languid and indolent, her muscles relaxing as the warm water in the spa pummeled them. She closed her eyes and lay there in lazy enjoyment.

What on earth was she going to do about Nikolai?

They'd woken this morning with limbs entwined, his morning erection nestling against her belly. It would have been so easy to lift her hips and join their bodies. She'd wanted to. Desperately. But something had kept her from the overt move. Instinctively, she'd known Nikolai had to make the first move. While he mightn't have objected at the time, later he'd have had second thoughts. She needed the skill and patience of a fly-fisher to hook the big, bad SAS man. Because if there was one thing she'd learned in the last twelve hours, it was that she wanted Nikolai in her life. These last few days without him she'd felt plain miserable.

A splash jerked her eyes open in sudden fear. She jerked upright. Her pulse only slowed again when she recognized Nikolai.

"Sorry. Didn't mean to frighten you. I should have called out." His eyes narrowed and a frown appeared. "You're naked."

Give the man a prize. Her pulse accelerated again, and it had nothing to do with fear. "Jake said he wouldn't be home until late. I assumed you'd be back the same time as him." Summer relaxed against the edge of the spa, and casually allowed a nipple to peep out from beneath the layer of bubbles. The combination of cooler air and the plain naughtiness of her actions drew her nipple tight. A corresponding jump low in her belly made anticipation leap to life. Nikolai hadn't taken his eyes off her. The spa didn't seem to be relaxing him. Summer bit back the need to laugh. What could she do next? The pleasant buzz spread downward into her pussy.

"Thank you for last night," she mouthed.

"I can't hear."

Good. Impish laughter tickled her insides. She'd have to move closer.

"Ah, Summer. Stay there." Nikolai sounded distinctly rattled. She pretended she didn't hear and shot across the spa pool to the molded seat right next to Nikolai. Jake must have had just this scenario in mind, she thought. She allowed her arms and thigh to trespass and bump into Nikolai. Suddenly seduction sounded like a damn fine idea. Her body craved him. She plain wanted him. They were consenting adults. No problem.

"How's the knee?"

"The medical people have told me to take off another two weeks," Nikolai said in clear disgust.

"You shouldn't have overdone it," Summer said.

"Don't nag."

"Fine." Summer pushed closer and let both breasts peep from the water. Encouraged by Nikolai's obvious interest, she stretched, arms rising into the air, basking in her feminine power.

"Thank you for helping me last night."

"No problem."

"Kiss me, Nikolai."

"Not a good idea," he muttered, ripping his gaze from her breasts.

"Why not?"

"We've settled why not."

Frustration made Summer testy. Irritation zapped through her, wanting an outlet, needing a vent. Then inspiration hit.

"I need sexual release," she stated. "If you're not interested then I'll use a toy." Summer stood, hoping like hell she'd drag a reaction from him because if he called her bluff, she had no idea what to try next. Somehow, the idea of a toy didn't do it for her, not when the real thing was inches away. "Or maybe one of the spa jets would do the job."

She peeped at him through lowered lashes. He wasn't moving. Bother. Summer turned to climb from the pool, lifting her legs and brazenly flashing her feminine folds as she stepped from the spa.

"Wait." Nikolai grabbed her arm and jerked her to a halt. She toppled off balance but he caught her, and dragged her into the safety of his arms. "I can make you climax."

"You sure can," Summer purred. Good grief. Where had this siren come from? At least her bright cheeks could be attributed to the spa. She batted her lashes at him. "And are you going to or are you all talk?"

Nikolai snorted right next to her ear. "Stop trying to push. If I decide to fuck you, I'll do it in my own good time. Not when you think I should."

His breath brushed across her ear and the tender skin of her neck. Summer bit back a pleased smirk. Fighting words. She had the big, bad SAS man on a hook—he just didn't like to admit he was caught. "So are you going to make love with me or do I need to get that toy?" She didn't bother telling him the toy was still in its original packaging.

Nikolai drew away far enough that he could see her eyes. "Baggage." A glimmer of humor lit his chocolate brown eyes, and she knew everything would turn out all right. Her body reacted swiftly, the slow burn of pleasure ignited with one look from Nikolai.

"This thing between us—it won't last. It can't."

Still fighting, she thought with a trace of irritation and sadness. Still thinking he knew what would be best for her. Oh, well. They had plenty of time until she returned to Eketahuna. She'd wear down his objections one by one. She wriggled around until she straddled his legs. All she needed was time.

Nikolai's eyes dropped to her breasts, the sensation of his gaze wandering her curves sending tendrils of pleasure fizzing through her. Summer cupped her breast in her hands and offered it to him. "Taste me," she whispered. "Make me feel good."

"You'd tempt a saint."

"You're not a saint," she countered. "And why would you want to be? I'd think someone who acts pure all the time misses out on a lot of fun. Go on, Nikolai. Taste me."

He lowered his head and laved his tongue the length of her distended nipple. "Any other instructions?" he asked with a wry edge to his tone. His teeth nipped at her flesh then he licked a wet path down her cleavage. His mouth alternated between breasts, sucking and licking until a whimper built inside her.

"No more instructions," she gasped out. "You have more experience. I'm willing to go with the flow."

Nikolai snorted again but at least he started to cooperate. With his mouth surrounding her nipple, warmth bloomed between her legs. Each draw of his mouth sent a bolt of sensation to her core. Summer parted her legs even wider, and squirmed closer to Nikolai until her pussy brushed the hard bulge at his groin. The spasm of flickering response that shot from her clit stalled her breath halfway up her throat. She threw back her head and rotated her hips so his erection brushed her clit again.

Nikolai surged to his feet without warning. Summer squeaked, thinking he'd drop her, but he held her easily without even breathing harder. While she clutched at his neck and had her legs hooked around his waist, Nikolai yanked his boxers down and stepped out of them. Then he sat again, strumming his thumbs over both nipples and staring straight into her eyes. She leaned closer and brushed her lips across his. A teasing kiss flared hot and serious. Tongues stroked and dueled as Summer squirmed closer. Craving swept the length of her body. Even though it had only been a few days, hunger gnawed at her mind, her body. She strained upward seeking a way to ease the emptiness between her legs. The warm pulse of the spa jets intensified the craving, the hunger, the desperate need to join with him. His cock brushed against her but not exactly where she needed him most. Just a fraction to the left. She slipped her hand between them and brushed her thumb over his tip. His eyes dropped to half-mast and a distinct shudder ripped through him.

"I've missed you," he murmured. "I tried not to."

Summer took pleasure from his raw honesty and stretched upward to reward him with a lingering kiss, the slow slide of his tongue against hers building the excitement. She leaned closer, brushing her breasts against his smooth chest, reveling in the drag of friction. "Ohhh," she groaned. The frisson of pleasure felt good but not as satisfying as Nikolai's cock. Without thinking, she guided his cock to her pussy mouth and sank slowly down. He was wide. Thick. So good as she slowly filled and stretched around him. Summer lifted her hips then sank back down, setting an instinctive rhythm. The powerful thrust of his body when he surged upward into her cunt sent desire flowing like honey. And it was just as sweet.

"Fuck." Nikolai grasped her hips and wrenched his cock from her.

"What are you — ?"

"No condom." His chest rose and fell rapidly as though he'd run a race. "Shit, I can't believe that just happened. I've never done that before. What was I thinking?" He swept his wet hair away from his face and met her frown unflinching. "That's it. We'll get married."

Summer felt her mouth drop open. Her head shook as if to negate his words, but she was pretty sure she'd heard correctly. "No. I don't think so." She scrambled off his lap and stood, darting out of reach when he tried to snare her. Summer climbed from the spa with more haste than dignity. "I'll go and get a condom. I brought some with me. Won't be long."

"Summer." The low masculine growl spurred her to speed rather than propelled her to obedience.

What was wrong with the man? Huh! Most men thought with their dicks or at least ceased rational thought when their members were involved. But not the big, bad SAS man. Oh, no! He had to be the voice of reason, Summer fumed as she stomped inside. She ignored the small voice at the back of her head that said she was being childish and that Nikolai was acting responsibly. *As he should.*

"Dammit, Summer. Come back here!"

Summer heard the splash of water then running footsteps across the wooden deck. She increased her speed while her anger grew. Pompous man! How dare he try to order her around? She was not going to marry him and that was that.

"Summer." A hand closed over her bare shoulder before she made it halfway down the passage, whirling her around to face him. "What's your problem?" he gritted out. "I thought females wanted marriage."

"They like to be asked," Summer snapped.

His dark brows furrowed. "So, I'll ask. Will you marry me?"

Fury, hot and savage, curled her hands to fists. If he uttered one more word, she'd deck him—right in the middle of his perfectly straight nose. "No. No, I will not marry you. All I want from you is a good, fun fuck. Is that plain enough? You told me before you didn't want responsibility. Fine. I'm taking you at your word. I don't want responsibility either."

"What if you're pregnant?"

"We're talking if." Summer felt as though he'd stabbed her through the heart. Thoughts whirred through her mind so quickly they tangled up in one confused mass. Not that she intended to scrutinize them too closely. Nikolai didn't really want marriage, and he'd only offered it to her because the thought of failing another child ate at him. If she got married, when she married, she wanted to know that she was loved. Cherished. The idea of being considered a duty left her cold and dead inside. Her nose rose in the air. "I'm only twenty-two. That's too young to get married. You said yourself that I'm too young for you. And here I thought women were meant to be the indecisive ones." Her hand closed around their allocated bedroom door. Summer jerked open the door and stomped inside with Nikolai a step behind.

Cold fear kicked him in the gut, but despite the terror inside, he could still appreciate a great ass when he saw one. Summer had a great ass. Tight and round, it begged to be fondled. He watched her bend over and flash the pink folds of her labia at him. Then she whirled about and slapped a small foil package in his hand.

"Now, can we have sex?" she demanded.

Her beautiful breasts rose and fell, distracting him for an instant. His eyes narrowed as he studied her flushed cheeks and swollen lips. The woman was marrying him if he had to drag her to the altar or before a justice of the peace.

While Nikolai debated his course of action, he peered at the condom wrapper. "Chocolate flavored. What happened to the glow-in-the-dark green?"

"I thought a change would be nice." Summer sat on the edge of the bed and primly crossed her legs. Pity the devilish glint in her blue eyes spoiled the pose.

Nikolai handed the foil package back to her. He wasn't adverse to sex, as his rampant penis indicated, but come hell, high water or local crooks, she would become Mrs. Tarei. "You can put it on." He dropped onto the mattress, calmly folded his arms across his chest and waited. A smirk built inside, just bursting to break out, but Nikolai remained impassive watching her hesitation through narrowed eyes.

"I've never done it before. Apart from the banana, and I suppose that doesn't count. Fruit isn't quite as distracting."

Good to know, he thought, unable to keep the smugness from his face. "It's not difficult. And if you want the bout of sweaty sex that you're so desperate for, you're gonna have to learn in a hurry."

"All right." Summer bounced to her feet, the sudden move sending her ripe, luscious breasts swaying gently. His cock jumped, his balls drawing tight and ready for action. Acute anticipation quickened his pulse rate as she turned away and bent to rifle through her bag. Summer pulled out the box of condoms. For a puzzled second Nikolai stared, then he got the picture. Summer was a librarian, trained to look up books, so if she wanted to learn a new skill, she read about it. Her pink lips moved as she mouthed the instructions and studied the diagrams on the enclosed leaflet. "Okay. I've got this sussed. I know exactly what I'm doing."

A chuckle burst from Nikolai. "Do your worst."

Summer tore open the wrapping, used her thumb to hold the end, and rolled it on as though she'd been applying condoms to men's cocks for years. "Ta da!"

The flush of achievement on her cheeks brought a wave of tenderness along with laughter. He wondered if she'd attack parenthood with the same single-minded determination. "Come here," he said.

"At last," Summer muttered. "Some action."

Nikolai lurched for her, grabbing and twisting her body so she fell flat on the mattress beneath him. He stared down into her flushed face. Hell, she aroused him without even trying. Nikolai bent his head, licking a few remaining droplets of water from the spa off her collarbone. Then he moved down her body to pay homage to her full breasts, drawing circles across the pale globes with his tongue. She tried to direct his mouth to her nipple by entwining her fingers in her hair and tugging. Instead, he licked and stroked his way down her smooth skin and the sweet dip of her waist to her belly button. She quivered with his ministrations, pleasing him with her responsiveness. Nikolai parted her legs and knelt between them. Placing his hands beneath her hips, he lifted her to his mouth.

Summer sucked in a harsh breath. "Don't make me wait too long. I've been thinking about sex with you for days. I'm so primed, I'll come if you breathe on my clit."

Nikolai parted her folds and took the time to study her pink labia and swollen bud. For some reason, the way she called what was between them *sex* rubbed him the wrong way. While he worried about the why, he trailed his fingers across her skin, damp with her arousal. Her hips jerked in his hold, and when he looked up, he saw she glared at him. He teased her feminine flesh with his fingers and savored her reaction. Open and honest with not a single pretence. Unlike Laura. Nikolai pushed the thought away to concentrate on Summer. She shuddered violently. He bent to rake his tongue along her cleft and clit. God, he couldn't get enough of the taste of her. She tensed at the touch, her eyes fluttered closed and a throaty groan escaped her. Nikolai watched the changes in her body with fascination. He'd never paid much attention or cared much after Laura. Summer was a real education.

"I thought I told you not to do that," she muttered, sounding cross. "I wanted you inside me."

"Ah, but now I've taken the edge off, I get to make you hot all over again. Let me tell you what I'm going to do to you."

"What?" she whispered, sounding enthralled. "Tell me."

Nikolai let her hips fall to the bed. "First, I'm going to tie your hands to the bed head so you can't distract me."

"Really?"

"Yeah. And because I know you'd cheat and open your eyes, you're going to lie facedown."

"You'll see my butt," Summer said.

"Yeah."

"It's daylight."

"You didn't seem too worried before when you pranced into the house ahead of me."

Summer groaned. "I was angry. I forgot. You know, it's not my best feature." She cupped her breasts in her hands. "Wouldn't you rather feast your eyes on these beauties?"

Damn, she made him laugh. He felt the corners of his eyes crinkle, and his mouth definitely quirked. "Next time. Turn over."

Summer resisted, a faint pucker between her brows. "Do you have to tie me up?"

Nikolai slid up the bed and pulled her into his arms. "We're not going to do anything you're unhappy with. Making love is about giving and receiving pleasure." He kissed her with an open-mouthed kiss, feasting on the curves of her lips and the minty moistness inside her mouth. When they parted, they were both breathing heavily. "It's about trust."

"It's not that I'm frightened you'll hurt me—"

"You like to stay in control." That made two of them. But she was so damned reckless at times, stubbornly trying to maintain power. Nikolai shook his head, knowing she was still in danger because of swapping that damned book. This marriage would be interesting. They might fight, but they'd have a hell of a time making up afterward.

"I don't like being told what to do. When I'm asked, that's different."

"So if I asked you to please turn over, would you do it?"

Her blue eyes were wide and dark with a trace of uncertainty as she studied him. Nikolai held his breath—waiting. She shifted, her belly rubbing the tip of his cock. A pained gasp squeezed between his lips, and he prayed she made up her mind fast.

"I'll do it on the condition that you let me tie you up in return."

"God, I've created a monster," he grinned, softening the words. "We'll save the tying up for an hour or so. Where's this toy I've been hearing about?"

Summer's curious gaze passed over his condom-encased cock and turned distinctly hungry. Her brows rose and fell in a comical manner, but yep, that look was predatory.

"Maybe a little later for that too?" she said.

"Good idea." Nikolai grasped her hips, positioned his cock at the mouth of her pussy and surged inside her tight, silken sheath with one seamless thrust. Hot pleasure spilled through him as he pumped his cock with slow, deliberate strokes. He bent to feast on her mouth, their tongues twirling together in an imitation of their lovemaking. Nikolai broke off their kiss, his hands tugging her brown and blue hair from the loose knot thing she'd tied it in. "That's better," he murmured, as damp locks of hair tumbled around her face. "Now you look like a fallen woman."

A gurgle escaped her right before she bit him on a biceps. Her sharp teeth sent a signal straight to his cock. He quickened his strokes, relishing the leap of pleasure and the powerful kick of sensation at the tip of his cock. It spilled through him in a steady stream, like nothing else he'd ever experienced before. Shit, he hoped she was close because he was going to come. He tried to slow his impending release, but his senses seemed heightened as he explored her curvy body. He savored the scent on her skin, the flowery smell of damp hair, the slide of their sweat-slicked bodies against each other, the salty taste when he scraped his teeth across the underside of her breast. He failed the quest for slow. *F for failure*, he thought, as he sucked a nipple into his mouth. The taste of coconut exploded on his senses as he drew hard on her flesh. The gnawing ache in his dick intensified.

"Nikolai," she gasped.

Thank you! Nikolai chanted silently. *Thank you*. His hands dropped to cup her buttocks and he lifted her to deepen the angle of his strokes. Flesh slapped. Quicker. Harder. Summer dug her nails into his back and tensed. He felt the tightening clasp of her womb and molten fire erupted from his cock. A dark sound squeezed past his clenched teeth seconds before his seed poured from him in a long, never-ending stream. He kept thrusting, short, hard jabs, until the last ounce of pleasure was wrung from him.

Nikolai came to himself again when Summer started to squirm beneath him. "Am I squashing you?"

"S'okay," Summer gasped. "Too many curves anyway."

He chuckled and rolled so she lay on top of him. "Sweetheart, I like your curves just the way they are. A good, big handful."

"Yeah, anywhere you choose to grab," she said, her tone rueful.

"I like it." Nikolai smoothed one hand down her back and squeezed her rounded butt gently. "A lot."

"You're good for a girl's ego." She looked up at him, a renewed flare of desire in her blue eyes.

He drew a breath, deep and unsteady. "I hate to say it, but I don't think I can manage another go-around. Not yet. The mind is willing. The flesh needs to recuperate."

"No problem," Summer said in a breezy voice that made the hairs at the back of his neck stand to cautious attention. She climbed off him, their joined bodies separating with a squelch that made her laugh. Once again, she bent over her bag to rummage through the contents, giving him a great view of her pussy and butt. He raked his gaze across her ample ass, his hands literally itching to touch. Shit, even better. He could sink his teeth in—he could bite. A surge of possessiveness flooded him without warning. Damn, he wanted to mark her fine-looking butt. He wanted his brand on her so no other man would make the mistake of thinking she was free.

A mischievous giggle drew his attention. She was busy watching him watch her. "Minx. Come here." Nikolai yanked the spent condom off his cock and put it aside. He held his cock in his hand and slowly pumped. His semi-erect dick reacted predictably to the stimulation.

"Ah-ha! There you are," she crooned, and she turned to Nikolai with a blaze of sexual heat in her face. As he watched, the soft tones of arousal crawled down her neck to her chest. "My toy." Summer yanked the wrapping off with all the enthusiasm of a child at Christmastime. Then she crawled across the bed to him on her hands and knees. Summer lay down across his chest, holding her toy up her him to see. "Feel how soft that is." Her hand caressed the red flexible skin, and Nikolai felt an answering surge in his cock as though she massaged him. "And look—it's got different speeds." A soft whine sounded. "But it doesn't grunt like you."

"You are in need of a good, hard spanking, Summer Williams."

"Okay," she said. "After we try the toy, and I tie you up."

Chapter Fifteen

"Summer!" a masculine voice hollered. The angry sound echoed and bounced off the walls in a too-familiar manner.

"Oh, no," Summer muttered. Somehow, she didn't think closing her eyes and pretending she was asleep would solve this one.

Nikolai slithered from the bed and pulled an ugly-looking gun from under the bed.

"Don't go. Did you lock the bedroom door?"

"No."

"Summer!" The second voice sounded a shade deeper but just as angry.

"Shit, there's two of them," Nikolai said, and he grabbed his jeans and yanked them on.

"Unfortunately."

Nikolai cast her a strange look, but the thump of heavy boots outside the bedroom forestalled his questions.

"Don't come in!" Summer shrieked. "I don't have any clothes—"

The door burst open and crashed against the bedroom wall. Two huge men paused at the threshold, and the four of them stared at each other with varying reactions.

"Fuck," Nikolai said in a fierce undertone.

Summer nodded. Yep, this was a situation that called for a stronger word than "shit". She tugged the covers up to her chin and considered crawling right underneath to hide. She thought about it for all of two seconds then cast the idea away. Someone needed to referee. She was the most likely candidate.

"What the hell are you doing?" Dillon, her oldest brother, roared. He balanced lightly on his toes, his biceps bulging beneath his T-shirt. His dark hair stuck up, appearing as ruffled as his temper.

Josh, her other brother, folded his arms across his broad chest. He didn't smirk but the glint in his baby blue eyes said he wanted to. "Oh, it's obvious what they've been doing," he drawled, confirming Summer's supposition. The louse thought this was funny.

"*Tarei.*" A vein throbbed at Dillon's temple, and he looked as though he wanted to haul Nikolai from the room and beat him to a pulp.

Summer swallowed despite her best efforts to keep her anxiety hidden. Her week just kept getting better. Murder, a little sex and a fistfight chucked in for good measure. She had it all. Who needed to read the Sunday tabloids?

"I don't particularly want to think about my sister and sex in the same sentence," Dillon snapped.

"Especially with him." Josh shifted his weight, and clenched and unclenched his fists. The ever-present humor in his baby-looking face riled Summer. Time to take control.

"Out," she snapped, trying to ignore the fine tremor of nerves that shook her limbs beneath the covers.

"Fine." Dillon glared at Nikolai. "He's got enough clothes on to come with us."

"I don't think so," Summer returned sweetly. If they laid one hand on Nikolai so help her… She'd learned a few moves at Tae Kwon Do that might surprise her two soldier brothers. "Nikolai stays with me."

Dillon and Josh exchanged a glance.

Summer narrowed her eyes. "He stays with me. He's seen me dress before."

"I don't think they want to hear that, sweetheart," Nikolai drawled. Black humor coated his voice as he sat on the bed at her side and waited.

"I'm trying hard not to imagine," Dillon snapped in a hard voice. He jerked his head toward the door. "Out, Tarei. You're coming with us."

"You know Nikolai?" Summer glanced from brother to brother. Their hard faces gave away little, but Summer knew them well enough that they weren't telling her something big. Fine. She'd worm the information from Nikolai the minute she got rid of her brothers. Which would be any time now.

Summer sat and made a show of grabbing the covers. They slipped dangerously close to flashing her nipples.

"Aw, Summer!" Josh said, starting to back away. He grabbed his brother's arm and yanked.

Dillon resisted until Summer made another move. He stirred then but it was unwillingly. "The kitchen in five minutes," he ordered. "A second longer and we'll come back and drag you out."

Her brothers exited the room, their remarks to each other peppered with enough swear words it was a wonder her mother didn't make an appearance with her bar of soap.

Summer scrambled from the bed and searched for some clothes. "I don't care what they said, I'm having a shower before I face them. And you are coming with me to explain what my brothers are talking about and why they don't like you. At least the bathroom has a lock."

Twenty minutes later, Summer sailed into the kitchen with Nikolai trailing behind.

"Coffee?" she asked Nikolai.

"Thanks."

"Don't think you can waltz in here and act like nothing has happened," Dillon snarled. He paced the length of the kitchen like a big cat confined to a cage. "Mum's not going to be happy when she hears."

Fury made Summer's jaw clench. "What? You gonna tell tales to Mum? It's about time you all realized I'm an adult. I'm not the sickly kid anymore. And I'll sleep with whomever I damn well want. If I want to sleep with an entire rugby team then I will."

"Over my dead body," Nikolai snapped, curling a possessive arm around her waist and hauling her against his side.

"For that, we might let you live," Josh conceded.

"But you can keep your hands off our sister."

Nikolai didn't look too perturbed at her brother's posturing, so Summer allowed herself to relax a little. She was old enough to make her own decisions, and if some of them were wrong, she'd deal with the consequences. *By herself.* Summer silently acknowledged her reckless streak, but she was working on that and trying to temper her reactions to new situations with thought first. *Lots of thought.* Sometimes that worked.

Nikolai ignored her brothers and brushed a lock of hair away from her face. He pressed a kiss to the spot of skin he'd uncovered, then captured one of her hands and traced the fine skin at the inside of her wrist. "We're engaged. We're getting married."

Summer was so busy concentrating on the fiery sensation racing from her wrist and down her body, she didn't register his words at first.

"Married?" Josh glanced at Dillon.

Summer's mouth dropped. Had he said married? She thought they'd discussed that earlier and come to an agreement. Summer was about to argue then decided silence might be the wiser course at the moment. When Summer witnessed the silent communication between her brothers, she knew it. She'd take issue with Nikolai and his high-handedness later.

"That's okay then." Dillon's grudging tone didn't fit with his words. "We'd better ring Mum and let her know the news."

Okay, that did it. "I'm not marrying Nikolai."

Silence fell. The only audible sound was the roar of the next-door neighbor mowing his lawn. Nikolai stiffened beside her, his hand gripping hers tightly. Dammit, she'd had enough of this. She'd pack her bag, call a cab and see if she could stay with one of her friends. She wrenched her hand from Nikolai's hold and stomped to the door. Summer flinched inwardly at the sudden heat caused by three big, bad SAS men glaring at her back. Too bad. They could settle their fight by themselves, and if they wanted to pound each other into the ground, let them.

"Summer!" Nikolai roared.

"I'm fed up with you all telling me what to do. I won't marry you. You haven't asked me." Was it too much to ask for a little romance? When had proposing on bended knee gone out of fashion? Dammit, she wanted it all. Summer kept walking and threw open the bedroom door. The rumpled bed reminded her of how good it felt when Nikolai was holding her, his cock tightly wedged in her pussy. Too bad memories would have to sustain her because she wasn't putting up with being told what to do and when to do it. They might belong to the army. She didn't, and it was about time they remembered.

Boots thundered on the wooden floor behind her. Great. The whole herd of big, bad SAS men had come to watch her pack. *Fine.*

"Care to offer suggestions as to the best place to pack these, boys?" Summer held up the box of glow in the dark condoms, with the label facing outward and clearly visible. Mrs. Ferguson would have been proud. She'd listened carefully during their marketing seminar.

Josh sniggered. "I wouldn't wear those if you paid me."

"He better have worn them," Dillon growled.

Nikolai tensed noticeably and shot an irritable look at Summer. "I didn't, which is why we're getting married."

"Bastard."

Dillon and Josh rounded on Nikolai. A fist flew. Summer wasn't sure which brother the punch came from but it connected with Nikolai's jaw. Before Summer knew it, fists were going in all directions along with all too realistic crunches and spurts of blood.

"Stop it!" she shrieked. Summer threw the box of condoms at Dillon's head. Green foil packets rained down, landing all over the floor. Something else to throw. But what? Summer grabbed the nearest thing to hand. The fly-fishing book. She heaved at Josh. Bull's eye! The book hit the back of his head and bounced off. It thumped to the ground. She searched for another missile.

Nikolai threw a punch at Dillon. Dillon's head snapped back. Her brother backed up to dodge a second punch, and his foot landed on the book. It skidded from under him, but Dillon balanced like the panther he resembled and kicked the fly-fishing book aside. It crashed against the wall.

The book. She'd heave it at her brothers again. When she scooped it up, a tightly wadded piece of paper fell from the damaged spine. Sudden excitement pounded through her. A clue as to why Dare wanted the book. "Nikolai!" she shrieked.

The three men ignored her. Summer scowled and wondered what else she could do short of throwing water on them. As she watched, Nikolai took a blow in the stomach then came up fighting. Dillon ducked, stepped back and bumped into Josh. Josh dodged out of the way but bumped into Summer and tripped her over. Summer squeaked in alarm as they both fell to the ground in a tangle of limbs and a loud thump.

"Get off me, you great big oaf!" Summer pushed at her brother, but he was slow to move and felt like a giant sack of potatoes draped across her chest. "Can't breathe."

"Get off her, dammit." Nikolai came to the rescue.

Seconds later, the weight was removed from her chest, and Josh was dumped on the mat beside the bed.

"You okay, sweetheart?" Nikolai helped her sit up and brushed her hair away from her eyes. "Do you need your inhaler?"

"Inhaler? God, Summer. You haven't used your inhaler for over a year," Dillon said.

"No, I'm fine. Josh knocked the wind out of me, that's all. Is he okay?" She peered past Dillon's worried face to study Josh who was rubbing the side of his head. He looked awfully groggy to her.

"Nah, he's got a hard head. He'll be fine," Dillon said. "I'm more worried about you. I thought you'd grown out of the asthma attacks."

"Dillon, for the last time, I'm fine. If or when I'm not feeling well, I'll take myself off to the doctor. I don't need my family treating me like a baby. Nikolai, look what fell out of the book when the spine broke. I didn't think of breaking the binding."

"We've got more important things to worry about than a damned book," Dillon muttered.

"Summer is in—"

Summer placed a hand on Nikolai's shoulder and squeezed hard. "I'll tell them since it was my fault. I've got myself in a spot of trouble—"

"Why didn't you call us instead of him?" Josh muttered. "We're family."

"She came to me," Nikolai snarled.

Summer drew in a sharp breath at the unspoken sentiment. Warmth tugged at her heartstrings. Maybe there was hope for this particular big, bad SAS man after all, if he thought of them as a unit. Summer pulled a face. No, not a unit! That smacked of army and military. Team? No. Perhaps she'd go for couple. Shying away from the idea, even though it made her warm and tingly inside, Summer unfolded the tightly wadded up paper.

"What trouble?" Dillon demanded.

"I met a man and—"

Dillon sliced a black glower in Nikolai's direction. "Him?"

"Will you let me finish? Five minutes tops. Then you can do your shouting when I've finished. More impact that way."

"Mum was too lenient with you," Josh muttered. "Should have paddled your backside."

"Nope," Summer said. "The only one who gets to do that is Nikolai. Do you want me to tell you or not?"

"Carry on," Nikolai drawled. "About the clotheshorse. Not the other. We'll discuss that later."

Summer brightened. "Tonight?"

"Enough," Dillon snarled.

Summer bit back the building grin. Her big brother looked distinctly uncomfortable, but he was playing dumb. Having a sex life helped in more ways than appeasing her curiosity. She made a mental note to use the ploy as a distraction again.

"Yeah." Josh sniggered. "I'm thinking this discussion doesn't have much to do with punishment."

"I met Dare Martin, and we went out together a few times. When I started getting serious about Nikolai, I told him I wouldn't see him again. It was strange," she mused. "He's not stupid but he acted thick as a plank of wood when I tried to break things off and made plans for dinner that night."

"You didn't tell me that," Nikolai growled.

"He knew I used to visit the same bookshop he did, and when he asked me to pick up a package of books for him now and then, I didn't think anything of it. But one night, I opened his package of books. The book inside was exactly the same as the very first one that I received by mistake. That's how we met," she added. "I thought it was strange so I found another one exactly the same and exchanged them. Then the owner of the bookshop was found murdered. Judging by the newspaper report, the police think it's a robbery gone wrong. I think it had something to do with me exchanging the books."

Josh groaned long and theatrically. "Jeez, Summer. Why didn't you just go and stick your hand into the lion's mouth?"

Irritation bloomed without warning. "Shut up, or I'll give you a matching lump on the other side of your thick head. I agree it wasn't the wisest thing I've done, but it's too late now. I need help, not 'I told you so'."

"Why didn't you control her?" Dillon growled at Nikolai.

"Excuse me?" Nikolai straightened. "We are talking about Summer here."

Dillon glanced at Summer, then shrugged. "Point taken. So, what do we do now?"

"I've already spoken to the police," Nikolai said, tugging the paper from Summer's hand. "Jake's brother is a cop. I'll take the book and the paper that fell out to him."

Dillon nodded.

Josh grunted his approval, and climbed up off the floor.

There was something wrong with this picture. What about her? As usual, they were treating her like a child, patting her on the head and expecting her to go along with their plans like a good little girl. Summer's mouth tightened to a mutinous line. "I'll go to the police with you. They'll want to talk to me."

Nikolai stood and frowned down at Summer who still sat on the floor. "No, it's too dangerous for you. I don't want to risk it."

Dillon and Josh repeated their nods and grunts of endorsement.

Summer scrambled to her feet and went back to her packing. Ignoring the big, bad SAS men, she picked up all the green foil packets and tossed them into her overnight bag. She crammed in her clothes and stomped down the hall to the bathroom to collect her toiletries. Somehow, without saying a word, Dillon and Josh had gotten to Nikolai, and he was backing off gracefully. She wanted to curse. She wanted to shout and punch. Instead, Summer did nothing and concentrated on packing.

"Good," Dillon said. "I'm glad you're packing. You can come with us."

Summer stilled. "Where?"

"We'll go to Uncle Henry's for tonight and back to Eketahuna tomorrow. You should be safe there."

"And what about my job?" Summer said. "If I leave, I won't get my certificate."

"You can do it another time," Dillon said.

Summer sucked in a deep breath, ready to shout, yell and hurl a few cuss words. Her job was important to her. She might not make world-altering decisions and save lives like them, but she made people happy. That had to count for something. She glanced at Nikolai, half expecting him to protest, but the stupid man didn't utter a word. *Fine.* Now she knew where she stood in his list of priorities.

* * * * *

Prison must be like this, Summer thought. Her two brothers hovered over her while she watered Uncle Henry's rose garden. They tensed at the sound of each car, generally making a nuisance of themselves, and making Summer want to scream. Frustration simmered as she turned off the water and rolled up the hose neatly on Uncle Henry's special stand.

"I don't think you should see Nikolai again," Dillon said without warning.

Even though she'd been expecting it, her brother's words still riled her, stoking the slow burning anger inside. "I don't think it's any of your business who I see. I wouldn't think of telling you not to go out with Suzie Daniels when you're at home on leave, even though she's a gossip and jumps into bed with Tom McPherson the minute you leave town. Nope, wouldn't even consider telling you that." Summer turned her back on her oldest brother, and came face to face with Josh's smirk.

"Help me out here," Dillon snapped. "You tell her since she won't listen to me."

The humor dropped from Josh, leaving an image of what he must look like in soldier mode. "Dillon's right. There are things you don't know about Tarei. Go home and go out with one of the boys there. I'm sure you're not lacking for offers."

Summer didn't dignify that with an answer. She stormed inside, sensing rather than hearing her brothers follow.

"His wife and kid died," Dillon said in a hard voice. "After that, he wasn't the same. That's what I heard. On his last mission, one of his men got hit. Tarei left him to die."

Summer yanked open the fridge and pulled out a bottle of wine. She pulled a corkscrew from a drawer and struggled to remove the cork.

"I'll do it," Josh said, coming up behind her and trying to take possession of the wine.

"No! I'll do it," Summer snapped, snatching the bottle from his grasp. "I don't care if it takes me all night to open the bloody bottle. *I will do it.* I'm sick of you all trying to run my life." Tears stung at the back of her eyes, and her voice took on a choked, thick sound. She glanced up to see her brothers look at each other in a sort of masculine, helpless panic. Give them a man with a gun and they knew what to do, but a woman in tears really put a spoke in their big he-man bravado. What did she have to do to convince them she didn't need looking after?

The phone rang, and Dillon went to answer.

"I'll get it," Summer snapped. "I can manage that without interference." She grabbed the phone on the eighth ring, after Dillon stepped away and gestured for her to take the honor. The theatrical gesture of his hand pricked her temper. "Yes?" she snarled, her narrowed eyes still on her brothers. This was what it must feel like to be incarcerated and watched 24/7. Well, they could shove it. As soon as she got the chance, she intended to blow this joint and go to confront Nikolai. *Probably exchanging two captors for another one*, she thought with a flash of black humor. "Hello?" she repeated on another impatient snarl.

"Girly, we know you have the book," a gruff voice said.

"What book? Is this the bookshop I did the special order at? The Pen and Quill?"

"Don't play dumb, girly. We want that book."

Her brothers closed in on her, one standing either side in silent protection. In this instant, it felt good to have them on her team, offering moral support. Summer took a deep breath, aware of the discrepancies in her thinking about her family and Nikolai. Something to think about. "Who is this?" she demanded, irritation mixing with a dose of healthy fear. They'd already killed once to get their hands on the book.

"Do you recognize the voice?" Josh whispered.

Only in her nightmares. Summer shook her head, unable to place the low, gritty voice.

"Put the book in the mailbox, and it will be collected with no questions asked."

"But I don't have—"

"Do it. Or else." The phone slammed down, the anger behind the crash echoing down the line and raising a rash of gooseflesh on Summer's arms and legs.

"He wants the book." Summer stared at her brothers. "What do I do?"

Dillon and Josh exchanged a glance then as one, they wandered away from her.

"What?" Summer stared after them. "Oh, I get it. I can't have it both ways. I can't expect help and push you away at the same time. Is that what you're trying to tell me? Fine." Enough. Summer turned and stomped from the kitchen. When she arrived at her bedroom door, she jerked it open, stepped inside and slammed it behind her. The room seemed to shudder at the force of her anger. A small bottle of perfume that balanced precariously on the edge of her dresser, because of the amount of important junk she'd tossed there, gave up the fight and toppled to the floor. Of course, she hadn't put the lid on properly and it parted company from the bottle. The perfume gushed out onto the carpet before she could grab it. The perfume's floral notes tickled her nose and a sneeze erupted.

Probably about time to tidy up, she conceded. Now was as good a time as any.

Summer sorted dirty laundry into a pile and consigned anything clean to drawers and the wardrobe. Instantly, the room looked better, tidier. She peered out the window at Nikolai's house. Before she'd even formulated the thought, she was at the window and sliding it up. At least this time her jeans offered better protection against Uncle Henry's rose bushes.

Summer slithered over the windowsill and dropped into the garden below. In the hour before darkness, the scent of roses filled the air along with the moist, damp soil. Summer felt another sneeze building at the back of her nose, and knew she needed to move fast before her brothers came to investigate.

For a moment, she thought she'd escaped the thorns until her shirt caught and a part of the rose bush shot under her shirt, the sharp thorns tearing the tender skin at the small of her back. Shoot. Summer extricated herself then frantically grabbed her nose. *Too late.* The sneeze escaped. A feeble one, but a noise nonetheless. She froze, waiting. When nothing happed, she let out a sigh of relief and crept across the open section of lawn before cautiously opening the gate and letting herself into Nikolai's property. The faint sound of an approaching car hurried her along. She didn't want to be seen. Summer hurried across the deck, dodging the broken board, heading straight for Nikolai's bedroom window.

A smile flickered across her face when she saw it was open, the net curtain dancing in the soft breeze. Summer slipped inside.

Chapter Sixteen

Someone tackled her. *Nikolai*, she thought with relief as she identified his soap and distinctive masculine scent. His hand curled around her breast before she could speak.

"Why Mr. Tarei, I do believe you have a breast fetish."

"Only for yours," he whispered, his hand shaping and testing the weight of her breast. He nuzzled the soft skin at the base of her neck and scraped his teeth across, taking a tiny nip. "God, I missed you," he said on a heavy sigh. He tugged at the cotton fabric of her shirt to expose more skin, then pressed a kiss to her collarbone.

Summer gave a breathless laugh, surprised by his admission.

"If you're pregnant we're getting married," he added in a suddenly tight voice.

It was as if he made the offer under duress and both his words and tone stung. "I never asked you to marry me. I don't want marriage." *Especially not if I'm ordered.* Was it too much to expect a little romance, a declaration of love? They were good together, if only he'd admit it and quit worrying about the age difference, and letting the past intrude on their potential happiness.

"You're right not to want marriage with me."

The hollow defeat in his voice made her want to shout in protest. "Are we talking about your wife?"

"Yeah."

"Sounded as though she was selfish—only thinking of herself and her own needs, instead of considering you as well."

"She was young, and I was away a lot of the time."

"Stop right there." Summer glared at Nikolai's face through the dim light. "Don't draw parallels. I am nothing like your wife. I have a job, friends, interests. I am not selfish and self-absorbed like your wife."

"No, you're not, but you're reckless. You leap without thinking. Do your brothers know you've left the house?"

"No," she whispered, guilt surfacing to replace her former anger. His accusation stung. "I'd better ring them. But I'm not going back. I want to stay with you and...talk."

A chuckled rumbled from deep in his chest. "Is talk an euphemism for sex?"

Summer closed one eye in a wink. "Could well be, if you play your cards right. Can I use your cell phone?"

Something that could have been approval glinted in his brown eyes as he tossed her the phone. Summer felt an answering warmth inside. Suddenly breathless, her hand shook when she dialed Uncle Henry's number.

"Dillon, it's me." Summer held the phone away from her ear and waited for her brother to stop shouting. When silence ensued, she put the phone back next to her ear.

"I am next door with Nikolai. No. You don't need to come and get me. I'm perfectly safe. And to be doubly sure, we'll use condoms." Her lips quirked as the inevitable shouting started again. "I love you too, Dillon," she said sweetly. "Seriously though, we have Nikolai's cell phone. If we have any problems we will call you."

"Sounded as if that went well." Nikolai leaned back against his pillows, his gaze skimming her face and coming to settle on her lips.

"Oh, yeah. And if I mention sex, that diverts the yelling."

"What about if I were to mention sex?"

Summer paused, then gut instinct told her to go with truth rather than coy. "I'd say 'good'." She stroked her hand down his cheek, across the dark stubble on his jaw and dallied to trace his lips with her finger. Nikolai opened his mouth and took her finger inside, closing his lips and surrounding her finger with warmth. A tingle sprang to life in Summer's breasts. She imagined his mouth drawing on her nipples instead of her finger and the tingle intensified to a pulse. A gush of juices moistened her lace panties, making her squirm. "And I'd say when are we getting to the action—"

Nikolai tugged on the fabric that clung to her hips. "You're the one with clothes on."

Summer bent up to brush a teasing kiss across his mouth then climbed off the bed. Her heart zinged at his teasing. She really liked him when he was in this mood. "You provide the music, and I'll strip."

Nikolai turned on his side and flicked on a radio. In dulcet tones, the female announcer read out the news. "Music," he said, his brows rising in a silent dare.

Summer smiled, blew him a kiss and wriggled her hips in a suggestive bump. Nikolai's eyes rounded slightly but zeroed in on her swaying hips and breasts. Huh! Didn't take much to snare a male's attention. She waggled her boobs, the heavy globes swaying beneath her cotton shirt. Then Summer reached under the fabric and flicked her bra open, spilling her breasts free from the lacey bit of nothing that she wore. Deft fingers separated button from buttonhole until her shirt gaped open, giving Nikolai peek-a-boo glances of the curves of her breasts and the occasional flash of nipple.

His intent gaze warmed her through until her body hummed and her limbs felt like warmed honey. Summer wandered a little closer, and a hum of approval sounded. A slow grin bloomed on his face, stoking her wavering courage. This stripper routine was harder than it had sounded. Her hands fluttered to the dome snap on her jeans and dealt with it swiftly before running the zipper downward.

Summer shimmied her hips and let the denim jeans slide down her legs. Then she hit a snag.

"Forgotten something, sweetheart?" Laughter echoed in his voice, bringing a wave of flustered color to her cheeks.

Hot damn. She'd forgotten to take off her shoes. Summer wrinkled her nose. *Back to stripper school for her.* Summer struggled like an ungainly stork, standing on one leg for a while, then gave up on the seductive front, and stooped to deal with the laces on her shoes and stepped out of her jeans. Right. She sucked in a deep breath and with a roll of her shoulders let her breasts flash. Yep. That got his attention all right. Summer strutted the length of the room, prancing like a show pony, keeping her eyes on Nikolai's face the whole time.

"Is that it?" A devilish grin twisted his lips. "All I've seen is a flash of tits. Can't see much else because of that shirt/dress you've got on." He made a tsk-tsking sound and shook his head in mock disappointment.

At least she hoped it was mockery. She'd hate to send him to sleep when she was starting to get off on this stripping game. "I obviously need training," Summer mused. "Perhaps I could get a job in a topless bar. There were ads in *The Herald* the other day."

Nikolai sat up so quickly a pillow flew to the floor. Brown eyes narrowed while his smile vanished. "I don't think so. I'm not having my wife pedaling flesh in a bar."

His wife. Damned presumptuous of him. He really had to control that character flaw, especially if he expected her to fight her reckless nature. Tit for tat, and all that stuff. Summer peeled back her shirt, baring her boobs. She glanced down then, peeked at Nikolai through lowered lashes. Mission accomplished. Definite interest. And definite distraction from the marriage record that seemed to have jammed. She was not marrying him, and that was final.

Suddenly tired of games, Summer flung her shirt off and let it drop to the ground. She pushed her panties down her legs, stepped out of them and kicked them aside. "Interested?" she asked, striking a pose then spoiling it by letting a giggle escape.

His eyes darkened as his gaze ran the length of her body. "Come here."

Summer strolled up to the bed, making sure she put an extra little wiggle in her walk. Her breasts swayed lightly while inside the sparks of desire grew. Summer launched herself at him, trusting him to catch her. He did. His arms tightened around her as their naked bodies aligned. He kissed her fiercely. Hungrily. Forcing Summer to concentrate on him, and leaving no room for distracting thoughts of marriage, crooks or family. The kiss softened, and his tongue darted inside her mouth to explore. Summer shuddered and undulated against him, savoring the bulk of masculine muscles and the fierce jut of his cock against her belly. Juices seeped from her body in readiness for his possession, her body softening, almost pleading for his hard cock.

Nikolai pulled away from her, breathing hard. He brushed the messy strands of hair from her face, his gaze somber, his eyes dark and hungry. "You're addictive. You know that? Lately, I can't stop thinking about you. About being with you. Being in you," he added fiercely.

His hands slid down her bare back in a long, luxurious stroke of fragrant, satiny skin. *It was true*, he thought. Each minute he spent with her seemed to draw him in tighter. Like a silken trap—that's what she was and somewhere along the line, he'd given up fighting for freedom. Each time he mentioned marriage, the word slipped easier off his tongue. Marriage to Summer Williams would be so different from his marriage to Laura. Summer would continue to fight for her independence. She'd expect it. When he left with his unit, Summer wouldn't pine away. She'd get on with her life. Yet knowing that didn't worry him. Despite her youth, Summer had integrity. He trusted her. Nikolai breathed in deeply, drawing a lungful of Summer essence and flowers. He'd always thought of flowers as girly. Now he thought of Summer. With his hands, he cupped her bottom then slid one leg between hers. He drew his leg flush with her feminine flesh, the heat he encountered sending a jerk of impatience the length of his cock.

"You want me," he whispered, part of him in awe. All they'd done was kiss, yet she was moist and ready for him. The knowledge made him feel like a god.

"Always," she said, running her fingers across his chest then dallying to finger his masculine nipple. The light scratching and pinching of her fingers sent a jolt of lust soaring through him. She massaged his chest with one hand, digging in and retracting her nails like a cat. And damned if he didn't want to purr.

Nikolai leaned over to jerk the bedside drawer open. He grabbed a condom packet, ripped it open and quickly rolled it on his penis. With one hard thrust, he slid into her tight channel. Summer clenched her inner muscles, making her womb tighten around him. A repeat of the move forced a groan past clenched lips. He withdrew and thrust, increasing his pace when Summer moved with him, clutching at his shoulders and still digging her fingernails into his skin.

Another thrust sent sensation rippling from his cock. He quickened his strokes, savoring the slap of flesh against flesh, the small pain of Summer's fingernails and the small sounds she made at the back of her throat. Nikolai gripped Summer's hips and pounded into her. He was so close to climax. He wanted to keep thrusting hard and fast until his seed spewed from him, but he wanted Summer's pleasure too. Desperately needed it. His hand slipped between them to dance across her swollen clit. He massaged lightly and gritted his teeth trying to hold back. A soft cry squeezed past Summer's lips.

"Come for me, sweetheart." His finger slid back and forth, round and round, and he couldn't prevent another thrust. One thrust was all it took for him to explode. Spasm after spasm shook his body. Then Summer tumbled into climax, gripping his cock in her tight cunt. Nikolai swallowed his groan at the tight vise of pleasure that gripped both his mind and his body. Man, he was in trouble here. Not only was he seriously thinking marriage, he was worried about his Summer addiction.

* * * * *

Nikolai woke alert and ready to fight. Training had taught him to assimilate the situation without moving a muscle. Nikolai listened intently trying to work out what had woken him. The moon shone through the window aiding his vision. Summer slept on, her mouth slightly open. Her chest rose and fell and a faint whistle sounded, followed by a snort. Nikolai grinned. She'd be mortified if she knew she snored. A floorboard squeaked, wiping Nikolai's grin clean. Someone was inside the house. He untangled his limbs from Summer's warm embrace, and grabbed up his jeans. His habit of leaving them on the floor right by the bed was coming in fine and dandy. Nothing worse than being caught with a bare ass. Except if it was Summer doing the catching.

"Nikolai?" Summer sat up in the bed and stretched with no pretence at modesty, her mouth split wide in a yawn.

"Someone's inside the house," he murmured.

Summer sprang from the bed and grabbed her clothes. "Dare?"

"Doubt it. He'd get someone else to do his dirty work."

Another board creaked at the far end of the passage.

"Ring your brothers." Nikolai didn't wait for her to answer, but opened the bedroom door and slipped out.

She strained to hear what Nikolai had heard. Nothing. Summer shoved her arms into her shirt, getting tangled in her haste. "Breathe," she muttered, giving herself an old, familiar lecture.

A crash reverberated from the far end of the house. A muffled thud. Anxiety for Nikolai hastened her speed. Once she'd scrambled into clothes, Summer grabbed the phone.

The bedroom door flew open before she could finish dialing.

"Put the phone down, girlie."

The man wasn't tall—about the same height as her—but his shoulders were bulky. When he switched on the light, she blinked. Her first clear look at his face didn't reassure. Mean and determined. Fear jumped squarely in the middle of her stomach. She backed up toward the window. She'd come in that way—maybe she could leave via the same route. Summer kept dialing, trying to concentrate despite the trembling fingers and her split attention. In a fight, she'd have her work cut out. Sparring in the gym was different from confronting a man.

"Put the fuckin' phone down." He had a smoker's voice, and it reacted on Summer like fingernails on a blackboard. She winced, trying to work out what to do. The crashes in the passage outside increased in intensity. Didn't take a rocket scientist to know Nikolai was in trouble.

The man snarled, a sound from deep down in his belly. "Girlie, don't make me tell you a third time." He kept approaching and closed the distance between them with a flying leap, snatching at the phone. Summer danced out of the way, trying to breathe through her panic. The rasp of her lungs indicated a need to calm herself, before she went into a full-blown asthma attack. If she did that, she'd be about as useful as a book with missing pages.

The wooden screech of a window being lifted sounded behind her. She whirled in time to see another man climbing through the window into the room. The smug expression on his freckled face fueled anger. Fine. She was cornered. She admitted it, but that didn't mean all was lost. She placed the phone down on the dressing table and stepped away.

The door opened without warning, and Nikolai was thrust through. A thin trickle of blood ran down one cheek and his hands were tied behind his back. Summer bit back a cry, knowing she needed to keep calm. *Breathe*, she reminded herself. Nikolai's calm demeanor helped her focus. Their gazes met in silent communication. Nikolai's eyes were hot with fury. Pissed, and in warrior mode.

Summer suppressed a swallow and looked away. Two men followed — one a stranger and the other very familiar.

Summer's chin jerked upward. "What are you doing here, Dare?"

"I want the book, Summer. I know you have it."

"The book I picked up for you? I gave it to the hostess at your restaurant. Didn't she give it to you?"

"Quit with the cute stuff, Summer. I know you have it — process of elimination. Give me the book and no one will get hurt."

Summer didn't believe him for a minute. Beneath the city gloss lurked a shark. She saw it now. Clearly, just as Nikolai had warned. Dare had killed already. Or one of his men had without giving a second thought to the victim or his family. Summer only hoped that the hostess at Dare's restaurant was alive to tell the tale.

"The book." Dare stepped up to her and slapped her across the face.

Summer stumbled back with the force of the blow. Nikolai growled and flung himself at Dare. He didn't get far. The freckled man kicked him in the stomach, and he fell to the ground.

Summer raised a hand to her hot cheek and glared at Dare. "I don't have your damned book."

"Come, my dear. You can do better than that."

"Boss, I'll make her talk," the freckled man said.

Summer darted him a look and inwardly shuddered. The way he looked her up and down sent loathing crawling across her skin. A combination of mean and stupid blazed from his open face. She didn't want to go near the man.

"I'd love to feel those tits of hers. Bet they're real. Not those false jobbies."

"Maybe later, Ross." Dare smirked at Summer, obviously sensing her unease and happy to foster her fear. "Give me the book, and I'll let you go."

"She said she doesn't know what you're talking about," Nikolai growled.

"I didn't ask you. Get him on his feet. We'll take him to the warehouse."

Summer's stomach lurched, the nagging knowledge that this situation was her fault making her feel ill. What should she do? Did she tell the truth? That the police had the book, or did she try to stall? Neither option looked good. Bottom line—the book wasn't hers to give.

But perhaps…

"The book is in my room next door," Summer said. And so were her brothers.

"Nice try, my dear. It's not. The house was searched last night, so we don't need to waste time searching again or bother about coming face-to-face with the two men currently in residence."

Summer wrinkled her nose and aimed for ditzy blonde. "If you've misplaced your book, why don't you buy another?"

"Like you did," Dare inserted smoothly. He studied her with a dispassionate look, unfazed by her act. "This is what we're going to do," Dare said after a long pause. "Take the boyfriend to the warehouse."

"What about me, boss?" the freckled one said. "What should I do?"

"Go with the others. One drive and the other two can sit in the back with him." Dare jerked his head in Nikolai's direction. "Make sure he doesn't get away."

"What about her?"

Summer held her breath. If Dare intended to send the others with Nikolai, she might have a chance to get free. A slim chance—if she kept her wits about her.

"Summer and I are going to have a little chat." Dare's face hardened with determination, giving Summer an inkling of his strength as a leader. In that instant, fear really took hold. Dare was determined to get his book back with the secret information it contained. Nikolai and her brothers were right. She was in over her head.

Chapter Seventeen

"Just showing you how serious I am, my dear."

Summer scowled, then bit down on her tongue to keep the horrified tears at bay. Dare's three men had hauled Nikolai from his bedroom unconscious and bleeding, and there hadn't been a thing she could do to stop the beating. "I am not 'your dear'."

"No," Dare said, prowling around her and looking her up and down like a piece of merchandise. "You're his whore."

The air whistled through her teeth as she sucked in an affronted breath. Who the hell was he to call her a whore when he was into crime and murder? Summer heard a car start and pull away. Gradually the sound faded, leaving her alone to deal with Dare. The irony of her situation brought a spark of humor. Damn, she'd wanted independence, and now she had it big-time, she wanted the comfort of her bossy, nosy family. And Nikolai.

"What? Nothing to say for yourself? You would have made a good wife for me Summer. Young. Intelligent. My parents liked you. You would have made a good mother for my children."

Dare sauntered around the bed, assured and confident in his ability to handle her. Summer waited until he was within range, her heart hammering with a combination of bloodlust and anticipation. Cocky little twerp. Nikolai was worth ten of Dare Martin.

"I wouldn't take you now if you paid me," he drawled.

Summer sprang at him, lashing out with a kick to the head and taking him by surprise. His head snapped back, and she gloried in the shock that rippled across his face. Grunting, she kicked out again and stomped on his glossy, black leather shoes.

She'd teach him to underestimate a woman. A balled-up fist to the stomach made him hunch forward.

"Bitch," Dare muttered, stepping back out of range.

"And proud of it," Summer snarled. "At least I'm not a coward."

Dare lunged at her, but Summer danced out of his way unscathed. She circled, watching his eyes, and feigned a punch to his upper chest in a move that would have made her teacher proud. Then she went low, sending a striking blow at Dare's groin. The animal scream of pain as he crumpled brought little satisfaction. Bastard. Summer rubbed her hands together in a job-well-done move. He deserved worse. Much worse, and by the time she was finished with him, he'd be sorry. Summer grabbed a belt and a black tie from the wardrobe and used them to bind Dare's arms and legs.

Keeping a wary eye on Dare, Summer hurried for the cell phone.

"Yeah?"

Her brother sounded alert as if he'd been awake for hours. Must be a SAS thing. "It's me. Nikolai's in trouble. They took him away to a warehouse somewhere."

"Josh and I will be there in five."

The phone slammed down, and Summer nibbled her bottom lip before coming to a decision. She checked the numbers Nikolai had stored in his mobile and rang Jake.

He answered on the first ring, just as alert as her brother. "Yeah."

"It's Summer. Nikolai's in trouble."

"The book?"

"Yeah."

"Louie and I'll be there soon. Don't do anything without us."

"Summer!" Her brother's holler echoed in the passageway. "Where the hell are you?"

"Down here."

Dare groaned, and Summer debated kicking him again. Perhaps this time with shoes on.

"The bedroom." Dillon snorted. "I should have known."

"Who's he?" Josh said. "Doesn't look too healthy."

"I kicked him in the testicles," Summer said with distinct relish. "Jake is on his way. I don't know where they've taken Nikolai. Or what they're going to do with him. He was unconscious. This is all my fault."

"Not now, Summer. Hold it together for Nikolai. He's tough. He'll survive," Josh said.

Summer turned to Dillon for added encouragement and found her brother glaring at the rumpled bed.

"Until I get my hands on him," Dillon snapped. He bent to check on Dare, then stood again. "Good job, sis. Doesn't look like he'll be going anywhere."

"But we need to find out where they've taken Nikolai," Summer said. "He can talk, right?"

"Go and wait for Jake and Louie. We'll talk to the clotheshorse."

"That's what Nikolai calls him," Summer said.

"We agree on something," Dillon said deadpan.

Summer rolled her eyes and walked from the bedroom without glancing back.

* * * * *

"What if we can't find Nikolai?" Summer demanded for about the fourth time. Worry furrowed her forehead as she looked from Dillon to Josh, who sat beside her in the rear of Louie's car. What if they'd hurt him even more? What if they'd killed him? She'd been so busy fighting for independence and playing games that she hadn't admitted how she felt about him. Summer attempted to swallow the huge lump of fear. What if it was too late?

"Can we gag her?" Josh asked.

Jake turned and grinned from the front passenger seat. "She's your sister. You gag her."

"Aren't you worried about Nikolai?" Summer snapped. "He was unconscious. They killed the owner of the bookshop. And we've got no idea where he is." Her sentence ended on a pained whisper. Summer sensed the men glancing at each other. "I'm not crying," she gritted out.

Jake's cell phone rang. "Yeah?"

Summer watched Jake's face closely as he listened, tension crawling through her stomach and hitching her breath. The tense set left his shoulders, and she let her breath ease out. They knew — or had a good idea — where Nikolai was.

"We'll meet you there," Jake said, confirming her guess. "East Tamaki. Cryers Road," he instructed Louie.

The car accelerated down the motorway.

Faster, Summer thought. Her hands twisted in her lap. Please let Nikolai be all right.

Summer thought about Nikolai's proposal of marriage. Again. Ever since she'd seen him being dragged from the bedroom like an ungainly sack of potatoes, she'd worried about not telling him of her feelings. Stupid and stubborn to the finish — that was her. *And don't forget reckless*, her conscience prodded.

"Why don't you kick a girl when she's down?" she muttered.

"Huh?" Josh said.

On her other side, Dillon's gaze pushed holes in the side of her face. Or at least it felt like it.

Summer turned to glare at him. "What?"

"Our sister is losing it," Josh muttered.

Summer's gaze jerked back to Josh, doing some eye boring of her own. "Your sister is in love with Nikolai Tarei," she snapped. "He's in danger because of me, and I'm worried sick."

"Go, Nik," Jake said from the front seat.

"What if something happens to him? It will be all my fault."

Josh groaned, long and loud. "Will you shut up?"

"But—"

"In the glove box," Louie said.

Jake didn't ask questions but bent to open the glove box as directed. He pulled out a navy blue silk scarf and turned round to the back seat with a grin. "A silencer," he said.

Dillon snorted. Josh chuckled, but Summer stared, momentarily diverted from her worries. She'd glimpsed a second blue scarf in the glove box before Jake slammed it shut. "Do you tie woman up with those scarves?" she blurted.

For an instant there was stunned silence, and all Summer could hear was the smooth purr of the car and the distant din of a siren.

"What kind of fool question is that?" Dillon demanded.

"Well, I don't know about you," Jake drawled, "but I'm kinda interested in the answer."

Josh stirred beside her. "Yeah."

The four of them stared at Louie. In Summer's case, all she could see was the back of his neck, but it was interesting to note the slow crawl of color and watch its progress down his neck.

"We're almost there," Louie said.

"Aw, come on, mate. You can't leave us hanging like that," Jake said.

"Don't answer," Dillon ordered. "Not with my baby sister in the car."

"She's not so little if she's doing the horizontal tango with Nik," Jake pointed out.

Both Josh and Dillon growled.

"That's enough," Summer said, placing a hand on each of them. "Louie, I'll discuss scarves with you later. Do you have any books on the subject?" she added.

Jake threw back his head and roared with laughter in the front seat. "Man, I'm not sure whether to feel sorry for Nikolai or envy him."

"You are not hooking up with Tarei," Dillon snarled.

Silence, tense and brittle, fell again. Summer's stomach hollowed out at the sudden chill inside the car.

Finally, Louie broke the silence. "Nik is our mate." The threat was implicit in his words. Do or say anything against Nikolai and suffer the consequences.

"He got a man killed. A good man," Dillon snarled. "Summer is staying away from him."

"I'm—"

"That's bullshit," Jake said in a quiet voice that made Summer shiver. He never came across as dangerous because he was always joking around. "You don't know what happened that day."

And don't judge, Summer thought. No matter what Dillon and Josh said about Nikolai, she wouldn't believe them. She knew him. He was gentle, and caring and loyal. And she loved him.

"I know enough," Dillon said.

"A good man died that day because Tarei left him," Josh snarled.

Jake scowled, and in that moment he looked like the dangerous hunter he was. "You weren't there. Everything you know is secondhand."

Summer suppressed a shiver at the unleashed violence in his words.

"Tell us then, because we sure as hell aren't letting our sister within calling range of him. He left his man to die. Teammates don't do that."

Summer straightened. "You can't send me home to Eketahuna. I won't go." Once Nikolai was safe, they were going to talk. Then once she'd sorted things to her satisfaction, they would marry. But first of all, she was going to tell him how much she loved him.

In the front seat, Summer noticed Louie and Jake glancing at each other. After a few seconds, Louie spoke.

"Nik had the choice of saving a woman and her three kids, or his man. He tried to do both and damn near killed himself. His leg is never gonna come right. Not one hundred percent."

"Do you have proof of this," Dillon demanded.

"Uncle Henry knows," Summer said with instinctive certainty. "But it doesn't matter. I trust Nikolai."

Louie glanced in the rear-vision mirror. "A Williams with commonsense. Thank you, God."

"Nikolai would give his left nut to save another life." Jake turned to fix her brothers with a steely glare. "Only old women listen to gossip. If you want the truth, ask Nikolai instead of condemning him without trial."

Summer laughed at Jake's fervent words while she felt her brothers wince at mention of the male anatomy.

"Good. We're all on the same page now. Nikolai and I are a couple."

"With an interesting sex life," Jake added.

"I find it interesting," Summer conceded. "I learn something new every time."

"Summer, button it," Dillon snapped.

"Boys, we're here," Louie said.

The men snapped into predator mode, and the tension ratcheted sharply upward inside the car.

"What if this isn't the right warehouse?" Summer asked.

Josh patted one jean-clad knee, squeezing in gentle encouragement. "If it's not the right one, we'll keep trying."

"It's the right one," Jake said. "My mate Dan sounded confident."

Louie slowed the car and drove past, then pulled up at the end of the street. "Anyone see life?"

A croak of protest leaked from Summer's tight throat.

"Sorry. Poor word choice," Louie muttered.

They climbed from the car, shutting the doors with careful thuds. The warehouse looked deserted, with broken windows high up on the graffiti-covered walls. Around the outside, scrubby-looking bushes grew amongst knee-high grass.

"Summer, stay with me," Dillon ordered. His expression told her he expected her to follow instructions to the letter. Summer jerked her head in compliance. Nerves jumped in her tummy. She had no experience in being a soldier, and was happy to follow instructions and do her part. At least he hadn't suggested she wait in the car.

"She should wait in the car," Josh said.

"No." Dillon gave her a hard look. "She'll worry. Summer's better off with one of us."

"Ready? Family conference over?" Louie demanded. When Dillon gave a curt nod, he said, "Jake and I will go right. You and Josh go left." Nikolai's two friends slithered along the side of the warehouse and disappeared around the corner with the stealth of a pair of cats.

A white car pulled up further down the street, followed by a police car.

"Do we wait for them?" Summer whispered.

"Nah," Josh said. "Let's go."

"Where are the doors? How do we get in?"

"Summer, shut up." Dillon squeezed her shoulder in silent comfort. "Don't worry. We'll find him."

Summer followed, right on Dillon's heels. They skirted the long grass and discarded litter, running low and keeping close to the rundown building.

"Keep up, Summer. Don't fall behind."

Summer grimaced at Dillon's broad back. Fine for him to say when he had long, ground-eating legs. She hastened her pace, breaking out into a trot. Her foot hit a hole and her ankle rolled.

"Shit."

Up ahead, Dillon and Josh froze. As one, they turned to her with their warrior faces in neutral. It took them a split second to analyze the situation, then their expressions turned from neutral to brotherly disgust.

Josh rolled his eyes and whispered in a low voice that Summer had to strain to hear. "I don't know why we didn't stroll up to the front door and knock. We might as well have with all the noise you're making."

"You're as bad as Nikolai," Summer snapped.

"Keep it down," Dillon murmured, his eyes assessing the area ahead and behind.

"Well, if you'd all let me in on your little games and give me some practice, I wouldn't blunder around like an elephant in ballet shoes. And thank you for asking, my ankle is fine."

Josh grinned. "Sis, you do have a way with words."

"If you two are finished, we need to move. Before the cops get here."

Josh and Summer sobered, and fell in behind Dillon. They moved quietly yet rapidly like snakes. When they reached the next corner of the warehouse, Dillon slowed and cautiously looked round the corner.

"Clear," he murmured. "Summer, watch where you put your feet and if there's any gunfire drop to the ground and crawl back in the direction we've come."

Gunfire. Mention of guns brought home the reality. They were all in danger. Tension tightened her belly in a vice-like grip.

They crept around the corner. At the far end of the warehouse, coming toward them, she saw Jake and Louie. Jake signaled with his hands. A foreign language to Summer, but Josh and Dillon seemed to understand.

As one, they moved along the rear of the warehouse to the open door.

Silly of them to leave the small, rear door open, Summer thought as Louie peered inside. Perhaps they felt safe because the huge roller door at the front of the warehouse was secured. Louie signaled with his hands, then moved back. He did another series of hand signals to Josh and Dillon.

Summer tugged on Josh's arm and stood on tiptoes to whisper in his ear. "What's going on?"

"Tarei knows we're here. He's going to distract them."

Summer's stomach hollowed out again. The perfect way to lose weight—live your life in fear. "How?"

Josh shook his head and squeezed her arms in silent encouragement.

Summer heard a loud crash inside the warehouse. It reverberated through her body, pushing fear along every nerve ending.

"Stay here," Dillon ordered.

Summer opened her mouth to argue.

Jake stopped her with a look. "Nikolai will worry. He needs to concentrate."

Summer's breath eased out and she nodded, albeit unwillingly. Now was not the time for being reckless. "I'll wait right here."

"Stay flat against the wall." Jake's face held approval.

Another crash sounded, followed by cursing. Her brothers and Nikolai's friends slipped through the door.

For a few moments, she stayed against the wall just as they'd told her, but the crashes and thumps coming from inside the warehouse got the better of her. She crept back to the door and peered inside. A hand snapped through the door and grabbed her shirt.

"Knew you couldn't resist poking your nose in," a familiar voice growled.

"Nikolai!" Summer flew through the door into his arms and hugged him tight. Then she stood at arm's length to survey the damage. She made a tsking sound and traced the swollen area around his eye. "You're going to have a black eye."

"Yeah." Nikolai grabbed her and hugged her tight as though he couldn't believe she was safe. He buried his face in her hair, and his chest rose and fell.

"Hands up. Against the wall." The harsh voice grabbed their unwilling attention.

"It's the cops," Nikolai murmured against her ear. "Follow their instructions. They're not sure who the bad guys are yet."

Summer glanced toward the door. The rigid stance of the cop in the doorway backed up Nikolai's words. A fair comment. Summer didn't want to get shot. She raised her hands slowly as did Nikolai at her side. His brown eyes bore silent encouragement and a trace of concern.

"I'm fine," she whispered. "Whupped Dare's hide and kicked him in the balls."

Nikolai's bark of laughter drew a frown from the cop who'd issued the instructions. "You two. Shut it."

Behind them, Summer saw that her brothers and Jake and Louie had overpowered Dare's cohorts. All four men stood to attention, their warrior's faces in evidence. Nikolai had his warrior's face on too. Summer stared at him, unable to look away. Dangerous. Hard. Without mercy. Then one brown eye closed in a wink. It was so uncharacteristic that Summer's mouth shut. Nikolai glanced at the cops then moved one hand off the wall. He traced the outline of her smiling mouth, his eyes dark and intent. Summer's pulse skipped in excitement. Oh, boy.

The cops entered the room cautiously—six of them—and fanned out. The last one through the door jerked his head at Jake in a gesture of greeting.

"Cuz. You've done our work for us." His wide grin told Summer his temperament was similar to Jake's—easygoing and fun.

"'Bout time you guys got here. Hey, love birds. Cut that out," Jake drawled.

Summer jerked her gaze from Nikolai's, and tried to control the burst of heat to her cheeks as she glanced around the cavernous warehouse.

Two of Dare's gang lay on the floor looking worse for wear. One groaned and attempted to crawl away until a policeman fastened handcuffs around his wrists and stood him up. The third man leaned against a wooden packing case, blood dripping from his face onto the concrete floor.

Nikolai curled his arm around her waist. He turned to Jake's policeman cousin. "Can we go?"

"We need them for questioning," another of the cops said.

Her brother Dillon prowled up to the cops. "Can you question them tomorrow? They've been through a fair bit today. We can answer most of your immediate questions. If they promise to drop into the Auckland Central station tomorrow, you could let them go home."

"Dillon," Josh muttered, a look of amazement on his face. "I thought we'd agreed."

"I've changed my mind. Summer is old enough to make her own decisions. We got into the habit of watching out for her when she was sick as a kid. It's time we stopped."

Josh's brows drew together. His head shook as he looked from her to Nikolai. "I don't think that Mum—"

"We're not telling Mum," Dillon said.

"No, I am," Summer said. Inwardly, she dreaded telling her parents, particularly her mother, that she intended staying in Auckland, but adults took responsibility. If she balked at telling her parents about Nikolai then what hope was there for their future?

Chapter Eighteen

"Will you marry me?"

Summer's blunt question echoed in the huge warehouse. The cops discussing whether they could go without giving a statement stopped to stare.

Jake tipped him a wink. Louie chuckled while Summer's brothers started to rumble like waking volcanoes.

Nikolai swallowed. It did nothing to disperse the lump of tension lodged in his throat. He ran his hand across her cheek and tucked a blue strand of hair behind her ear, the familiar action relaxing him. "Are you pregnant?"

The rumbling from Summer's brothers grew louder, but he ignored them to focus on Summer. His lover. And now — his wife-to-be. A month ago, the thought would have scared him spitless. But today a surge of anticipation throbbed through him.

"Well?" Dillon demanded. "Are you pregnant?" His disapproval bled through into his expression, making him look tough and mean.

"None of your business," Summer inserted smoothly into the pulsing silence left while her brother scowled. "In other words, butt out."

A laugh sounded from one of the policeman, abruptly cut off when Dillon's attention focused on him.

Nikolai decided it was about time he took control. He cupped Summer's elbow and exerted a little force. No way was he baring his heart in public or airing their sex life. It had aired enough already. "We'll see you tomorrow," he said to Jake's cousin. "Around ten?" After receiving a nod of approval, he urged Summer out the door despite the glare burns he felt smoldering in the middle of his back. He gritted his teeth, trying to ignore the shooting pain from his knee. Summer didn't need to know that Dare's goons had done a good job on roughing him up.

"Good exit," Summer said once they were out of sight. Humor lurked in her beautiful blue eyes, and Nikolai forgot the jagged pain. "But how are we going to get home? We don't have a car."

The last thought on his mind was a car. His gaze traveled her face. Her blue eyes sparkled with life and humor. Her pink lips curved in a secret smile. A jolt of pure lust laced with possessiveness raced through his body, stirring his cock to life. She didn't look like a woman who had to get married. Confidence and assurance blazed from her. She looked like a woman with sex on her mind.

"Wait there, and I'll grab Louie's keys," Nikolai said. "Then we need to talk."

"Are you sure you're all right?" Summer said when he returned.

"Why, don't you want to marry an old crock like me? You gonna change your mind?"

Summer stopped beside Louie's car. "Not only am I not going to change my mind about marrying you, I want to have your children too." A challenging glint glowed in her blue eyes.

Nikolai stared, mesmerized by her beauty. *His woman.* He ran his fingers down her silky cheek, trying to ignore the throbbing bumps and bruises on his ribs, inflicted by the clotheshorse's thugs. "As long as you agree to marry me, you can have anything you want."

"But not straight away, please. I want to have you to myself for a few years."

Nikolai grinned suddenly. "Not finished with your research yet?"

"That's right," Summer said with an enthusiastic nod. "I found this neat book in the secondhand book shop. A bit racy for the library," she added.

"I love you."

"I know," Summer said in a smug tone. "I finally worked it out. The feeling is definitely mutual." Summer paused, her forehead puckering into a cute frown. "Except when you try to boss me around. I don't like being told what to do. I like—"

"To be asked," Nikolai finished. Okay. He could learn to do that. It looked as though this babysitting assignment was turning into a permanent one. Who'd have thought? But the idea of waking up each morning beside Summer didn't scare him. Nikolai smirked as he pressed a kiss to her mouth. Not too much, anyway.

"Just remember that I like to be asked for my opinion and our marriage will be a big success." Summer reinforced the sentiment. As the sound of voices grew louder, she glanced toward the rear of the warehouse then back at him.

Nikolai moved toward the car in silent accord. "I think we should disappear before they come out and decide to keep us here."

"You just want to have your wicked way with me."

Nikolai opened the door for her and then climbed into the driver's side. "Damn straight," he said and leaned over to kiss Summer, and cop a feel of her beautiful breasts at the same time.

A full-time commitment with Summer.

A wife.

His wife.

The thought should have terrified him. Knowing Summer, he'd suffer a few gray hairs in the process, but he wouldn't have it any other way.

Nikolai winked at her, a sense of rightness settling in his heart. "Sure do."

"Let's go then," Summer said, lifting her chin and staring at him in clear challenge.

"Good idea," he said, a grin of real anticipation curling across his face. Nikolai fired up the car and pulled away from the curb. "I'm ready to go home and get horizontal. After all, we have new positions to try."

Enjoy this excerpt from
Talking Dogs, Aliens and Purple People Eaters

"We're gonna crash. Buckle up."

"What?" Janaya spun around to gape at her aunt, Hinekiri. One look told her the truth. Hinekiri wasn't teasing.

Janaya gulped and scowled out a porthole at the rapidly approaching blue planet and muttered a succinct curse, trying to halt her escalating panic. Tendrils of icy fear curled around her insides. Her worst fear come to life. "I thought you said this…this antique had plenty of life yet." She fumbled with the harness straps and another weak curse slipped out when the ship plunged into white, fluffy clouds sending her stomach swooping toward her toes.

"Ah, good." Her aunt's voice held satisfaction, despite their impending doom. "You worked your way through the Earth-speak tapes."

Janaya stared at her aunt, speechless for an instant, before her gaze slid past the porthole once more. She swallowed and imagined shaking Hinekiri until her teeth rattled and good sense reigned. The image didn't ease her panic any.

"We're gonna bloody crash," Janaya shrieked. "Pay attention. What do I do? I don't know anything about flying this bucket of bolts. I'm a bodyguard."

"Yes, dear, and I'm very proud of you."

"*Hinekiri!*" The only reason she'd boarded this ship was because fear for her aunt's life was greater than her dislike of flying. She was beginning to regret her impulse big time.

"I said we were crashing," her aunt said. "I don't believe I mentioned death."

"You… When we land, I'm going to damage you," Janaya gritted out.

"Tsk-tsk." Her aunt waggled her forefinger while nonchalantly maneuvered the manual steering controls. The ship groaned in loud protest and if anything, they picked up in speed. "I thought you stowed away to protect me from the bad guys." A teasing grin flashed, lighting up her lined face. "Not do their dirty work for them."

"Tell. Me. What. To. Do." They were gonna die. Janaya was sure of it. She'd never live to set foot on Dalcon again. She'd never get the captain's promotion she was aiming for, the promotion she'd earned by sheer hard work. And Santana would find someone else.

"Harness up and let me concentrate."

Tension seeped through Janaya's body, finding an outlet in her white-knuckled grip, as she watched her aunt calmly prepare to crash.

"I thought you said most of the Earth's surface is water," she blurted, her gaze darting from the porthole on her right to her aunt and back.

"That's right, dear."

"Are we going to land in water?"

Her aunt looked up from the panel of controls and frowned. "Can't you swim?"

Janaya bit her bottom lip to keep the curse that trembled on her tongue contained. "Yes, I can swim." The quirk of Hinekiri's top lip gave her away, and Janaya's shallow breaths eased out with a relieved hiss. Chances were good that her aunt was…ah yes…pulling her leg. When she stood with both feet firmly on the ground again, she'd feel more in charge. After an aggrieved glare at her aunt, she amended the thought. Maybe not.

"Assume crash position."

Janaya stared at her aunt. Then with morbid fascination, her gaze drifted to the bridge view port. Instead of the water she'd expected, she saw land. Flashes of green, trees then a sea of gold.

The initial impact jolted her body and clacked her teeth together. Behind her, something crashed to the floor — probably one of the stupid Earth-speak tapes her aunt had insisted she view and assimilate. The ship hurtled off the ground then hit again.

"He-haw!" her aunt shouted, one hand raised in the air, her wiry body riding the impact despite the constraints of her harness.

Janaya lacked the same exhilaration as they bounced across the ground barely missing a large tree. The sturdy branches gouged the protective outer shell of their ship as they zipped past.

"I'll try for up in those hills." Her aunt jabbed at the controls, and the ship responded sluggishly before hurtling to the ground again. Trees and hills passed in front of Janaya's horrified eyes.

What felt like hours later but was probably only a matter of minutes, they settled feet short of a dilapidated building up on the hill. The stench of metal fatigue lay heavy in the air.

"I need to stand on the ground," Janaya muttered. "*Now.* Is it safe?" Nausea worked up her throat. In a panic, clumsy fingers clawed at the restraining harness. In the end, her aunt leaned over to release the lever.

"No problems with the atmosphere here," her aunt said. "New Zealand, according to my charts. Clean and green."

Janaya needed no further urging. She stumbled out the door, dragging in huge breaths of fresh air until her lungs ached. Gradually, the panic attack subsided leaving her shaky and embarrassed. Make that mortified. Thank the Gods her aunt had been the only witness.

Hinekiri strode down the narrow exit steps from the ship and stopped beside her. She patted Janaya on the shoulder in a silent gesture of comfort. "Janaya, we need to camouflage the ship so the Earth people don't stumble across it."

"All right. I—" The small hairs at the back of her neck prickled to life. Janaya stilled, her eyes narrowing as her gaze swiveled to survey the area around the ship. Her hand slid toward her hip.

"Back on the ship," she snapped to her aunt as she pulled her weapon free. "Now."

To her right, the leaves of a fern shuddered. Janaya scented the air. Sweat. Torgon sweat.

"Come on out with your fingers poked inside your ears," she ordered, aiming her neutralizing weapon at the dark green bushes that had moved.

"That would be, hands in the air," her aunt said.

Janaya shrugged, not taking her eyes off the leafy plant. "What ever. I have a weapon. Come out."

The fern leaves shook, dried leaves crackled underfoot. Janaya's outstretched hand never wavered, the heavy weapon still pointing at the bushes.

"Don't shoot." A black nose thrust past a lacy fern leaf.

Janaya's eyes widened.

A black face with black eyes poked into view. "Are ya gonna shoot?"

"Janaya put the weapon down. It's a dog. Nothing to get trigger happy about."

"Yeah," the little dog said. It stepped into full view. The dog stood below knee height and had white fur peppered liberally with black spots. It trotted closer, tail wagging. "Do ya have any food?"

Janaya reholstered her neutralizer and rolled her eyes. "Talking animals?"

"I never met a human who talked back," the little dog said. "Food? Do ya have any?"

Janaya glared. "The sooner we leave this blue planet the better. How long will it take for the ship to be repaired?"

"Two, maybe three—"

"Days? Cool."

"Months."

"Months!" Janaya saw her promotion chances slipping away. After five Earth days, she'd be missed. Especially with the big mission coming up. They'd declare her AWOL. Janaya swallowed her regrets. The protector would become the hunted.

"Parts are hard to get. Besides, I intend to sightsee while I'm here. I'm not slaving over a smoking space ship without a little fun. And I'm not leaving Earth until I see what I came for."

"Yeah." Janaya sighed, having heard the refrain all the way to Earth. No matter how logical her arguments were Hinekiri never wavered from her goal. "The migration of the wildebeest."

"I didn't ask you to come. It was your idea to stow away."

"The Torgon want your galaxy exploration charts and your journals. And once they get them, they won't care if you're dead or alive. They've put a mercenary contract out on you."

"Contract, somtract. They've got to catch me first."

"Someone's coming," the little dog said. "Perhaps they'll have food."

Janaya scented in the direction the dog had lifted its nose. She felt a curious swooping pull that zapped all the way to her clit. Excitement sparked within. Her heart thudded and she shifted, uneasy with the sensation and the way her new Earth clothes clung to her breasts.

A steady, buzzing drone sounded. Janaya frowned, every instinct hyperaware of the new threat of danger. A clean scent drifted to her on the breeze, one that reminded her of the mountains and spruce forests of home. Then her eyes focused on a small dot on the horizon at the bottom of the hill. The dark blue dot grew steadily larger, her apprehension growing in direct proportion.

About the author:

Shelley lives in Auckland, New Zealand, with her husband and a small, bossy dog named Scotty.

Typical New Zealanders, Shelley and her husband left home for their big OE soon after they married (translation of New Zealand-speak: big overseas experience). A year-long adventure lengthened to six years of roaming the world. Enduring memories include being almost sat on by a mountain gorilla in Rwanda, lazing on white sandy beaches in India, whale watching in Alaska, searching for leprechauns in Ireland, and dealing with ghosts in an English pub.

While travel is still a big attraction, these days Shelley is most likely found in front of her computer following another love—that of writing stories of romance and adventure. Other interests include watching rugby and rugby league (strictly for research purposes *grin*), being walked by the dog, and curling up with a good book.

Shelley Munro welcomes mail from readers. You can write to her c/o Ellora's Cave Publishing at 1056 Home Avenue, Akron OH 44310-3502.

Why an electronic book?

We live in the Information Age—an exciting time in the history of human civilization in which technology rules supreme and continues to progress in leaps and bounds every minute of every hour of every day. For a multitude of reasons, more and more avid literary fans are opting to purchase e-books instead of paperbacks. The question to those not yet initiated to the world of electronic reading is simply: *why?*

1. *Price.* An electronic title at Ellora's Cave Publishing and Cerridwen Press runs anywhere from 40-75% less than the cover price of the <u>exact same title</u> in paperback format. Why? Cold mathematics. It is less expensive to publish an e-book than it is to publish a paperback, so the savings are passed along to the consumer.

2. *Space.* Running out of room to house your paperback books? That is one worry you will never have with electronic novels. For a low one-time cost, you can purchase a handheld computer designed specifically for e-reading purposes. Many e-readers are larger than the average handheld, giving you plenty of screen room. Better yet, hundreds of titles can be stored within your new library—a single microchip. (Please note that Ellora's Cave and Cerridwen Press does not endorse any specific brands. You can check our website at www.ellorascave.com or

www.cerridwenpress.com for customer recommendations we make available to new consumers.)

3. *Mobility.* Because your new library now consists of only a microchip, your entire cache of books can be taken with you wherever you go.

4. *Personal preferences are accounted for.* Are the words you are currently reading too small? Too large? Too…**ANNOYING**? Paperback books cannot be modified according to personal preferences, but e-books can.

5. *Instant gratification.* Is it the middle of the night and all the bookstores are closed? Are you tired of waiting days—sometimes weeks—for online and offline bookstores to ship the novels you bought? Ellora's Cave Publishing sells instantaneous downloads 24 hours a day, 7 days a week, 365 days a year. Our e-book delivery system is 100% automated, meaning your order is filled as soon as you pay for it.

Those are a few of the top reasons why electronic novels are displacing paperbacks for many an avid reader. As always, Ellora's Cave and Cerridwen Press welcomes your questions and comments. We invite you to email us at service@ellorascave.com, service@cerridwenpress.com or write to us directly at: 1056 Home Ave. Akron OH 44310-3502.

Discover for yourself why readers can't get enough of the multiple award-winning publisher Ellora's Cave. Whether you prefer e-books or paperbacks, be sure to visit EC on the web at www.ellorascave.com for an erotic reading experience that will leave you breathless.

www.ellorascave.com